FALKLANDS OR MALVINAS?

Conrado Etchebarne Bullrich

FALKLANDS OR MALVINAS?

Grupo Editor Latinoamericano

1ª edición

I.S.B.N.: 950-694-614-0

© 2000, *by* Conrado Etchebarne Bullrich
© 2000 de la primera edición *by* Grupo Editor
Latinoamericano S.R.L., Hipólito Yrigoyen 1994 - 2º "3"
(1089) Buenos Aires, Argentina.
Tel./Fax: 4952-9638

Queda hecho el depósito que dispone la ley 11.723.

Impreso y hecho en la Argentina. Printed and made in
Argentina.

Colaboraron en la preparación de este libro:

Diseño de tapa: Pablo Barragán. Composición y armado: José
Luis Servicios Gráficos. Impresión y encuadernación: Edigraf.
Películas de tapa: Tango Gráfica. Se utilizó para el interior papel Obra Boreal de 80 g y para la tapa cartulina de 250 g.

Two islanders sheltering from the wind behind a Gaucho's hut made of peat and straw with a cattle hide roof. (Photograph: A. Cameron)

INDEX

Prologue		11
Author's Prologue		13
Introduction		15
I.	Description of the Islands	19
II.	Historical Background	45
III.	Argentine Period	89
IV.	The British Occupation	107
V.	The Argentine Claim	145
VI.	The 1982 Conflict	165
VII.	The Seduction Policy	203
VIII.	The Islands Today	235
IX.	Falklands or Malvinas?	253
Annex: The Bullrich-Forsyth Proposal		281
Bibliography		285

PROLOGUE

During my time as Foreign Minister, I have given priority in our foreign policy to the Falkland Islands issue. At the end of the mandate entrusted to me by President Menem, I believe that we have advanced in creating better conditions for the dialogue on the sovereignty dispute that will enable future administrations to make further progress.

The first step has been taken. We now have communication between the Islanders and Argentines. We also have an open channel with the United Kingdom, which is the only interlocutor in the discussion over the sovereignty dispute. We hope that these two paths may converge into a *"third way"*; that of dialogue and mutual understanding which will allow us to find, in a cooperative and well-balanced fashion, a definitive final solution for this century old dispute.

There has been, and there will continue to be, much speculation about the final juridical status of the Islands. The efforts undertaken and the course of events will dictate the direction and progress of the debate over what the future may bring. In this regard, this book examines the problem from a personal perspective and is highly provocative.

Although it should not, under any circumstance, be interpreted as a form of support to the author about the likely outcome of the story of the Falklands, I believe that, as Conrado Etchebarne Bullrich has done, it is necessary for all Argentines to be able to analyse, debate and propose solutions to this longstanding dispute.

Guido Di Tella

Minister of Foreign Affairs of
The Republic of Argentina

Buenos Aires, December 6th 1999

Author's Prologue

Exactly ten years ago I published my first book *"Americanos del Sur en el Siglo XXI"*. It was the result of many years of efforts to write a doctoral thesis which would once more give shape to the unrealised dream of unity for the countries of South America. Years later Mercosur was created, the most realistic and successful project yet to pursue this goal.

There are two remaining European colonies in South America: French Guyana and the British Falkland Islands. They are two unacceptable anachronisms in the 21st century that create aditional difficulties to the dream of an united South America.

The sweeping changes that marked the end of the European colonial empires after the Second World War, together with the old imperial powers' longing for their glorious past, mean that they are painstakingly holding on to the last few remains of their lost empires.

To this one must also add the new and more

sophisticated forms of colonialism, neo-colonialism and peripheral globalisation that are being taken forward into the 3rd millennium. It is therefore even more difficult to find a solution to these inequities today than it was decades ago.

In the case of the Falklands, the existence of a local population, albeit small, with clearly different interests and objectives from the colonial power, must be taken into account. Additionally there are still strong, passionate feelings after the unfortunate war of 1982. Nevertheless, there is a light that allows us to see a satisfactory solution for all the parties involved.

Let us then delve into this fascinating history.

INTRODUCTION

> *"We acquired our Influence and Possessions by force, it is by force we must maintain them"*
> James Lawrence[1]

The Falkland Islands have always had an emotional connotation for the Argentine people. Perhaps because of the Hispanic heritage that was transmitted by word of mouth amongst the first settlers or the stories from Peru that reached Buenos Aires with gruesome details of English pirates attacking Spanish ports in the Caribbean and the Pacific or even the centuries of hostile Anglo-Hispanic relations.

This was later followed by the reality and the legends of the English invasions of Buenos Aires. English merchants and travellers, the slave settlement in Retiro,

---

[1] *The Making and Unmaking of British India,* Lawrence, James; ed. Abacus, London, 1998, pág 42.

bootlegging and trade, the English ships, a powerful presence which awoke the imagination of the *"Porteños"* and allowed them some relief from the monotony of the Pampas. The British appropiation of the Falkland Islands in 1833, after the attack of the American corvette *"Lexington"*, and the Anglo-French Blockade of the River Plate, helped to foster the legend.

By the time of Rosas' dictatorship, there was already the dictum of a love-hate relationship. This was clearly reflected in the literature of the River Plate, in books such as the *"Inglés de los guesos"* by Benito Lynch and *"Long Ago and Far Away"* by William Hudson.

This was followed by a long period of Argentine growth. From 1860 to1930 a successful and wonderfully balanced Anglo-Argentine relationship flourished. Business was booming, the Falklands, so remote, were forgotten.

In the 1930's, the military coups began, together with nationalism, populism, flirtations with the Axis and State intervention. All of these helped to create a stagnant and backward Argentina. The Falkland Islands, little by little, began to have a privileged place in Argentina's foreign policy, eventually dominating it completely. The United Nations, the *"third position"*, the confrontation with the United States and finally the madness of the conflict with Great Britain in 1982.

There was also dabbling with the non aligned countries in the first years of rediscovered democracy.

Finally, in the 1990's, and with a complete change in direction, Argentina aligned with the United States, the victors of the Cold War.

Introduction

By then firmly in British hands, the Falkland Islands awoke, thanks to fisheries and the dream of oil millions. Within this context, Foreign Minister Guido Di Tella personally undertook a new and imaginative policy of the Islanders and the continent *"drawing closer"*, known popularly as the policy of seduction.

"Falklands or Malvinas", is an impartial attempt to see today's Falkland Islands.

A typical rock formation, similar to those which produce the "stone runs".

I

DESCRIPTION OF THE ISLANDS

> *"...nothing could be less interesting. The country is uniformly the same; an undulating moorland; the surface with light brown withered grass, and some few low shrubs growing out of an elastic peaty soil...Few sorts of birds inhabit this miserable looking country; there are many flocks of wild geese feeding in the valleys, and solitary snipes are common in all parts."*
>
> Charles Darwin[2]

No doubt Darwin's description is still the impression given by the Falkland Islands to observers today, both from Europe or more exuberant countries such as Brazil. To this description one must add the constant winds and the lack of sun, certainly not very attractive to a Southamerican.

For those of us who come from the flat pampas, the hills and rolling countryside of the islands seem like high

---

[2] Charles Darwin, quoted by Patrick Armstrong in *Darwin's Desolate Islands*, Pictron Publishing, Chippenham, 1992, p. 42.

mountains. Those of us familiar with the dull and monotonous and almost fastidious Argentine coast, the fjords of the Falklands, their many islands, peninsulas, inlets, promontories, cliffs and beaches are fascinating.

To those coming from the dry Patagonian desert, the Islands are a veritable orchard, with no shortage of grass or water. It is not surprising that the Islands were already inhabited and had plenty of cattle by the end of the 19th century, while in Argentina the desert frontier remained at the coast of Rio Salado, near Buenos Aires, until well into the 19th century. Patagonia was only truly populated in the 20th century.

The journey to the Islands in itself, has always been an adventure. One can arrive by boat, after sailing the roughest and windiest seas in the world. The well-built ports are, and have always been, a refuge for sailors. Hundreds of ships, destroyed by the winds and southern storms, have found their eternal resting place in the natural harbours of the islands. The remains of shipwrecks are to be found by the dozen.

For seventeen long years since 1982 the lack of communication between the Islands and Argentina made it impossible to get there other than by airplane from Punta Arenas (Chile) in a small twin engine aircraft[3], or

---

[3] Over two years ago LANChile inaugurated a weekly Boeing 737 flight from Punta Arenas, which replaced the twin engine Twin Otter aircraft operated by DAP that had previously provided the weekly service from Punta Arenas. These flights were cancelled for 6 months at the beginning of 1999, as a Chilean reprisal against the detention of General Augusto Pinochet in London. In August 1999 flights from Punta Arenas were reinstated. In October 1999 one flight each month was authorised to stage through Rio Gallegos.

Solitary petrel standing on a small islet surrounded by kelp.

via Ascension Island in a British Royal Air Force Tristar. Only since October 1999 has a regular LANChile flight connected Rio Gallegos with the Islands.

The trip to the Islands from Punta Arenas in a small twin engined aircraft is always exciting. The plane usually takes off with strong tail winds on a sunny day and, after three hours flying over the South Atlantic, reaches the Islands, which are covered with a blanket of cloud. From the air they are beautiful. The white sandy beaches and the different shades of the sea, ranging from the white crests of the waves to the deep blue ocean, passing through a variety of pale blues and turquoise tones, give one the erroneous impression of flying over a Caribbean island. But the cold felt in the cabin, the ice on the wings of the plane, and the desolate steppes of the Islands abruptly brings one back to reality. The chains of mountains, the lakes, the bays and headlands are powerfully attractive for those travelling by air.

The journey from London is an interminable military flight, with only one stop on Ascension, which gives the impression of having travelled to the end of the world. The crossing of the North and South Atlantic, with no alternative stop-overs, is almost palpable proof of the absolute isolation of the Falkland Islands.

Darwin's description is only a half-truth. In the Falkland Islands the untouched landscape can be seen in all its splendour, the grandeur of the Southern Ocean, the majestic *King* and *Emperor* penguins, the charming *Magellan* and *Rockhopper* penguins, the attractive flight of the albatross and petrels, the docile *Upland Geese*[4]

---

[4] The most typical Falkland Islands bird.

An impressive "stone run" at Darwin

and the murmur of the wind and sea, all confirm the impression of entering a wonderful world ruled by mother nature.

Geographic Location

The Falkland Islands are an archipelago formed by some 420 islands, located in the South Atlantic between latitudes 51° and 53° south, and longitudes 57° and 62° west [5].

The Islands are situated on the Patagonian continental platform, approximately 200 miles from Staten Island, 250 miles northeast of Tierra del Fuego, 300 miles east of the Patagonian coast and 1,900 miles south of Buenos Aires.

The Islands have a surface area of approximately 4,700 square miles, extending 160 miles from east to west and 80 miles from north to south. Eighty percent of the surface area is distributed between East Falkland with 2500 square miles and West Falkland 1,750 square miles, separated by the Falkland Sound. Amongst the smaller islands, the most important are Weddel Island with 105 miles, Saunders Island with 47 miles, Pebble Island with 40 miles, Lively Island, Speedwell Island, Beaver Island, Keppel Island and Bleaker Island.

To have a clearer understanding of the comparative size of the Islands, useful points of reference are that they are somewhat smaller than Hawaii (6,200 square

---

[5] Destéfani, Laurio; *Historia Marítima Argentina*, Cúantica Editora, Buenos Aires, 1981, p.192 onwards.

miles), and larger than Jamaica (4,200 square miles), Cyprus (3,600 square miles) and Puerto Rico (3,500 square miles).

Geological Origin

The Islands owe their existence to sweeping movements of sedimentary rocks during the Paleozoic and Mesozoic periods.

These geological contortions formed the main mountain ranges on the Islands. The *Wickham Heights*, which follow a slightly curved line from East to West on the Northern half of East Falkland *(Isla Soledad)*, and include *Mount Usborne*, 2,310 feet, the highest point on the Islands. The heights of the peninsular Byron Heights, *Mount Adam* (Cerro Beaufort) and *Mount Robinson* to the north of the West Falkland (Gran Malvina) also run from east to west. Finally there is the *Hornby Range*, which includes the second highest peak and Mount Maria, almost 2,200 feet high.

The Islands are marked by successive periods of glacial activity, which, because of the maritime influence, was not as pronounced as in Patagonia.

The northern part of East Falkland is characterised by the harshness of its rock formations, which are crested with high peaks amongst which tumble the well known *"rock runs"*, described by Charles Darwin and whose origin is still unknown. The structure of the rocks in this region is of Paleozoic sedimentary origin, with deposits of quartz and granite. The southern part of East Falkland includes the great Lafonian Plains, located at an average of 100 feet above sea level, which, together with the neighbouring islands, are formed by more modern structures of the Mesozoic age.

By contrast the mountain ranges on West Falkland have smoother shapes and rounded peaks, the oldest of which appear to date from the Paleozoic period.

The existence of permanent glaciers on the Islands has not been proven, although it is likely that they did exist during the last glacial period approximately 30,000 years ago. Only 1,000 feet above sea level there are clear traces of ancient glaciers and ice fields. On Mounts Usborne, Adam, Robinson and María, remains, including lakes and lagoons of clearly glacial origin, can be found.

It is believed that the remarkable *"stone runs"*, the most unusual geological formations on the Islands, were formed during the post-glacial thaw when the Islands were apparently also affected by the movements of the earth's crust. These extraordinary accumulations of slabs or split rocks, ranging from 10 to 30 inches in diameter, and even larger in some cases, are spread over many kilometers, descending from the highest peaks to the valleys. The rocks are mainly white with some staining and were seemingly the remains of mountain peaks that crumbled under the force of nature. No explanation has been found for their formation. Recent theories indicate that they flowed together with melting ice and mud.

The main characteristics of the Islands' coast are the number of fjords and convolutions, the 100 feet high cliffs, especially on the western islands, and the beautiful beaches with their coarse, white sand. There are also many pebble beaches. The highest and most impressive

Macaroni penguin.

cliffs, in some cases over 300 feet high, can be found south of West Falkland, perhaps due to the effect of the permanently southeasterly winds and seas.

Innumerable small lakes, lagoons and streams are to be found all over the islands.

Soil[6]

A generous blanket of damp peat covers the surface of the Islands where the native grasses and shrubs grow. The few plains with good organic soil and the rocky peaks alternate the monotony of the superficial layer.

Peat bog, which covers almost 70% of the Islands, is intensely acid, affecting the quality of the grass. This type of soil is known locally as *"soft camp"*[7]. It is deep and moist soil with a pH that can vary from 3.3 in the coastal regions where the tussac grass grows, to 5 on the plains near the farms. Despite the abundance of nitrogen, little can be utilised naturally by the plants. The levels of potassium and magnesium are adequate for vegetal growth, but in most cases the soil is deficient in phosphorous and calcium. These soils almost exclusively produce what is called *white grass*. It could be described as undulating moorland.

There is a small percentage of what is known locally as *"hard camp"*[8], which are soils of mineral origin

---

[6] The Department of Agriculture, Falkland Islands Government, *Annual Report 1996-97*.
[7] Sp. "campo blando".
[8] Sp. "campo duro".

Flock of albatross flying over the sea.

derived from sands and granite. These are the only soils with agricultural potential. Lastly, there is ground with a high stone content that is useless for agricultural purposes or cattle raising.

Climate [9]

The Falkland Islands have a cold, windy and damp oceanic climate. The winds blow predominantly from the west and southwest, although it is not unusual to have winds blowing from the four points of the compass on the same day.

The Islands are situated on the northern limit of the depression, which is commonly located to the east of the Drake Passage. For this reason the islands suffer constant climatic changes, as the relatively hot air mass alternates with the fronts coming in from the south.

The climate is very similar to that encountered in the northern part of Staten Island and the southeastern part of Tierra del Fuego. As the Falklands are located several degrees to the north, its climate can be slightly milder.

There is not much climatic variation between winter and summer. In winter, of course, days are shorter and nights are longer and colder. During January and February the average temperature is 9°C, while in June and August it drops to 4°C. The constant wind is a characteristic of the Islands, except in the early morning

---

[9] Bernhardson, Wayne Bruce; *Land and Life in the Falkland Islands*, Dissertation, Graduate Division, University of California, Berkeley, 1989.

Description of the Islands

and at sunset when it is calm, and also during some sunny days in winter. The average wind speed is 16 knots. In spring it is not unusual to have winds blowing at speeds of over 40 knots. Fog is rare, nonetheless on West Falkland it is generally misty in the mountain ranges and on the coastal regions. Because of the influence of the nearby continental mass the western islands have a better climate, with more sunshine and less humidity. The northeast of West Falkland only receives 430mm of rain, while in Port Stanley, to the east of East Falkland, rainfall can reach 650mm annually. The difference in the hours of sunshine accentuates the climatic variation.

In the summer, the winds blow almost constantly from the west, at an average of 4 on the Beaufort scale. Calm days are limited to an average of one during the summer season and there are approximately five storms per month. Twenty percent of the time the waves are over 4 metres high.

In winter, the winds and currents calm down, but the number of stormy days increases.

Coming from the continent either by air or sea it is easy to spot the Islands from quite a distance as they are covered by a layer of clouds in contrast with the clear Patagonian skies, which continue out over the Atlantic until shortly before reaching the islands.

Snow is rare on the islands, and accumulations are exceptional. Only in the high regions does it remain after a snowfall.

Maritime Influence

The Islands are situated some 60 miles inside the eastern border of the Patagonian continental platform, which surrounds the archipelago.

This location generates a rich habitat for a great variety of fish species and sea mammals, which in turn are a source of nourishment for the numerous birds on the Islands.

The Antarctic current, the most powerful in the world, runs constantly from west to east around the Antarctic, with no continental mass to interrupt it. It only narrows and speeds up between the Antarctic Peninsula and Cape Horn. This in turn produces an alternate route towards the north known as the Falkland current. The average speed when it reaches the Islands is about 2 knots, which means it flows at a speed of almost 50 miles a day. The water takes less than a week to travel from the eastern limit of Staten Island to the extreme south of the Falkland Islands.

The archipelago, with its numerous islands and islets, forms a natural barrier for the current, which in addition to the tides creates a favourable environment for plant and animal life.

The algae or *kelp* surround the islands, the *tussac* grass surrounds the coast, and countless schools of *Argentine Illex* squid and *Martialia Hyadesi* are found in these waters. Southeast of the archipelago, near the edge of the continental platform, lies Beauchene, the last island, surrounded by a singularly rich environment for marine life, particularly the *Loligo Gahi*.

Petrel.

The whole of this area forms part of the Sub-Antarctic environment, with a colder Antarctic region to the south of the Islands. As a direct consequence of Antarctic thawing, the waters are less saline than those to the north and are richer in phosphorous and minerals as well as *plankton* and *krill*.

Water temperatures reach an average of 2°C in winter and 5°C in summer.

But undoubtedly the most remarkable characteristic of the marine life that surrounds the Islands is the *kelp*. These gigantic algae form flexible stems and grow in depths which may vary between 4 and 40 metres, and extend hundreds of metres from the coast, traditionally posing a threat to boats as they can get tangled up with propellers and rudders. They also mark the existence of submerged rocks and basins, which is why seamen always avoid them. there is The usually submerged *Tree Kelp* and the *Durvilea Antarctica* grow in the deeper waters. Sea lettuce *Ulva Sp* and goose weed can be found in the inland bays.

The algae calm the waters and create an ideal environment for marine species and the birds that feed off them.

The Terrestrial Habitat [10]

There is a variety of microclimates in the Falklands. The variations are caused by the influences of the

---

[10] The following are the most common species: Poa pratensis (Kentucky Blue Grass), Agrostis capillaris (brown top), Lolium perenne (ryegrass),

Gentoo penguin.

geographic conditions, the different geological formations of the various islands and the changing vegetation, which in turn is influenced by the natural fauna and sheep, cattle and horses introduced since the arrival of man. The latter is especially so in the larger islands. The smaller islands, where cattle have not been introduced, maintain their natural habitat. On the main islands intensive grazing by sheep has been the main cause of erosion and the destruction of the natural habitat over the past hundred and fifty years.

The soil on the main islands is generally cold and acid, a peat bog with low fertility. The characteristics of the peat bog can differ. It is more consistent and dry in the high areas and softer and muddier in the low regions. This is known on the Islands as *hard camp* and *soft camp*. In the higher regions there is no peat bog, but a mixture of stony ground and clay. In some valleys and coastal regions, probably due to years of natural fertilisation, peat bog has been replaced by fertile humus.

Soil with poor drainage is generally covered by *white grass*. A typical example of this would be the Lafonia plains in southern East Falkland. In areas with drier soil, shrub vegetation can be seen. *Diddle Dee, Mountain Berry and Brown Swamp* also grow there. The streams that

---

Phleum pratense (timothy), Festuca pratensis (meadow festue), Dactylis glomerata (cocksfoot), Ulex europea (gorse), Cytisus europea (broom), Lupinus eurpaus (lupins), Parodiochloa flabellata (tussac grass), Oxalis enneaphylla (scurvy grass), Empetrum rubrum (diddle dee), Myrteola nummularia (teaberry), Gunnera magellánica (pig wine), Chiliotrichum diffusum (fachine), Taraxacum officinali (dandelion), Cordaria pilosa (whitegrass), Juncus scheuzerioides (native rush), Calandrinia feltonii (feltons flower) Picea jezonensis (jeno spruce), Nothogagus spp (southern beech), Cupressus macrocarpa (Ciprés de Monterrey).

Description of the Islands

flow into the sea are usually bordered with *Juncus scheuzeroides*, which creates a better habitat for the local fauna, birds particularly, than the windy plains. The *Upland Goose* is possibly the most typical of all Falkland Islands birds.

The *tussac grass* was, until the introduction of cattle, the main indigenous plant for the habitat of the local fauna. It is still found today on the coast where there are greater concentrations of wild birds, especially penguins.

There are almost 300 smaller islands where tussac grass is still plentiful. These plants can reach a height of two metres, offering protection from the cold and wind and where many birds build their nests.

The farms have created small, protected microclimates thanks to the planting of windbreakers made of *Ulex europeus* and *Cupressus macrocarpa* species. The *Boxwood* species, a native shrub, is also used successfully for the same purpose. This slow growing plant can reach a height of 3 metres.

There are no native trees on the Islands and those planted on farms, especially cypress trees, have grown with great difficulty. The lack of sun and adequate soil and the constant wind and saline environment all conspire against healthy tree growth.

It is difficult to determine precisely the variety of fauna on the Islands before the arrival of Bougainville in 1764.

The only mammal which existed on the islands, the

Upland Goose grazing in Stanley.

Description of the Islands

Warrah, or Island fox (*Dusicyon antarticus*) became extinct last century. It was probably not a native species, and although it could have been introduced from the Magellan region, it is still not certain how. Curiously it was only found on the two main islands. It is a species very similar to the dogs of the Yaghan indians *(Duicyon culpaelus)*. These Indians travelled in canoes through the Fuegian channels and it is possible that they landed on the Falkland Islands as a consequence of the storms and currents. However, no evidence or remains have been found. The Falklands current takes only 7 days from Le Maire strait to the island. It is known that the Yaghan indians used to cross the strait from Tierra del Fuego to Staten Island.

South Georgia [11]

The island of South Georgia was for many years, considered a dependency of the Falkland Islands by both Argentines and Britons. Hence its inclusion in this work.

South Georgia is an isolated island, surrounded by some islets, located in the extreme south of the Atlantic Ocean, some 850 miles northeast of the Antarctic Peninsula, 1,050 miles east of Staten Island and 2,700

---

[11] Headland, Robert; *The Island of South Georgia*, Cambridge University Press, Cambridge, 1992.
  Brown, Nan; *Antartic Housewife*, Hutchinson, Victoria, Australia, 1971.
  Poncet, Sally; *Destination South Georgia*, Simon & Schuster, New York, 1995.
  Sewall Pettingill Jr, Olin; *Another Penguin Summer*, Charles Scribner & Sons, New York, 1975.

miles southeast of the Cape of Good Hope. It is located at latitude 53°56' South and between longitude 34°45' and 38°15' West. Its half moon shape extends from northeast to southeast along 100 miles with a width that varies between 2 and 20 miles. It extends over a total surface area of 1,500 square miles. South Georgia has been described as the *"Alps of the South Atlantic"*, as the entire island is nothing but a chain of mountains which protrudes from the bottom of the sea with only the peaks of the mountains visible above the water. In fact, it looks much more like the southern Chilean Andes than the Alps, and effectively they are part of the submarine mountain range that joins the Antarctic Peninsula with the southern Andes. The South Sandwich and South Orkney Islands are part of this same geological range.

The most noticeable of the smaller islands are Bird Island and Willis Island to the northeast, and the Annenkov, Pickergill, and Cooper Islands further south. South Georgia also includes the Black Rocks 140 miles in the direction of the Falkland Islands and the Clerke Rocks 40 miles southeast.

The highest peak is *Mount Paget*, nearly 9,000 feet in height. Other important mounts are the *Nordenskjold Peak* (7,000 feet), *Mount Carse* (6,900 feet), *Sugar Loaf Mount* 6,800 feet (2200m). These tall mountains are located almost in the centre of the island, creating a natural barrier against the strong and steady freezing winds, which assail the island from the southeast. It is thus how the western coasts are much more inhospitable that the eastern ones. Fjords, glaciers, cliffs and strong waves characterise the western coasts. To the east, on the other hand, the coasts are relatively more tranquil, there are less glaciers, and good harbours can be found.

Emperor penguin colony.

There are only two plains of some importance on the island. One of them is in the Cumberland Bay and the other in the *Bahia de las Islas*. The island has only two rivers worth mentioning. These are the Penguin River and the *Río de la Esperanza*. The permanent snow begins at only 600 feet above sea level on the western coast and 1,200 feet above sea level on the eastern coast. The island also has a dozen lakes.

The climate in winter is damp, windy and extremely cold. But during the short summer season, the sun shines quite regularly. Captain James Cook, in his description of the island, when he took possession of it, considered that it was the most desolate of all those previously discovered.[12]

Trees do not grow on the South Georgias. The lower lands and the coastal region, especially on the eastern side and in the two plains mentioned above, have abundant vegetation, mainly grass and lichen. The most common being the *tussac* (Parodiochlia flabellata) and the *festuca austral*, (Festuca contracta). Other varieties include the *Acaena magellanica*, the *Ranunculus biternatus*, the *Colobanthus quitensis*, the *Cystopteris fragilis*, the *Ophioglosum crotalophorides*, and the *Cladonia rangiferina*.

Animal life is limited to seals, sea lions and birds, including various species of penguins. Over thirty bird

---

[12] "The wild rocks raised their lofty summits till they were lost in the clouds and the valleys laid buried in everlasting snow. Not a tree or shrub was to be seen, no not even big enough to make a toothpick. I landed in three different places and took possession of the country in his Majesty's name under a discharge of small arms..." quoted by Richard Hough in *Captain James Cook*, Hodder & Stoughton, London, 1994.

Description of the Islands

species inhabit the islands. There are even two species exclusive to the Georgias. They are the "Pipi of the Georgias" *(Anthus antarticus)* and the South Georgia Duck (*Anas georgica*). Seagulls, sea petrels (*Oceanites oceanicus*), snow petrels (P*agodroma nivea*), giant petrels (M*acronectes giganteus*), ducks, cormorants, albatross, (*Diomedea exulans*) and penguins, all can be found here. Amongst the penguin species, there are large colonies of King (*Aptenodytes patagonicus*) and Macaroni Penguins (*Endyptues chrysolophus*). On the rocky coasts, particularly if they are covered in tussac, sea lions (*Mirounga leonina*) and sea elephants *(Arctocephalus gazella)* can be found along with Weddel seals (L*eptonychotes weddelli*).

Herds of deer, (particularly the *Rangifer tarandus*), can be found grazing on the islands, as well as horses, wild pigs, mice and rats. However all these animals have been introduced by man and are not native species.

The South Sandwich Islands

These are considered by both Argentines and Britons as falling within South Georgia's jurisdiction. They are included in the sovereignty dispute between the United Kingdom and the Argentine Republic, which is why these lines are dedicated to them.

The South Sandwich Islands are the most easterly of the Sub-Antarctic islands. There are eleven main islands accompanied by islets and minor rocks, located approximately at 56°14' Latitude South and 27°35'

Longitude West. They are located 1,300 miles southeast of Staten Island, 900 miles southeast of the Falkland Islands, 500km southeast of South Georgia, and 2,000 miles from the Cape of Good Hope.[13]

The Sandwich Islands are within the scope of the Antarctic convergence, the climate is very cold, and during most of the year they are surrounded by ice. Fog, mist and snow are almost continuous.

These islands emerge abruptly as spiky volcanic cones from the seabed that is between 6,000 to 9,000 feet deep. Only 70 miles away there are trenches on the seabed down to a depth of 21,000 feet. The South Sandwich Islands are volcanic in nature, and one of them, the Zavodoski, has permanent volcanic activity.

Vegetation is reduced to moss and lichens in the more protected regions, which are precisely those chosen by penguins to settle down and where they are fertilised by the same guano of the birds. As well as penguins, seals, sea lions and sea elephants, bird species such as albatross, petrels and seagulls can be found inhabiting the southern seas.

---

[13] Destéfani, Laurio H.: *Historia Marítima Argentina*, Cúantica Editora SA, Buenos Aires, 1982, Volume I, p. 214 onwards.

II

HISTORICAL BACKGROUND

The Discovery. Different versions

Uninhabited Islands

It is not certain how, and when, and by whom, the Falkland Islands were discovered. What is certain is that they were the last territories of the American continent of any size to be discovered and inhabited by man.

Most scientists agree that the American continent was the last to be inhabited. The origins of the indigenous settlements go back to the migrations across the Bering Straits from Asia approximately 25,000 years ago. During the last glacial period the low level of the oceans allowed the crossing of the first immigrants on a natural bridge of land and ice. It is likely that some small groups crossed during the previous glaciations some 40,000 years ago. Lastly, it is believed that almost 2000 years ago, groups of Polynesians arrived by boat on the western coast of the continent. Perhaps 1000 years ago Viking groups did the same in Greenland and the extreme northwest of North America.

This indigenous population was scattered all over the continent and islands from Alaska to Tierra del Fuego.

The Europeans who arrived on the American continent after the discovery made by Columbus on 12 October 1492, found only the Galapagos Islands in the Pacific (today a part of the Republic of Ecuador) and the Falkland Islands in the South Atlantic, uninhabited.

On the Falkland Islands –which were partially and temporarily united with the American continent during the last ice age– the European explorers did not find any signs of either human occupation or Patagonian mammals. Only the Falklands Fox (now extinct) –a close relative of the Fuegian Fox– established some connection (terrestrial, ice or vessels) with the continent.

Diverse theories –none of which have been proven– have attempted to explain the arrival of this fox, the Wanah, to the islands because their isolated and independent evolution is highly unlikely. The predominating winds and currents make it quite possible that the ancestors of the Falklands Fox could have come from Tierra del Fuego or Staten Island during the last glaciations on drifting ice blocks or on lost indigenous vessels.

It is also possible that indigenous groups could have arrived in the Islands in their canoes and were not able to survive. This is highly probable because the currents from the Le Maire Straits lead directly to the Falkland Islands and the natives of the Feugian channels were accustomed to navigation in canoes in those latitudes. With favourable winds and currents, a lost canoe in the Le Maire Straits would only take a week to arrive at the Falklands. Notwithstanding the fact that there are no archeological remains, it is a field that needs further investigation.

Typical Falklands ducks.

Discovery

The Spanish and Portuguese were the first Europeans who set out to discover the world. The almost simultaneous discovery of America and the Cape Good Hope obliged both countries to reach an agreement about how the newly discovered lands and those yet to be discovered should be divided between them.

That was why, at the request of the Crown of Castilla, Pope Alexander VI (at a time when all of Europe was Catholic) by means of the *Bula Inter Caetera* in 1493, granted Spain all the lands located west of an imaginary line drawn 100 leagues west of the Azores, and Portugal all those to the east. The same Papal Bull prevented other nations access to those lands without the prior consent of the favoured countries.

In those days, the Pope not only had religious authority, but also temporal authority in areas of international law amongst the Christian nations of Europe. Throughout the Middle Ages, the Pope's temporal authority replaced the former Roman Imperial authority.

Because of the difficulty in drawing a line and due to pressure from Portugal, who considered the limit to be too near the African coast –or perhaps because they expected (as it later transpired) to occupy a part of the new continent, the Treaty of Tordesillas was signed on 7 June 1794. The new agreement established a new line 370 leagues west of the Cape Verde Islands.

This Papal ruling, following the discovery of America

A gaucho corral.

by the Crown of Castilla, and the access to the Indian Ocean by Portugal was in principle accepted by the Christian kingdoms of Europe.

Nevertheless, a few years later, François I –King of France– opposed the legitimacy of the Papal ruling. In 1515, he openly encouraged French expeditions to explore the new continent. England, on the other hand, while under the rule of Henry VII did not question it. Only after Queen Elizabeth I, who advocated the principle of *mare apertum**, came to power, did they begin, timidly at first and more aggressively later –to challenge the Spanish rule over the Americas. Nevertheless in 1616, John Seldon –secretary of the King of England– proclaimed the theory of *mare claussum*.

Religious reforms, the religious independence of Northern Europe, the rejection of Papal authority, and the defeat of Phillip II's Invincible Navy in English waters in 1588, all contributed to ending the Iberian monopoly of the new world.

However, the Spanish possessions to the south of the equator were recognised by all the European powers until the middle of the 18th century.

It is not clear who were the first to discover the Falkland Islands. From a juridical point of view however, this issue is not essential, as only a sighting or discovery, without occupation and formal acts of possession, were insufficient to acquire sovereignty over a territory. This issue has always been a part of the Argentine-British dispute over the sovereignty of the Islands.[14]

(*) Open seas, freedom of the seas.
[14] Dolzer, Rudolf; *The territorial status of the Falkland Islands*, Oceana Publications Inc., 1992, New York, p. 23.

Historical background...

Both Great Britain and Spain upheld that the mere discovery was insufficient and that to claim sovereignty required effective occupation. Great Britain maintained this argument during a dispute in 1561 with Portugal over Guinea. Spain, on the other hand, in a dispute with Portugal over the Mollucas Islands, sustained the theory that acquisition of a territory required its effective occupation.[15]

The maps and nautical charts of the 16th and 17th century were not sufficiently accurate to indicate with any precision where the Islands had been sighted in unknown seas. Nautical technology and the lack of points of reference made many navigators' mentions of the Islands vague and imprecise, which in the end made it impossible to know who had discovered them. The longitude was especially difficult to calculate, because of the lack of chronometers, and could only be estimated. This often led to ships being wrecked.

There is no doubt that those who travelled the South Atlantic in the 16th century were mostly Spanish. Américo Vespucio, considered by some to have made the first sighting during his famous voyage in 1501-2, does not appear to have navigated that far south. If Hernando de Magallanes discovered them during his circumnavigation in 1515-16 we will never know, as no mention of the Islands appears in his notes. Esteban Gomez, a deserter from Magallanes' expedition, could have passed close by, but again his notes make no mention of a sighting.

---

[15] In 1982 a representative of the British Foreign Office expressed his opinion before the committee of the House of Commons, that the facts relating to the discovery were not clear. Foreign Office Memorandum, House of Commons Foreign Affairs Committee, Section 1982-83, Falkland Islands, Minutes of Evidence, 17-1-83.

It is more than likely that the Islands were sighted by Spanish navigators, especially those who were unable to make the passage around Cape Horn, as the winds and currents of the Le Maire Strait would have pushed their ships in their direction. The Islands can also be seen from a great distance, not only because of their 700m mountains, but also because of the bank of clouds that almost permanently cover them, calling the attention of all those travelling from the windy clear skies of the Patagonian coast.

The first maps to show details of islands in these latitudes were the charts of Diego de Rivero dating from 1527 and 1528, which show some islands named *"Sansón"* or *"de los Patos"*[16], but which correspond to the location of the Falklands. Another sighting could have been described by one of the ships of the Camargo expedition under the command of Fray Francisco de Ribera which makes mention of islands at a similar latitude and longitude to the Falkland Islands.[17]

Only by the end of the 16th century, did British vessels begin to travel to the region. A ship under the command of John Davis, which had deserted from an expedition led by Sir Thomas Cavendish, sighted islands close to the location of the Falklands in August 1592. As there are no other islands in the area, it is probable that these were the Falklands. In 1594 another Englishman, Richard Hawkins, also sighted islands in this area.

It is more than likely, given the difficulties in crossing

---

[16] *Duck Islands*, perhaps in reference to the Upland Goose, so numerous on the islands.
[17] Destéfani, Laurio; *Las Malvinas en la época hispana*, Corregidor, 1981, Buenos Aires, p. 56.

Herd of criollo *horses grazing in the Falklands.*

the Pacific, the rough seas around Cape Horn and the constant and powerful southwest winds, that many of the numerous deserting ships –from either Spanish or British expeditions– had sighted the Islands on their return journeys to Europe. But none of them either occupied the Islands or took possession of them. In reality no exact descriptions exist, although seafarers of the time appear to have known of the existence of some islands to the northwest of Staten Island in a location that clearly coincides with that of the Falkland Islands. It is well known that in those times it was common to conceal the existence of islands to avoid them being used by enemy powers or even by other ships flying the same flag.

On 24 January 1600, the Dutch vessel *"Geloof"*, commanded by Sebalt de Weert, a member of the ill-fated expedition of Admiral Jacob Mahu, discovered three islands at a latitude of 50° 40' and named them the *Sebaldinas*. From then onwards the Islands regularly appeared on nautical charts of the South Atlantic.[18]

It would seem that only a few expeditions put in to the Falklands during the 17th century. Amongst the most notable was the Dutch flotilla of Isaac Le Maffe and Wilhem Shouten who passed through the Islands in 1616. A ship from John Cook's expedition, under the command of Ambrose Cowley, put in to the Islands in January 1684. In 1690, during a period when Spain and Great Britain were allies, Captain John Strong's ship *"Welfare"*, stopped at the Islands and for the first time gave the name Falkland (apparently in honour of Viscount Falkland) to the channel that separates the two main islands, which he named

---

[18] Destéfani, Laurio, ibid., p. 59.

Historical background...

Hawkins Land. Up to that time the Islands had been known as the *"Sebaldinas"*.

The 18th century is characterised by the advance of French mariners in the waters of the South Atlantic. In February 1701, the ship *"Phllypeaux"*, under the command of Captain Jacques de Beauchesne Gou'm, from Saint Maló, after an eventful journey around Cape Horn, discovered the small island of Beauchene in the south of the archipelago, and also explored the main islands. Beauchesne's reports reached the St Maló company, which organised a series of expeditions to the South Atlantic. In 1704 Lepine's expedition of four ships discovered the Sea Lion Island in the south of the archipelago and also stopped to re-provision there. There were other expeditions by St Maló mariners in 1706 and 1708.

The absence of information about the region, led some French and Dutch seamen to believe that they had discovered new islands which they called respectively the *Isles Nouvelles* and the *Belgis Australis.*[19]

The 17th century had been characterised by the aggressive advance of Portuguese *bandeirantes*[19bis] towards the west of Brazil beyond the Tordesillas line. The most troubled situation was that of the River Plate with the foundation of Colonia de Sacramento on the *Banda Oriental*[19tris] of the river in 1680. After an attack from Buenos Aires, the Treaty of Lisbon was signed in 1681 between Spain and Portugal by which Colonia was returned and the border situation was regularised.

---

[19] Destéfani, Laurio, ibid., p. 67.
[19bis] Brazilian slave traders.
[19tris] Eastern Shore -now known as Uruguay.

The weakness of the last Kings of the Austrian Empire, exacerbated the Spanish decline at the end of the century. The death of Charles II "the Bewitched", extinguished the House of Austria, and began the long Spanish War of Succession which caused from 1700 to 1713. The Bourbons victory and the Treaty of Utrecht put an end to the war and Felipe V assumed the Spanish crown. However, great concessions were made to England including the ceding of Gibraltar and rights over the slave trade in Hispanic America. The arrival of slaves in the River Plate was a consequence of the Treaty and represented the beginnings of British commercial activities in the River Plate, both legitimate and illegitimate.

England and Spain fought successive wars in 1719 and 1739. During the latter, Richard Walter, a member of the expedition commanded by George Anson, recommended that Britain should set up a base to protect navigation in the South Atlantic. In the meantime, due to the Treaty of Utrecht, all journeys from St Maló to the Falklands had been suspended. The treaty had resolved to acknowledge the *status quo* of all Spanish dominions in America as they existed prior to the War of Succession.[20] It was the same treaty that required Spain to cede the Rock of Gibraltar to England.

In 1749 Spain opposed British preparations to establish a base in the Falklands. England desisted temporarily.

---

[20] The correspondence between B. Keene, British Ambassador to Spain, and the Duke of Bedford can be found in the *Collection of Documents Relating to the History of the Falkland Islands*, Introduction by Ricardo Caillet Bois, University of Buenos Aires, 1957, volume I, pp. 16-21.

Historical background...

The Portuguese advance in the River Plate continued. The Treaty of 1750 ceded the eastern Jesuit Missions to Brazil and returned Colonia.

The First Settlers.
France, Great Britain and Spain.
The Founding of Fort San Louis.

The 1763 Treaty of Paris, which put to an end to the 7 Year War, required Spain to cede Florida and other North American territories to Great Britain. However, the *status quo* of the other territories remained unchanged. The same treaty obliged France to withdraw from Louisiana, leaving North America in British hands. On the other hand, the familial pact of 1761 between the Bourbons of France and those of Spain, partially allowed the Spanish colonies to trade with the other powers and permitted visits by its ships.

Louis Bougainville, who was forced to leave French Canada, made his first journey –with the support of the French Crown– with the objective of occupying the previously uninhabited Falklands. Thus, in 1764, with various members of the St Maló crew, and the ships *"L'Aigle"* and *"Le Sphinx"*, making a stop to re-provision in Montevideo, disembarked in the Islands which they called *Les Malouines* and founded the small Fort Saint Louis on East Falkland.

It is noteworthy that at the time there was no Spanish population either in the Falklands, Southern Patagonia, the Magellan Straits or Tierra del Fuego. It is true though, that all european powers recognijeo those lands as part of the Spanish Empire. The southern lands of the continent had been inhabited by wild indians who lived by hunting and fishing. In the Falklands there had been no previous settlement. The feeling of solitude must have been overwhelming among the first settlers.

On 5 April 1764, Captain Louis Antoine de Bougainville, took formal possession of the Falklands in the name of the French King Louis XV and established the first settlement on the Islands at Fort Saint Louis. He named his cousin Bougainville de Neville Governor over a total population of 27 French settlers, including 5 women and 3 children.

The families came from the Canadian Atlantic coast, which had been left in British hands. This was precisely the reason for the emigration to Canada in the first place: they had no desire to live under a British flag.

The French government issued a public declaration formally announcing the occupation of the Islands in the name of France.[21] The following year the population had grown to 80, crops had been planted and the rearing of horses and cattle had begun. Although the crops failed, the cattle and horses were raised successfully. By the next year the population had grown to 136.[22]

The decision to establish the Port of Saint Louis on the most important bay to the northeast of East Falkland had been essential given the predominantly southwesterly winds. It was considered the location with the best climate

---

[21] Dolzer, Rudolf, ibid., p. 26.
[22] Destéfani, Laurio, *Las Malvinas en la época hispana*, Corregidor, 1981, Buenos Aires, p. 94.

Historical background...

and calmest waters. It was the northest port on the western coast. The bay is some 15km wide and is surrounded by low hills, which protect its islands and islets from the wind.

It was undoubtedly a good choice, being one of the most welcoming places on the Islands with abundant fresh water, good grazing and easy access.

In February Bougainville sent *"L'Aigle"* to the Magellan Straits in search of firewood and saplings for planting. The ship encountered the British expedition led by Commander John Byron who had already travelled the region with Anson's flotilla (1740-44).

In April 1764 Louis Bougainville, after having established the fort and leaving 79 people in the colony, returned to St. Maló and, during the austral winter, prepared his return with reinforcements and provisions. In January 1765 he returned to Port St Louis and found a colony making progress but not without some problems. Particularly the absence of trees and firewood, the constant winds, the damp and cold of winter, the difficulties in growing vegetables, the ungerminated wheat and the few existing heads of cattle had roamed all over the island. The settlers also claimed the need for a small boat to travel among the different islands and islets.

Apparently no further contact was made with the British expedition. The winter of 1765 was very hard for the settlers.

When in February 1766 the ships "L'Aigle" and "L'Etoile" returned they found that the settlers had run out of provisions and were surviving on hunting and fishing. After finding more wood and trees on the Magellan Straits and increasing the population to 136, they returned to France.

Port Egmont

On 15 January 1765, almost a year after the French settlement, the English Commander John Byron, in the *"Dolphin"* and with the support of the *"Tamar"*, arrived in the Falklans after a stop in the Magellan Straits. Although it is likely that the expedition had been planned some considerable time beforehand, according to the report left by the Anson expedition, the truth is that the founding of Port St. Louis by the French probably hastened their plans.

After travelling along the western coast of the Islands he discovered a natural harbour northwest of West Falkland, between Saunders and Keppel Islands, which he called Port Egmont. On 23 January the Commander and his officers disembarked on Saunders Islands, raised the British flag and took possession of the Falkland Islands in the name of King George III of England. Later Admiral Byron continued his travels around the world through the Pacific.

In February 1766, Commander John Mac Bride on board the frigate *"Jason"* and supported by the *"Carcass"* and the *"Experiment"*, founded Fort Egmont.

In the meantime the French colony of Port St. Louis had built a small sloop, called *"La Croisade"*, with which

Historical background...

they travelled and explored different islands and rediscovered the natural harbour which had been named Port Egmont by the English.

The British government, by now aware of Byron taking possession of the Islands and of the advantages of the natural harbour, and also of the existence of the French settlement, ordered Captain John Mac Bride to found a permanent settlement. Thus Mac Bride, in the *"Jason"*, *"Carcass"* and *"Experiment"* arrived at the *Sebaldes Islands* -which he named Jason- in 1766.

This was the only period (1766-70) of the history of the Falklands when the western and eastern islands fell under the control of two different authorities. With the exception of those years, the Islands have always been a single political unit, albeit under successive and different authority, French, Spanish, Argentine and finally British. In every document, every piece of correspondence and every exchange of letters between the various controlling powers, the archipelago has always been referred to as the *Malouines, Malvinas or Falkland Islands*.[23]

Mac Bride's arrival was not a matter of chance. For more than two decades British colonial policy had had its eye on the Falklands. From a strategic standpoint, the Islands were considered especially important in view of the existing dispute with Spain over freedom of navigation in the Pacific and the Caribbean.

Already in 1748, the expedition led by Admiral Anson had explored the Patagonian coast in search of a suitable base. Given that the Portuguese, who were traditional

---
[23] Dolzer, Rudolf, ibid., p. 35.

allies of the British, did not support their expansionist policy in these waters, such a base was doubly important. Anson believed that the acquisition of the Falklands would be beneficial for British development in the Pacific.[24]

The proximity of the Islands to Cape Horn made them a key strategic point for British plans, similar to Gibraltar's importance, from 1713, in controlling access to the Mediterranean and Cape Town's comparable role with regard to the Indian Ocean, as well as Hong Kong and Singapur on the China's seas.

The British Crown rapidly accepted Anson's proposal to colonise the Islands. The good relations that formally existed in those days with Spain led them to consult with Madrid, but the roundly negative response they received resulted in Great Britain proceeding independently with her plans.[25]

This period of Anglo-Spanish friendship ended in 1762 when Spain joined France in the 7 Year War (1756-63). After the Treaty of Paris (1763), France was left out of the American continent and the relations between a declining Spanish empire and an increasingly powerful British empire deteriorated.

In 1765 Lord Egmont said, *"This station (the Falkland Islands) is certainly the key to the whole of the Pacific Ocean. These Islands dominate all the trade through the ports of Chile, Perú, Panama and Acapulco; in short, all the Spanish trade from the Pacific ports."*[26]

---

[24] Walter, William, *Voyage around the world*. London 1748-1753, p. 153.
[25] J. Goebbel, *The Struggle for the Falkland Islands*, 1927, p. 198.
[26] W. Down, *The Occupation of the Falkland Islands and the Question of Sovereignty*, 1927, p. 239.

Historical background...

The British and French settlements had not been in contact. So much so that a report from London dated 17 March 1766, informed Mac Bride, for the first time, of the presence of a French settlement on the eastern island. This led Mac Bride to mount further expeditions. Thus the *"Jason"* arrived at Fort St. Louis. After the initial surprise and with no exchange of gunfire, the French and British Commanders met, both ratified the rights of their respective Kings and, after inviting the French officials on board the *"Jason"*, he withdrew from the port that day and left the area the following day. The fact that Mac Bride had only 25 settlers in Port Egmont and the absence of a warship in Port Louis avoided a confrontation.

The Spanish Ambassador in Paris, Conde de Fuentes, who was informed of the events, protested before the French government, maintaining that the Islands, despite being uninhabited, belonged to Spain, being an integral part of the Spanish possessions in South America, due to their proximity to the continent.

Under pressure from the French government to negotiate with the Spanish, Bougainville travelled to Spain in April 1766 and claimed an indemnity for his expenses in establishing Port Louis, which the government of Madrid accepted.

Simultaneously, in May 1766, France notified Great Britain of the transfer of the settlement to Spain. Compensation of *"616,108 libras tornesas, 18 sueldos and 11 dineros"*[27] was agreed, paid partly in Paris and partly in Buenos Aires.

---

[27] Destéfani, Laurio, Ibid, p. 101.

In September 1776, Great Britain was notified that the cession would take place in accordance with the terms of the Treaty of Utrecht. Formally, on 4 October, France ceded all its rights over the Islands to the Spanish Crown. The British government did not react formally. After the transfer of Fort St. Louis, Madrid concentrated its efforts on the British settlement. For three years correspondence was exchanged between the two governments without any advance being made.

The French and British settlements cohabited peacefully despite not acknowledging each other's rights.

On 4 October that same year, Felipe Ruiz Puente was named Governor of the Falkland Islands under the dependency of the Government of Buenos Aires. After a meeting in Buenos Aires with Governor Francisco de Paula Bucarelli, Ruiz Puente sailed via Montevideo on 21 March with the ships *"Liebre"* and *"Esmeralda"*.

After the French-Spanish agreement to restitute the Islands to Spain was formerly accepted, Captain Felipe Ruiz Puente was named Governor of the Falkland Islands, under the dependency of the Government of Buenos Aires.

In January 1767, Bougainville and Ruiz Puente met in Montevideo, from where they travelled to Buenos Aires to see the Governor, Francisco de Paula Bucarelli. Not only did Ruiz Puente depend on Bucarelli, but also some of his troops were recruited in Buenos Aires. There was also part of the indemnity to be paid to Bougainville in Buenos Aires.

On 25 March 1767, the Spanish expedition, with a

Historical background...

total of 62 people and 100 head of cattle, disembarked in Port St. Louis. Ruiz Puente would stay on in the Falkland Islands until 1773. On 1 April Bougainville withdrew together with 94 Frenchmen, leaving Ruiz Puente as Governor of the colony from 2 April 1767. There were 37 people left from Bougainville's colony, which with the newly arrived settlers amounted to 118. Those who departed had given up after three tough years, where the cold, damp, winds, lack of sun and the impossibility of growing cereals or trees had discouraged them completely. The Fort and the Governor's house were made out of stone, the remaining thirty houses only of mud and straw, like the typical *"ranchos" of the Pampas.*

This was the most southern settlement of the River Plate, and of the entire Spanish Empire and also the most southerly in the whole world. There were no settlements either in southern Patagonia or in Tierra del Fuego. The native Indians in the region –*Alacoofs*, *Onas* and *Patagones*– were nomads with no established villages.

On 25 January 1768, the frigates *"Aguila"* and *"Liebre"* arrived at Fort St. Louis with a statue of Nuestra Señora de la Soledad*, sent by Governor Bucarelli, to become the Patron Saint of the settlement. The port was therefore christened Nuestra Señora de la Soledad.

In the meantime, the British presence continued in Port Egmont.

The European situation in those times was

(*) Our Lady of Solitudes.

complicated. Great Britain, under the rule of George III, had consolidated its position as the strongest naval power. Its fleet was double the size of those of Spain and France together. Russia, under the reign of Catherine II, was becoming the leading power of Central Europe. The incipient industrial revolution was leaving Spain behind, and the difficulties in defending its empire in the Americas were increasing year after year.

Carlos III, with the aim of strengthening his power in the Americas, expelled the Jesuits in 1767, this led to the weakening of the borders between the River Plate and Brazil.

The winter of 1767 was a particularly difficult time for the Spaniards in Port St. Louis, who were left almost without provisions and no ship of any size. Only two schooners and a small sloop, which could only be used to navigate the surrounding islands. Nevertheless, the first chapel on the Islands was built. In January 1768, the frigates *"Aguila"* and *"Liebre"* arrived with supplies from Buenos Aires. During that summer and the next, further exploration of the islands was carried out, although it was impossible for them to explore the Magellan Straits and Tierra del Fuego. The ships sent from Buenos Aires had to return to the River Plate without having fulfilled their mission.

In the meantime in Europe, Spain had filed complaints to the British government demanding their withdrawal from Port Egmont. The British refused unless the ransom for Manila was paid to them first. The ransom, which had nothing to do with the Falklands, originated from the price agreed between Spain and Great Britain to avoid the pillage by British

Historical background...

sailors of the capital of the Philippines. Spain had refused to pay this sum, arguing that Manila had been pillaged anyway.

The British colonies of Fort George and Port Egmont were visited regularly by British ships and received supplies of wood from the Magellan Straits. Similar to the situation in the Spanish colony, their crops had failed, fut the cattle did not reproduce. They hunted geese and ducks, and the native fox. The foxes soon disappeared from the area.

On 28 November 1769, the first encounter took place between the Spaniards and the British, when the Spanish boat *"San Felipe"* and the British frigate *"Tamar"* met in the San Carlos Strait. The British warned that reinforcements would soon be sent and to withdraw their settlement. Governor Ruiz Puente sent the boat back with the message that it was the British who should withdraw as they were in Spanish waters. It was only on 16 December that *"San Felipe"* discovered the British settlement.

It is not surprising how long it took them to discover the British colony. Not only are the islands irregular, but Port Egmont was not on any of the two main islands, but on a smaller island northeast of the archipelago.

In February 1770, a Spanish three-ship flotilla sent from Buenos Aires with the mission of evacuating the British from the Islands arrived at Port Egmont. The Spanish Captain protested the British presence and demanded that they withdraw from the domains of King Charles III of Spain. On their part, the British replied that the Islands had been discovered by and belonged to His Majesty the King's government.

In April, the ships stopped in Port Louis without having tried to evacuate the British colony by force. Up to that moment both parties had issued only formal protests.

Finally on 9 June 1770, a Spanish fleet commanded by Captain Juan Ignacio de Madariaga, sent from Buenos Aires by Governor Bucarelli, demanded they hand over the port. The British, after a few skirmishes but without any casualties, surrendered to the Spanish forces. The following day the surrender was signed and the Spanish allowed the British to withdraw honourably. The Spanish then re-named the port *Puerto de la Trinidad* and left a small garrison of 26 men.

The Anglo-Spanish Agreement

In September 1770 Spain notified France of the expulsion of the British and informed Britain that Governor Bucarelli of Buenos Aires was solely responsible for the decision of occupying Port Egmont.

Arduous negotiations between the three countries began, with the advantage that they all wished to avoid war these far away islands. King George III of England only requested that Bucarelli be disenfranchised. In November 1770, Lord North informed the Spanish envoy in London that the King did not wish to hold on to the Islands, but insisted on a reparation of British honour affected by Captain Madariaga's actions.[28] The Spanish

---

[28] Goebels, Julius, Ibid, p. 346.

Historical background...

also sought apologies for the British ultimatum in February 1770 to withdraw from Port St. Louis.

Though no formal treaty was signed, after five months of negotiations an agreement was reached on 22 January 1771. Spain issued a formal declaration in July 1770, which disavowed the use of force, voluntarily undertook to re-establish the *status quo* and explicitly reserved Spanish rights over the Islands. For their part, the British declared that they considered the Spanish declaration sufficient redress and omitted any reference to Spain's reservation of its rights.

The Spaniards accepted the redress and returned to the *status quo ante*, because according to the international law in force at the time, the expulsion of the British in peacetime and without diplomatic negotiations was not lawful. Thus Port Egmont was returned to the English in a formal ceremony on 15 September 1771.

In the British Parliament there was strong criticism of the government because the opposition believed that British rights had not been safeguarded in the agreement. Interestingly, the exchange of declarations made no reference to Port St. Louis, neither did it mention English sovereign rights. It only made reference to the offence suffered by His Majesty.

Simultaneously with the exchange of declarations, there also existed a complimentary agreement, which assured the English withdrawal once a Spanish apology was forthcoming. The existence of this secret agreement has not been proven, however nearly three years later, on 11 June 1774, the British government informed the

Court in Madrid of its intention to abandon the Islands citing economics as the reason for the decision.

These three years were not easy for the Spanish colony. In 1771 the lack of fresh food resulted in an epidemic of scurvy which affected almost half the population. Governor Ruiz Puente, dispirited by the climate and the lack of natural resources, repeatedly asked to be relieved of his post.

In January 1773, he was replaced by Captain Domingo de Chauri from the garrison in Buenos Aires. In January 1774 Chauri returned to Buenos Aires and was in turn replaced by Captain Francisco Gil de Lemos y Taboada who had participated in the evacuation of Port Egmont.

Throughout this period Lieutenant Samuel Clayton was in charge of Port Egmont (on Saunders or Trinidad Island) with a population of 50 and a small skiff, the *"Penguin"*, for transportation. In April 1774 the frigate *"Endeavour"* arrived under the command of Captain Gordon, who brought orders to evacuate Port Egmont. The evacuation was completed on 20 May of that year.

Before their departure, the British left a lead plaque as a symbol of possession, which read *"The Falkland Islands, including this port and all its bays and inlets are the property of his most sacred Majesty George III, King of Great Britain".*

In January 1775 a Spanish official removed the plaque to Buenos Aires (Great Britain made no protest) where it stayed until the English invasion of 1806, when General Beresford removed it to London.

Historical background...

When the British Colonial Office searched for the plaque in 1832, it could not be found.

The Vice-Royalty of the River Plate

The Spanish Crown was concerned about adequately defending the territories of the Government of the River Plate. In the face of Portuguese advances in Brazil and to reaffirm its presence in the South Atlantic, it therefore created the Vice-Royalty of the River Plate, which included all Spanish territory south of Peru and east of the Andes and with its capital in the city of Buenos Aires. On 1 August 1776 the Vice-Royalty came into being and the Viceroy, Don Pedro de Ceballos, arrived in command of a powerful fleet of some 20 warships and 8,000 men to recover the city of Colonia in the *Banda Oriental* and to expel the Lusitanians back to Brazil.

Ceballos' actions allowed Spain to sign the Treaty of San Idelfonso with Portugal in 1777, which set the frontiers between the Vice-Royalty of the River Plate and Brazil.

1776 was also a significant year for Great Britain. On 4 July, the United States of America proclaimed its independence and began a war which was concluded in 1783 with the defeat of the British and the recognition of an independent United States of America. France and Spain both intervened in the war on the side of the North Americans without realizing that the breaking of the *status quo* in the American continent and the support of a republic against a European monarchy would, in the long run, be detrimental to them.

During the course of the war the Spanish unsuccessfully attempted to regain Gibraltar from the British, who defended it at all costs.

Also in 1776 Adam Smith published his famous work *"The Wealth of Nations"*, that had an enormous impact on the traditional colonial and monopolistic mercantile systems of the times. Thus on 12 October 1778 the Spanish Crown established the *"Royal Regulations on Tariffs and Free Trade"* that, for the first time, allowed legal trading from the port of Buenos Aires and acted as an incentive for the British traders in the River Plate area.

There was also a relatively unsuccessful attempt to colonize the then uninhabited Patagonia. In 1779 settlements were founded at San José (quickly abandoned) and Carmen de Patagones (still existing today) on the banks of the Rio Negro, and in 1780 at Puerto Deseado (re-founded in 1789) and Floridablanca (abandoned in 1784). A naval station was also created at Montevideo to protect the waters of the South Atlantic.

In 1777 Gobernor Gil de Lemos was replaced. His efforts during these difficult years were later recognised and he was appointed to the Vice-Royalties of New Granada (1778) and Peru (1792).

Difficulties of every kind forced the majority of the colonists to return to Buenos Aires and Port St. Louis became almost exclusively a military outpost concerned with controlling, with little success, the growing illegal activities of North American whalers and sealers.

In January 1781, the *"porteño"*, Jacinto de Alto

Historical background...

Laguirre was designated as the new Governor of the Falklands, tasked with replacing the previous outpost. By then the colony had 103 inhabitants (including 40 convicts) who lived in some twenty houses (some of stone and others of mud and straw) together with 40 horses and about 500 cattle.

There followed a succession of governors of the Islands. In April 1783, Captain Fulgencio Montemayor became Governor and a year later was replaced by Lieutenant Agustín Figueroa.

He in turn was succeeded in 1786 by Captain Ramón de Clairac y Villalonga. His term was marked by the pursuit of ships acting illegally in the surrounding waters and important advances in the exploration of the Islands. Cattle and horse rearing also continued to grow.

Lieutenant Pedro Pablo Sanguinetto became governor in 1791. During his term of office, it was estimated that the cattle population rose above 6000 head. During those years, there were regular contacts with the only two existing Patagonian settlements: Carmen de Patagones and San José.

Lieutenant José de Aldana became Governor and Naval Commander of the Falklands in April 1794.

In March 1798, Captain Francisco Javier de Viana, born in Uruguay, became Governor of the Islands.

During these years, while time seemed to stand still in the Falkland Islands, Europe underwent important transformations and changes.

(*) Inhabitant of the port of Buenos Aires.

The war against England had weakened and indebted France. Louis XV had lost control of the situation and the French Revolution took place on 14 July 1789. A year previously, in 1778, Carlos IV had replaced Carlos III in Spain.

In 1790, Great Britain and Spain signed the *"Nootka Sound"* convention which recognised England's right to establish themselves in the Pacific Ocean whilst requiring them not to establish settlements either on the American coast or off-shore islands.

And finally, the battle of Trafalgar on 21 October 1805 signalled the end of the Napoleonic wars, the full recuperation of Britain's power, and the beginning of the end of the Spanish Empire.

In the first ten years of the 19th century, there were five Spanish Governors of the Islands. It was the period of the Napoleonic wars, the English invasions of Buenos Aires, and finally the May Revolution and the separation of the South American colonies from Spain.

The South Georgia Islands

It is not clear which was the first ship to see these islands, but it is quite unlikely that is was Americo Vespucio's in 1501. Other Spanish and English sea captains reported sightings in the area during the 16th and 17th centuries but with little precision.

Captain James Cook who is considered to be the first to disembark in 1775, made the first map of the Islands but left no one there.

Historical background...

Sealers and whalers of various nationalities frequented the islands regularly throughout the 19th century, but without any formal authorisation to do so.

In 1892, the Argentine government authorised a concession to Jullu Popper, a Romanian immigrant, to take possession of the islands and to begin their exploitation. This never took place for various reasons. In 1898, a second attempt was made because there were prospects of the existence of coal on the Islands. This attempt also proved fruitless.

The first human settlement on South Georgia was that of the Argentine Fishing Company, which, in November 1904, founded Grytviken, the capital of the island.[29] This company, founded in February 1904, had its headquarters in Buenos Aires.

The first hydrographic survey of the islands was carried out by the Argentine Navy in 1905, in the ship *"Guardia Nacional"* contracted by the Argentine Fishing Company.

An Argentine post office also started at this time, but was not recognised by Great Britain, which brought about Argentine protests in 1927 at the International Postal Bureau and in 1934 in Cairo where the convention on international post was ratified.

A meteorological station was founded in 1905 by Captain Larsen who was then the head of the Argentine Fishing Company, but was transferred to the Argentine

---

[29] Headland, Robert; *The Island of South Georgia*, Cambridge University Press, Cambridge, 1984, p. 238.

National Meteorological Service in 1907. This station functioned uninterruptedly until 1 January 1950 when it was taken over by the Falklands Islands Dependencies Survey. This action resulted in a protest by the Argentine Ambassador in London, who reiterated the sovereignty claim of his country.

That same year, 1950, the British ship *"Polar Maid"* was obliged to pay import tax in Argentina, having refuelled on the Island.

In 1909, the United Kingdom formally created within the Falklands government, the position of magistrate who exercised control over the whaling stations of different nationalities that had been established on the Island. This situation continued until the 1982 Conflict.

The principal activity on the Islands was whaling. In 1909, various different factories had been established at Bird Island, Olaff Bay, Leith in South Bay, King Edward Point and others. At its peak the population exceeded 700 with the greatest activity taking place during the 1950's. The language of the Islands was a mixture of Norwegian English and Spanish.[30] The life of the whalers was tough, spending up to 18 months on the Islands (two summers and a winter), with no women save for some very rare exceptions and very little or no entertainment outside work. The Argentine Fishing Company had a chapel in Grytviken and organised annual football championships amongst the various whaling factories during the summer months. Since the

---

[30] "Language presented no problem, the unique South Georgia Jargon, a mixture of English, Norwegian and Spanish..." Brown, Nan; *Antarctic Housewife*, Hutchinson, Australia 1971, p. 91.

Historical background...

prohibition of whaling in 1966, the Island has become deserted with the exception of about a dozen scientists. Only after the 1982 war a small British ganison was established. It was closed by the end of 1999.

The Islands became known worldwide in 1915 as a result of Shackleton's failed Antarctic expedition and his epic journey in an open whaling boat from the Antarctic to South Georgia Island. He successfully rescued the whole expedition without the loss of a single life.[31]

The South Sandwich Islands

These islands were discovered by Captain James Cook on 31 January 1775. The name Sandwich was chosen in honour of England's then First Lord of the Admiralty. They remained uninhabited for many years. In 1908, Captain Larsen of the Argentine Fish Company landed on the islands but left no permanent settlement. From 1951 the Argentine Navy undertook scientific investigation in the area and installed beacons. On 7 November 1976, the Corbeta Uruguay Scientific Station was built on Thule Island. In 1971 Argentina took possession of South Thule in the South Sandwich Island Group, considered part of the jurisdiction of South Georgia Islands by both the Argentine and British. The occupation was limited to a Naval Meteorological Station.

Great Britain tried to obtain Argentine recognition of their sovereignty over the Islands, but was never

---

[31] Berguño Jorge; *Las 22 vidas de Shackleton,* Santiago de Chile, 1985.

successful and on numerous occasions (all before the signing of the Antarctic Treaty in 1959) suggested sending the dispute to the International Court of Justice.** This was not accepted by the Argentine government, which has always insisted that the British must withdraw.

As a result of the Falklands Conflict of 1982, the British evicted the Argentine Base and, since then the islands have remained occupied by Great Britain and administered as part of the South Georgia Islands. However, the Argentines maintain their sovereignty claim.

A British Ocean

For many years, the South Atlantic was a de-facto Portuguese ocean. This was the first interpretation given of the Treaty of Tordecillas, which explains why the port of Buenos Aires was practically closed until 1778. Brazil, Portugal's heir in the South Atlantic, still occupies all the off-shore islands around its coastline, including the San Pedro and San Pablo Rocks on the equator, and 300 miles to the northeast of Fortaleza, the Fernando de Noronha archipelago, some 120 miles northeast of Natale, and the Martin Vaz Islands, situated 500 miles northeast of Rio de Janeiro.

Only after the Spanish occupation of the Falklands,

(*) Norway was the country of origin of the greater part of the island's population.
(**) The International Court of Justice has normally favoured the european powers with its rulings. Third World countries distrust the ICJ.

Historical background...

the Islands of Fernando Poo and Annabón and the creation of the Viceroyalty of the River Plate, did the Spanish Crown decide to partially occupy this vast ocean.

But simultaneously the British began to take an interest in the South Atlantic ocean. After the productive occupation of Cape Colony, a few years later they sought to occupy Buenos Aires, Montevideo, and the Falklands.

The British failed in both Montevideo and Buenos Aires, but in only a few years were successful in occupying the Falkland Islands, the South Georgia and South Sandwich Islands, as well as St. Helena, Ascension, Tristan da Cunha and Diego Alvarez. This constituted all the islands of the South Atlantic that are not situated on the continental shelves of South America or Africa. The only exceptions were the Falkland Islands, located well inside the Patagonian Shelf.

For the British Empire, at a time when neither the Panama nor the Suez Canals existed, the South Atlantic was the route to India and to the Pacific and Oceania. Hence the strategic importance.

Fernando Poo[32]

There is an incredible and forgotten story that is an exception in a British ocean: the African colonies of the River Plate. The story refers to the African territories

---

[32] Etchebarne Bullrich, Conrado; "Las Colonias de la Reina del Plata", *La Nación*, Buenos Aires, 24 August 1997.

that fell under the jurisdiction of the Viceroyalty of the River Plate.

Under the terms of the Treaty of San Idelfonso, signed by Spain and Portugal within one year of the creation of the Vice-Royalty of the River Plate, the Spanish Crown received from its Iberian neighbour the islands of Annabón and Fernando Poo, in the Gulf of Guinea, on the east coast of equatorial Africa.

Thus it was that the recently appointed Viceroy of the River Plate, Lieutenant General don Pedro de Cevallos, was charged in 1778 with taking possession of, and administering from Buenos Aires, the new colony. Count Argelejo, who was put in charge of the expedition, fell victim to malaria after a troubled journey. The second commander of the expedition, Lieutenant Colonel Don Joaquín Primo de Rivera was not dispirited by the difficult circumstances and continued to carry out the mission requested by the Viceroy. In December 1778 he took possession of Fernando Poo, which was ruled from Buenos Aires for decades until it was abandoned during the Napoleonic Wars. Buenos Aires' independence in 1810 marked the end of its interest in the colony.

Great Britain, on the other hand, had decided to occupy the enormous void of the South Atlantic, an undertaking that came to a head in only a very few years. In 1827 Great Britain occupied Fernando Poo. Spain, having recovered from the Napoleonic Wars and longing for its past empire, again took the island in 1843 through an expedition led by Captain Juan José Llerena. This action was reaffirmed by the expedition of Captain Chacon in 1858, which ratified Spanish sovereignty. Fernando Poo and Annabón remained a Spanish colony

Historical background...

until the territory became independent in 1968 and became known as the Republic of Equatorial Guinea. Argentina and Great Britain who had long since abandoned their sovereignty claims, recognised the newly independent and poverty-stricken state.

St. Helena [33]

The island of St Helena was discovered on 21 May 1502, St. Helena Day, by the Portuguese Commander Juan de Nova Castella on his return journey from India. The Portuguese did not occupy the island, but left supplies of provisions and, later landed sick or mutinous sailors there. The island was free of malaria, which was of great importance to those circumnavigating Africa in the days before the discovery of quinine.

A famous exile was the Portuguese nobleman Fernando López, who had deserted his country while in India and became a renegade. He was captured in Goa, had his nose, ears and right hand mutilated and was abandoned on the island. Four years later he was given permission to return to Portugal. Portuguese ships regularly visited the island, but its existence was kept secret.

It was re-discovered by the English, on 8 June 1588, during Captain Cavendish's circumnavigation of the globe. He found various Portuguese buildings including a chapel in an excellent state of repair. The only inhabitants were three abandoned slaves. The English did not take possession of the island.

---

[33] Bain, Kenneth; *St Helena*, Wilton, York, 1993.

In 1645 the island was occupied by the Dutch and then promptly abandoned when they established a settlement at the Cape of Good Hope. The English surreptitiously occupied the island in 1661, but were expelled by the Dutch in 1665. In 1673, when the Dutch had again abandoned the island, the English re-occupied it and it was administered by the East India Company until 1834, when it came under the direct rule of the British Crown.

The island was important as the gateway to the South Atlantic. It was used in the slave trade. In 1676 the astronomer Halley, who was then studying at Oxford, visited with the intent of studying the stars of the Southern Hemisphere. Captain Cook also landed on the island in 1771 and 1774, as did Darwin in 1836.

Undoubtedly the island's real fame lies in the fact that Napoleon, after his final defeat, was exiled there until his death [34]. Many Boer colonists and Zulu chiefs captured by the British were also sent to St. Helena. For decades the island was administered from Cape Town.

Thus it is that the local population has mixed African, Boer and Indian blood.

Since 1982 the British have sent St. Helenians to work in the Falklands to replace the Chilean workers who spoke Spanish. This immigration served two purposes; it helped to "Anglicise" the Falklands and it reduced unemployment on St. Helena, an island with practically no natural resources. Of the current population of 5,000 St. Helenians, almost 400 live on the Falklands.

---

[34] Local stories claim that he was poisoned.

Historical background...

Ascension Island

Ascension Island was discovered by a Portuguese seaman, Juan de Nueva Castilla on Ascension Day in 1501. This volcanic island was uninhabited until the British imprisoned Napoleon on the neighbouring island of St. Helena in 1811. A small British garrison was established there to prevent its occupation by another European power, and as part of their strategy to occupy the whole South Atlantic.

For over a century it was considered a possession of the British Navy and was administered by the Admiralty until 1922, when it became a dependency of St. Helena. Ascension is strategically located half way between Brazil and Angola at latitude 8° South. The island is an important centre for military communications. It has been partially ceded to the United States which, since 1966, has set up a military satellite communications centre that is used to guide and track intercontinental missiles. It is also used as a support centre for NASA.

The island does not have a native population. Currently, apart from the British and US military staff, there are 800 St. Helenians who live in Georgetown, the only town. It is a volcanic island without natural resources and with a central volcano rising to 900m. The United Kingdom exploits the fish stocks of its territorial waters and its exclusive economic zone. The stocks are not abundant as the waters deepen abruptly and the area of the continental shelf is very small.

Ascension is part of Britain's defence network in the

South Atlantic. During the Falklands Conflict, it was used as a support base for the British Task Force campaign, and since then it has become the mandatory stop for the communications flights between the Falklands and the United Kingdom. It is worth pointing out that St. Helena does not have a landing strip. Ascension is the only stop made by the Royal Air Force Tristar during its twice-weekly flights to the Falklands.

Tristan Da Cunha

The Tristán Da Cunha group includes three small islands: Tristán Da Cunha, Inaccessible and Nightingale. The last two are uninhabited.

Tristán Da Cunha is a small volcanic island without natural resources, and is only 1 mile wide and 5 miles long. The volcano reaches a height of 6,000 feet and can therefore be seen from great distances, serving for years as a point of reference for navigators. For many years there have been British and South African meteorological stations on the islands.

These islands, situated half way between Buenos Aires and the Cape of Good Hope, were discovered by the Portuguese Admiral, Tristán Da Cunha at the beginning of the 16th century. However, they remained uninhabited until the Dutch unsuccessfully tried to settle them in 1656 and the East India Company tried equally unsuccessfully thirty years later. It was only in 1816 that the British consolidated their dominion over the islands

Historical background...

by establishing a garrison there. There were no native inhabitants. But over a period of years, the population grew as a result of various shipwrecks, St. Helenian slaves moving there, and also through the descendents of pirates. In 1886, there were about 100 inhabitants living mainly in Edinburgh, named after the Scottish capital and from whence came the first immigrants.

By 1961, the population had increased to more than 250 people, but a volcanic eruption then forced the complete evacuation of the island. The inhabitants were only able to return in 1963.

Gough (Diego Alvarez)

Nearly 300km to the southwest of the Tristan Da Cunha group, on the same latitude as Bahia Blanca and at longitude 10° West is the island of Diego Alvarez or Gough. It was discovered by Portuguese navigators in 1505 and then rediscovered by Captain Gough in 1731. Since 1930, together with the Tristan Da Cunha group and Ascension Island, it has been a dependency of St. Helena. For many years there have been British and South African meteorological stations on the island.

---

[35] Braun Menéndez, Armando; *Pequeña Historia Antártica*, Francisco de Aguirre SA, Buenos Aires, 1974.
Moneta, José Manuel; *Cuatro Años en las Orcadas del Sur*, ed. Peuser, Buenos Aires, 1944.
Fraga, Jorge A.; *La Antártida*, ed. Instituto de Publicaciones Navales, Buenos Aires, 1992.
Casellas, Alberto; *Antártida, un malabarismo político*, Instituto de Publicaciones Navales, Buenos Aires, 1981.

Conrado Etchebarne Bullrich

The South Orkney Islands[35]

The southern ocean, meaning that which surrounds Antarctica, to the south of the Atlantic, was discovered and explored, almost privately, by whalers and sealers. This activity was at its peak at the beginning of the 19th century. Many journeys to the southern oceans were made from Buenos Aires. Amongst them were those made by the sealing ships the *"Mercurio"* and the *"San Juan Nepomuceno"*. There were few records of their journeys, the principal reason being to avoid giving away the locations where they found their catches.

In the context of these voyages, Captain Smith discovered the South Shetland Islands in 1819, very close to the tip of the Antarctic Peninsula. On 6 December 1821, Captains Powell and Palmer discovered the South Orkney Islands, located half way between the Antarctic Peninsula and the South Georgia Islands. James Weddel made various voyages between 1820 and 1824 with the support of the Royal Geographic Society and inaugurated a series of scientific voyages to the Antarctic region that lasted throughout the 19th century.

The South Orkney Islands form a part of this story as the result of a fortuitous rescue. In March 1902, the Swedish whaling ship the *"Antartic"*, became trapped in the ice and subsequently sank. The crew was rescued by the Argentine corvette the *"Uruguay"*, awakening Argentine interest in these desolate regions.

Thus, in 1904, an Argentine settlement was founded

Historical background...

on Laurie Island in the South Orkney archipelago, which remains occupied to this day.[36]

Because the South Orkney Islands lie within the Antarctic sector, and since the Antarctic Treaty in 1959, all sovereignty disputes within the zone have been frozen, they now share the same fate as the Antarctic. Consequently this southern archipelago does not form part of the present Anglo-Argentine dispute over the Falkland Islands, the South Georgia Islands and the South Sandwich Islands.

---

[36] Braun Menéndez, Armando; *Pequeña Historia Antártica*, ed. Francisco de Aguirre SA, Buenos Aires, 1974, p. 95.

Foremen with their dogs inspecting the farm.

III

THE ARGENTINE PERIOD

The English Invasions and the Independence of the River Plate

The victory over Napoleon converted Great Britain into the superpower of the 19th century with dominion over all the oceans.[37]

The control of the South Atlantic was a fundamental part of the expansionist imperial policy. This was so because the South Atlantic was the only route to the Pacific, to the eastern coastline of the American continent, to Asia, to the Indian Ocean, and to the east coast of Africa. Before the Suez and the Panama canals, the South Atlantic was the key to the world.

Great Britain already had under its dominion the island of St. Helena. In 1804 it took Cape Colony, in 1805 Ascension Island and, in 1806 and 1807, it invaded Buenos Aires and Montevideo with the clear objective of controlling the extreme south of the American continent.

---

[37] English schoolchildren were taught that 40% of the world was under the control of the British Empire.

Buenos Aires had been founded for the second time in 1580 after the unsuccessful first attempt in 1536. For nearly two centuries the future Argentine capital remained at a subsistence level without major development or growth.

But, from the creation of the Viceroyalty of the River Plate in 1776, and the passing of the Free Trade Regulations of 1778, Buenos Aires became the capital of the River Plate, and grew and modernised at a staggering rate. The security of the Spanish Empire's southern frontier and the border with Brazil, was defended from Buenos Aires. Buenos Aires governed the *Banda Oriental*, the Alto Peru*, Cuyo, Paraguay, Cordoba, Salta, Tucumán, and the old Jesuit missions. From being the last town of the Spanish Empire, Buenos Aires became the centre of an important territory that included the Falkland Islands in the South Atlantic across to the Island of Fernando Poo (Bioko) in the Gulf of Guinea on the east coast of central Africa.

Because of its military weakness the River Plate was a great temptation for the expansionist British Empire. However, thanks to the courage and decisiveness of its inhabitants and the leadership of people like Santiago de Liniers, the English Invasions of 1806 and 1807 represented major defeats for the British Crown.

The *Criollos*, conscious of their own strength and the weakness of the Crown of Castille, took power into their own hands and displaced the last Viceroy in 1810. This resulted in a long and difficult period of civil wars, the first against the Spanish Royalists, who wanted to

---

(*) Nowdays Bolivia.

The Argentine period...

maintain the Empire, and then amongst the *Criollos* themselves. Independence was declared in 1816 and fighting with Spain ended successfully in 1824.

In 1823, the United States of America decided to support the independence movements in the former Spanish colonies through the Monroe Doctrine –"America for the Americans"– and to put end to the new expansionism of the European Crowns that had been united in the Holy Alliance since 1815.

In 1825, Great Britain recognised the independence of the United Provinces of the River Plate and signed a treaty of peace and friendship. The falklands were peacefully occupied and governed from Buenos Aires since 1820. The United Kingdonw did not make any reservation on the friendship treaty.

The Last Years of Spanish Administration

The Spanish authorities in Montevideo, pressured by the revolution in Buenos Aires in 1810, decided at the beginning of 1811 to withdraw the garrison from the Falkland Islands to reinforce the defences of Montevideo. Despite this the city finally fell into the hands of the patriots on 23 June 1814.

Thus it was that on 13 February 1811, the last Spanish Governor of the Falklands, Second Pilot of the Royal Navy, Don Pablo Guillén withdrew from the Falkland Islands with his complete garrison of 46 men. They closed down the buildings, released their livestock and left a lead plaque, as proof that the Islands continued to belong to the Sovereign Don Fernando VII, King of Spain and the Indies.

For nearly ten years, the Islands were abandoned, except for occasional visits by whalers and sealers from North America, Great Britain and the River Plate. There were also various shipwrecked mariners who were forced to remain on the desolate Islands temporarily.[38]

Malvinas Argentinas

"Declaration of Argentine Sovereignty in the Falklands

Frigate Heroine in Puerto Soledad, Falkland Islands, 2 November 1820.

Sir:
I have the honour to inform you of my arrival at the port, to take possession of these islands in the name of the Supreme Government of the United Provinces of South America. The ceremony was publicly performed on the 6th day of November and the national standard hoisted at the fort, under a salute from this frigate, in the presence of several citizens of the United States and Great Britain. It is my desire to act towards all friendly flags with the most distinguished justice and hospitality, and it will give me the pleasure to aid and assist as many require them, to obtain refreshment with as little trouble and expenses as possible. I have to beg of you to communicate this intelligence to any other vessel of your nation whom it may concern. I am Sir, your most attentive and humble servant,

David Jewett"

---

[38] Captain Charles H. Barnard, *Marooned*, Syracuse University Press, New York, 1986. A fascinating book which describes the adventures of a group of shipwrecked sailors in the Falklands. The story is also related by David Miller in *The Wreck of the Isabella*, Leo Cooper, London, 1995.

(Text of a letter given by David Jewett to all North American and English fishing and sealing boats encountered in the Bahia de la Anunciacion).

The Argentine period...

During the wars of independence, the various patriot governments established in Buenos Aires, granted several corsair licenses to adventurers, sailors, and to French, English, Irish and especially North American pirates. Although the corsair war against the Spanish Navy mainly took place between 1816 and 1818, there still was some fighting going on in 1821, when all licences were cancelled to bring the situation back under control.

David Jewett, an American corsair from the port of Baltimore, who had actively participated in the American corsair war against Great Britain in 1812-1814, offered his services to the patriot governments established in the Southern Cone. He thus obtained corsair licenses from Chile, the United Provinces of the River Plate, and Brazil.

Back in Buenos Aires, after the corsair campaign fought with his brigantine the *"Invincible"*, he reached an agreement with Patricio Lynch, who had obtained a corsair license for his frigate *"Heroine"*. Jewett was appointed Captain of the frigate, which, with its 475 tons, 34 cannons, and almost 200 crew members, was one of the most powerful ships to leave the port of Buenos Aires. At the beginning of 1820, the Supreme Director José Rondeau granted him the rank of Army Colonel in service of the Navy. He thus received instructions to fly the national flag over the abandoned Falkland Islands, and deposit a group of convicts there.

In March 1820 the *"Heroine"* headed north in search of Spanish captures. After a difficult journey and having previously re-provisioned on Trinity Island and Cape Verde, they reached European waters and were able to capture the Portuguese corvette *"Carlota"*. While scurvy was spreading amongst the crew, the lack of discipline made it impossible to continue their corsair campaign. Therefore, in September 1820, Jewett decided to head back to the Falklands to fulfill his official mission, and allow his crew to recover. After a tough journey through many storms, he arrived in the Falklands in October during the windy season. He reached *Bahia de la Anunciacion*, where they found the ruins of Puerto Soledad, known today as Port Louis. His frigate was in a desperate condition and only 70 of his men remained alive.

There he met the British explorer James Weddel, and several North American sealing ships that were wintering on the Islands. Jewett's crew disembarked to recover and by means of a diet based on native vegetables, were eventually cured of the scurvy. It is a little known fact that the many grasses and wild fruits of the Falklands are edible. The *gauchos* on the islands who had settled during the Spanish period had become used to preparing jams and jellies with *Diddle Dee* (a small wild red berry), to eat *tussac grass*, (whose meaty part is an ideal source of food for hungry mariners) and especially *Scurvy Grass*, (with a high content of vitamin C and excellent for treating scurvy). Another nutritious source of food for the recovering crew was the wild cattle left behind by the Spanish.

Jewett's crew's health improved, but their indiscipline only became worse. During the whole of the Argentine period, the lack of discipline was a constant factor. The English, after 1833, resorted systematically to whippings and hangings –in moost cases without a fair trial– for all the gauchos who caused problems or fell out of favour with their British masters.

The Argentine period...

Nevertheless, on 6 November 1820, David Jewett formally took possession of the Falkland Islands in the name of the government of the United Provinces River Plate the South, and raised the Argentine flag, which he saluted with 21 cannon shots. Several British and American sealing ships witnessed the event. Jewett notified James Weddel –famous for his expeditions to the Antarctic Continent– and the remaining ships' captains in the surroundings, that he had taken possession but that he had no intention of disturbing their activities. No foreign country or State contested the public and peaceful taking of possession, even though it had been published in "El Redactor" of Cadiz and The Times of London in August 1821. In Buenos Aires, the news was only published in November that year. The treaty of Friendship and Free Trade signed with Great Britain in 1825 acknowledged *de facto* the Argentine sovereignty over the occupied territories at that time.

The difficulties of the weather, the state of insubordination of the troops as well as the non-existence of Spanish ships to capture and make Jewett's expedition profitable, all led him to request his replacement. In Buenos Aires Jewett did not enjoy a good reputation, particularly amongst the community of North American residents who considered him to be a bandit and a pirate. John Murray Forbes[39], who was head of the US diplomatic delegation in Buenos Aires from 1820 to 1831, wrote several letters to the North American Secretary of State, John Quincy Adams, complaining about Jewett's activities, whom he accused, amongst other things, of using corsair licences of convenience

---

[39] John Murray Forbes, *Once años en Buenos Aires*, Emecé, Buenos Aires, 1956.

from Buenos Aires or from the Uruguayan caudillo Artigas and also of changing the flags on his frigates to suit his own purposes.

In May 1821, Jewett was replaced by Guillermo Mason, who became commander of the corsair ship *"La Heroina"* and who later left for the Falklands, and from there in search of booty in a new corsair campaign, flying the Argentine flag.

Jewett, for his part, returned to Buenos Aires where he survived different accusations, but in the face of the bad feelings that Forbes had generated against him, he decided to move to the Brazilian Navy, where he fought various successful campaigns and rose to the rank of Rear-Admiral.

He died in 1842 in Rio de Janeiro at the age of 70.

Shortly after the end of Forbes' mission in Buenos Aires, and not by chance, another North American adventurer, Captain Silas Duncan, commanding the corvette *"Lexington"*, and with the support of the new US Consul in Buenos Aires, Mr. Slacum, attacked the Argentine outpost at Puerto de la Soledad and proceeded with the cruelty characteristic of pirates to sack and burn the Argentine installations, establishing a precedent for the English invasion the following year.

Louis Vernet

Louis Vernet was born in Hamburg in March 1791, the son of a French Hugenot family exiled in Germany.

The Argentine period...

He arrived in the River Plate in 1817 after years of successful business. A little later in 1819, he married a Uruguayan, Maria Saenz, and settled in Buenos Aires.

In 1823, Louis Vernet became associated with the Buenos Aires businessman, Jorge Pacheco. On 5 August that year, the two partners signed a contract in which Pacheco undertook to request a concession from the Government of the Province of Buenos Aires for the exploitation of the existing wild cattle on East Falkland. The concession was similar to that given to the cattle herders south of the Salado River in the Province of Buenos Aires. In return for the right to exploit the cattle and horses, he was tasked with renovating the existing buildings in Port Saint Louis. Governor Martín Rodríguez and his Minister Bernardino Rivadavia –the future Argentine President, signed the decree authorising the concession. Pacheco, already 62 years old– an advanced age for those times –and Vernet had other businesses including his sister's estancia south of the Salado River, and a salting house on the Valdés Peninsula in Patagonia.

It was therefore decided to subcontract the livestock exploitation on East Falkland to an Englishman, Robert Schofield. Retired Captain Pablo Areguati, a Guaraní born in the eastern missions close to the brazilian border in 1887, was also contracted as military commander to defend the territory. The Governor of Buenos Aires Province, Martín Rodríguez, approved his nomination.

Captain Areguati arrived on the Islands on 2 February 1824, and, in a situation aggravated by the scarcity of resources, began his difficult task.

Emilio Vernet, Louis' nephew, and Schofield arrived at the end of March on board the English brigantine the *"Antilope"*. Things were very difficult to begin with. In spite of the estimated 20,000 head of cattle and many wild horses on the islands, there was a lack of tame horses, the majority of which had died on the journey or shortly after arriving on the Islands. This first attempt at colonisation failed. *"La Rafaela"*, which was the only ship that was left in the Islands, was lost. The *"Fenwick"*, which had made many journeys from the River Plate was sold to cover the losses. Schofield, who had a serious drinking problem, died after only a short time on the Islands.

Louis Vernet was not dispirited and decided to continue with the business. He re-negotiated the partnership with Pacheco, contracted a new ship, the brigantine *"Alerta"*, and at the beginning of 1826 he embarked for the Falklands, running the Brazilian blockade of Buenos Aires. He succeeded in taking 50 broken-in horses, he reorganised the workforce and explored a large part of East Falklands. On his return journey he was surprised by strong storms that virtually destroyed the *"Alerta"*. He undertook further journeys in the brigantine *"Iris"*, and asked for government support for his company.

The Governor of the Province of Buenos Aires issued a decree on 5 January 1828, authorised additional benefits to Vernet, including all the land of East Falkland, with the exception of that land previously granted to Pacheco, and an area of 10 square leagues in the Strait of San Carlos. He also authorised fishing rights in all the Falkland Islands and on the continental coast south of Rio Negro and Patagones. In these years

The Argentine period...

Vernet made various journeys to the Islands, delivering more people, including some thirty black slaves.

Numerous foreign sealing and whaling boats, and some merchant ships, passed through the Islands. Vernet organised a register, which shows that in 1826, nine ships called in, in 1827 twenty-two ships, and in 1828, eleven ships put in to harbour. The vast majority were American sealers, the others were English and French.

On 10 June 1829,[40] Governor Rodriguez* issued a decree creating the position of political and military Commander of the Falkland Islands and the same day named Louis Vernet as the first incumbent. His area of responsibility included Staten Island.

Great Britain, which had made no protest when Jewett was made the Argentine representative on 6 November 1820, nor had made any reference to it when signing the Treaty of Friendship, Trade and Navigation in 1825, protested on 9 August 1828, through Mr. Woodbine Parrish, their representative in Buenos Aires, at the creation of the Political/Military Headquarters. The protest was not answered by the Government of Buenos Aires.

Vernet, who was essentially a businessman, had meetings with Parrish in May 1829, where he stated, as Parrish reported to London, his willingness to accept

---

[40] This is the official date of "Dia de las Malvinas", a national holiday in the Argentine Republic.

(*) Martín Rodríguez was Gobernor of the Province of Buenos Aires. The Falkland Islands were under his jurisdiction.

British protection. The British did not pay attention to his suggestion.

On 15 July 1828, Vernet arrived on the Islands with his wife, his children and 15 English colonists, 23 Germans, as well as gauchos and indians to work on the land. He made various changes to the names on the Islands; *Puerto Soledad* became again *Puerto Louis* and *Bahia de la Anunciación* became *Bahia Louis*[41]. Puerto Hermoso (later Port Stanley) became Puerto Williams.

The Islands underwent a period of rapid development, the like of which had never been seen previously. Cattle and seal lion hides were exported, and salted meats, fat and dried, salted fish were sold to passing ships. A ship, the *"Aguila"* was built for inter-island travel. Vernet also mapped Staten Island.

Captain FitzRoy, of the later famous voyage of the *"Beagle"*, expressed his surprise at having encountered a civilized settlement on the islands when he expected to find only sealers.[42]

Vernet felt his colony was threatened by the mainly American ships that hunted sea lions illegally and also killed the livestock. At the beginning of 1831, he decided to put an end to the situation and resolved to capture three American schooners, the *"Harriot"*, the *"Breakwater"* and the *"Superior"*. The *"Breakwater"* escaped and the other two submitted themselves to Argentine jurisdiction. The North American consul in Buenos Aires, George

---

[41] Louis Bougainville's original placenames.
[42] FitzRoy, Robert; *Narrative of the surveying voyages of HM Ships Adventure and Beagle,* London, 1934.

The gaucho *customs still survive amongst the Islands'
farming community.*

Slacum, sent a protest note which was rejected by the Minister of Foreign Affairs, Tomás Manuel de Anchorena.

The North American naval frigate, the *"Lexington"*, that was then in the port of Buenos Aires under the command of Captain Silas Duncan, with the agreement of the American consul, and having previously advised the Buenos Aires government, departed for the Islands to avenge the capture of the two American ships. The *"Lexington"* arrived in Port Louis on 28 December 1831 and, in a typical act of piracy designed to mislead the settlers, raised the French flag. Having encountered no resistance they disembarked on 31 December, and destroyed the Islands' defences including the artillery and the gunpowder magazine. They also burnt houses, stole hides, skins and other goods and left the settlement in a state of desolation.

After an exchange of letters of protest with the North American representative in Buenos Aires, the latter withdrew thereby breaking diplomatic relations between the two countries.

That same month, December 1831, the government of Buenos Aires recognised the new British Envoy Mr. Henry Fox, as the Minister Plenipotentiary of Great Britain.

Whilst Vernet was in Buenos Aires, the government of Buenos Aires named Sergeant Major José Francisco Mestivier, as the new military/political commander of the Falkland Islands on 10 September 1832. On 29 September, Mr. Fox protested in the name of the British Government.

The Argentine period...

Simultaneously with these events, on 30 November 1832, the Falklands garrison led by a black soldier, Manuel Saenz Valiente rebelled, committing several murders, including Sergeant Francisco Mestivier.

With the support of the French frigate, the *"Jean Jacques"*, Juan Simón, Vernet's French foreman, successfully captured those guilty of Mestivier's murder.

At the end of December, Lieutenant Colonel José Maria Pinedo arrived on the Islands in the schooner *"Sarandí"*. He disarmed the remaining members of the garrison and arrested Gomila, who had been the second in command.

The British Corvette "Clio"

On 2 January 1833, the British corvette *"Clio"* arrived in Puerto Louis. Its commander, Captain John James Onslow, notified Pinedo in writing that, the following day, he would raise the British flag and demanded the lowering of the Argentine flag and the withdrawal of all Argentine government forces.

Pinedo, with inferior forces, did not resist and withdrew on 3 January. He arrived in Buenos Aires on 15 January.

The Buenos Aires government immediately constituted two councils of war. One to judge Pinedo, who was found guilty and dismissed; and the other to judge the mutineers, those found guilty of the murders were condemned to death and Gomila was sentenced to a year on the frontier.

On 22 January, the Argentine government protested formally to London. The Argentine argument, as presented by Pedro de Angelis, had solid grounds which were expressed by Manuel Moreno to Lord Palmerston on 17 June 1833. Having had no response, Moreno reiterated his protest to the Duke of Wellington on 29 December. Never again did the British accept juridical negotiations on the rights and wrongs of the issue, which they resolved only on the basis of military supremacy.

In 1839, when relations with the United States were re-established, the Argentine representative in Washington, Carlos Maria de Alvear, renewed the claims against the attack on Puerto Louis committed by Captain Duncan. Daniel Webster, the Secretary of State responded by letter on 4 December 1841, saying that the US Government had decided to suspend any decision on the matter until such time as an agreement had been reached between Argentina and Great Britain over the jurisdiction of the Falkland Islands. The matter remains unresolved to this day.

The Rebellion of the Gaucho Rivero

The people taken to the Islands by Vernet remained there with no form of government, as the British had expelled all the authorities. Power in the Islands rested with Brisbane, Vernet's administrator. William Dickson was in charge of the store and the supplies and Juan Simón was the foreman of the gauchos. The population of the Islands had been reduced to only 14 gauchos and 18 Europeans.

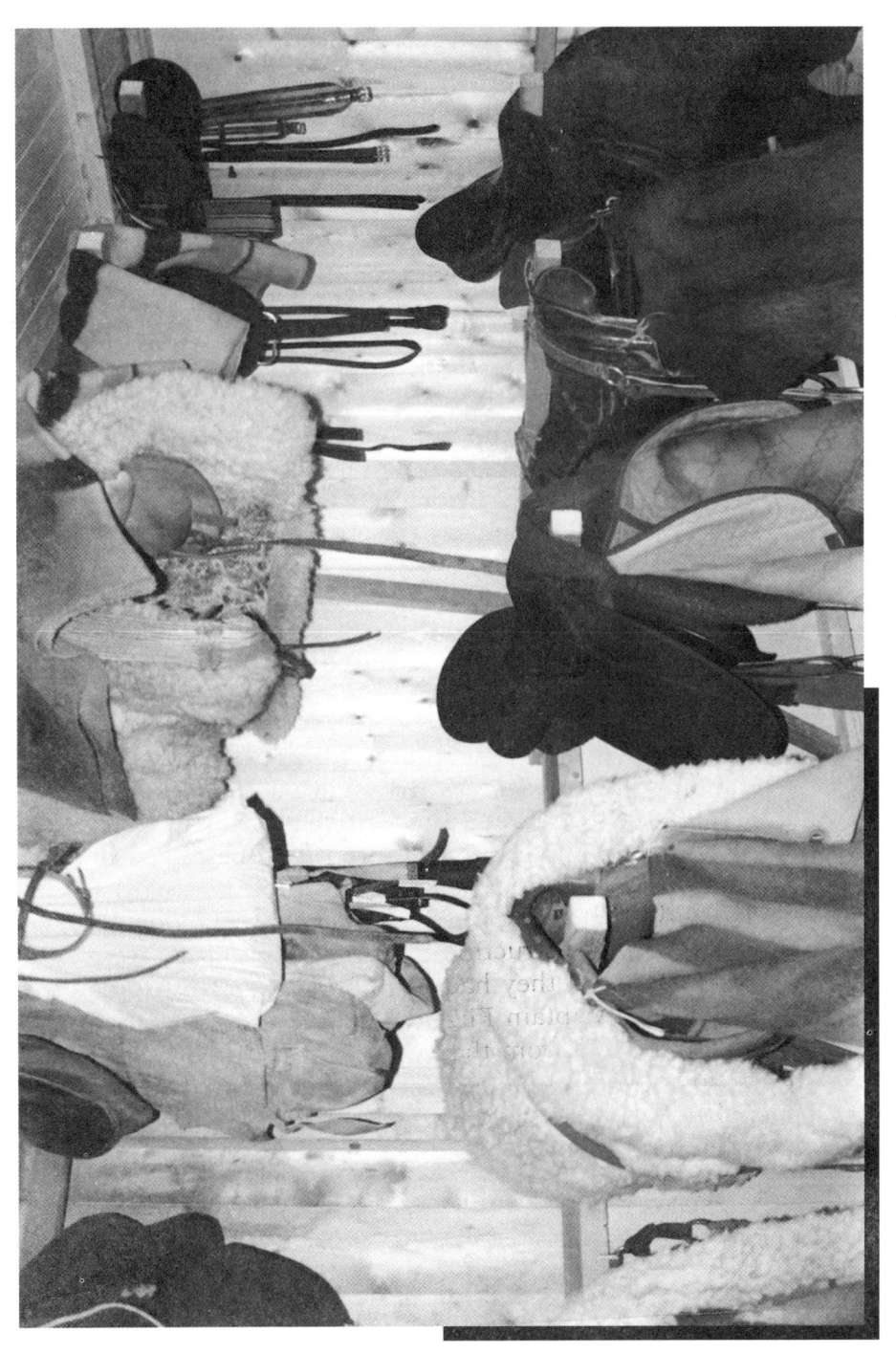

English saddles and criollo *riding gear side by side on an Estancia.*

The situation of the Islands was aggravated by the feeling of abandonment and by the circumstances in which the workers received their salary, which was paid in the form of vouchers signed by Vernet, but were no longer accepted by Dickson. Discontent spread, they slaughtered the tame cattle instead of the wild ones, they would no longer break in the new horses and finally, faced with so much hardship, the gauchos, led by Antonio Rivero, rebelled on 26 August 1833. The foreman Juan Simón, the administrator Brisbane and the Spaniard Ventura Paso were murdered. Dickson also died trying to defend the British flag, which was lowered by the rebels and replaced by the Argentine flag.

On 23 October 1833, the British ship *"Hopeful"*, under the command of Captain Prior, arrived in the Islands and the British flag was raised once more. Prior then sent a report to his superiors.

Two months later, Rear Admiral Seymour, commanding the *"Challenger"* arrived at Puerto Louis. On 10 January 1834 he raised the British flag again, after the gauchos had apparently removed the one raised by Captain Prior. Lieutenant Smith disembarked with 6 men, with instructions to impose order in the colony. By March 1834 they had captured all the rebels. They were taken in Captain FitzRoy's brigantine *"Beagle"* to Rio de Janeiro and from there to London where they were tried and absolved due to the lack of British jurisdiction over the Falkland Island. They were then returned to the River Plate, arriving in Montevideo in the middle of 1835.

IV

THE BRITISH OCCUPATION

> *"No native, however high his rank, ought to approach within a yard of an Englishman; and every time an English shakes hands with a Babu he shakes the basis on which our ascendancy in this country stands"*
>
> James Lawrence [43]

Organization of the Colony

The British, after the removal of the Argentines at the beginning of 1883, left the Islands in a state of total abandonment for approximately 10 years.

There is no doubt that, during the first half of the 19th century, this part of the world had no importance

---

[43] Lawrence, James; *The making and Unmaking of British India;* ed. Abacus, london, 1998, p. 157.

(*) (British exports to the countries in the Southern Cone during this period never exceeded a million pounds a year).

for the British economy.* Neither did it have any strategic defence importance for imperial territories, although it was clear to everyone that in the future it would have a significant role to play.[44]

During these years some Argentine gauchos who had not been deported with Rivero's group, stayed on the Islands. A small force of British marines under the command of Lieutenant Henry Smith was established. Smith was replaced by Robert Lockway in 1838 and then by John Tyssen in 1839.

The semi-abandoned state of the Islands concerned London, because of the development of affairs in the River Plate, which led to the later establishment of a French blockade (1838-1840) and the establishment of a British Naval force in the River Plate.

Thus, Lieutenant Governor Richard Clement Moody was appointed on 23 August 1841. One of his first decisions was to organise the sale of land.**

In 1843, Port Stanley, named in honour of the Minister of the Colonies.***

Despite the notorious illegality of the British settlement, one must emphasize the enormous difficulties that confronted the first British pioneers.

---

[44] McLean, David; *War, Diplomacy and Informal Empire*, Ed. British Academic Press, London, 1995, p. 1.
(**) The British Crown had appropriated all the lands belonging to Vernet.
(***) Lord Edward Smith Stanley, was founded and became the Island's capital.

The Islands' criollo horses, a result of interbreeding between English and criollo blood.

The site chosen for the capital was inferior to Puerto Louis. The land was worse, the distances to the cattle pastures were greater and the climate was wet and windy. The place had been chosen, not with the criteria of establishing a farm, as Vernet had done, but solely because it had the best harbour in the Islands.

The British decision to occupy the Falklands was based on its role as a strategic port between the Atlantic and the Pacific and not because of any plans to develop livestock farming.

Governor Moody wanted to organise the new colony of the Empire. He realised there was a large quantity of wild cattle descended from the cattle brought from the River Plate, and decided to support their exploitation.

In 1844, Samuel Fisher Lafone, an English businessman resident in Montevideo, bought land on the Islands with the objective of establishing a farm. The British Crown also granted him approximately 200 leagues of *camp* that included everything south of the Choiseul Strait[45] on East Falkland.

In 1848, Lieutenant Moody was replaced by Governor George Rennie, who like Vernet, decided to control the North American sealers. From then on, they stopped visiting the Islands, at least in the way they had up to that time. The colony by then consisted of 300 people, including English, Scots, as well as Argentine and Uruguayan gauchos.

In 1851, a new phase began in the Islands, when the

---

[45] Foulkes, Haroldo; *Los Kelpers*, Corregidor, Buenos Aires, 1961, p. 46.

The British Occupation

recently created Falkland Islands Company obtained the lands of Lafone with the objective of raising sheep and producing wool. The workforce, the majority of whom came from what is now Uruguay, were subjected to iron discipline which, when necessary, included whipping and hanging. On 18 March 1853, a gaucho, Hilario Córdoba, was summarily hanged on the orders of the Governor.[46]

In 1855, Governor Thomas Moore assumed charged and gave a new impulse to the exploitation of wool. This period was very hard and in his first year an epidemic struck.

To this day one can see in the oldest part of the Stanley cemetery, the tombstones of those first families who died in this tragic way.

The records talk of a "putrefying pestilence of the throat". One example is the family of John and Esther Smith who in only a few months lost their son, George, aged 6, then Edwina aged 8, followed by the 5 year old Esther, and finally John, the eldest aged 12. Something similar happened to the family of John and Margaret Yates, who lost their children Lavinia, aged 14, Augustus aged 8, Maria aged 12, Emma aged 16, Alice aged 15, and Sara aged 10, all in less than two months. This happened in the terrible winter of 1855. A few years later the Governor lost his wife, Emma who died in August 1859 at the age of 43.

At the end his period of office in 1862, the population had grown to 600 people and nearly 20,000 sheep.

---

[46] Smith, John; *Those Were The Days*, Ed. Falkland Islands Trust, Bluntisham, 1989, p. 11.

Classic shipwrecks around the Islands.

The British Occupation

Only in 1867, was West Falkland colonised when Mr. John Waldron began farming in Port Howard. Over time this was to become one of the most important Falklands farms.*

The Gauchos who stayed and their legacy

Once the British had successfully imposed the *Pax Britanica* in the Islands, and after the repatriation of the gaucho Rivero and his companions out of necessity, they allowed the gauchos who were not openly involved in the rebellion to remain on the Islands.

But Governor Moody realised the need to keep the gauchos because *"the cattle of these Islands are all very wild and very difficult to capture, but I am inclined to think that the typical gaucho of the Pampas, on horses trained for the task, will not find it so difficult nor dangerous as I have been informed"*.[47]

In contrast, all Louis Vernet's properties, goods, houses and belongings were confiscated.

Charles Darwin had the opportunity to live through the transfer of the Islands from the Argentines to the British. He visited them twice, in April 1833 and in March/April 1834. On both occasions he was on board the *"Beagle"* commanded by Captain FitzRoy. He

---

(*) It is now onwed by the see brothers and it is perchaps the best managed farm in the Falklands.
[47] Solari Yrigoyen, Hipólito; *Malvinas, lo que no cuentan los ingleses*, El Ateneo, Buenos Aires, 1998. p. 13.

described with admiration in various writings, the abilities of the gauchos to move around the Islands, to capture the cattle, to cook in the *camp* and especially their riding abilities.[48] Captain FitzRoy considered the gauchos to be excellent inhabitants of the Islands.

Among the other Argentine inhabitants who stayed were Antonia Roxa, Gregoria Madrid, Carmelita Penny, Pascual Ricano, José Espino and Manuel Coronel.[49]

In 1851, when the British colony had become firmly established, there were 51 adults and 18 minors of either Argentine or *Oriental* (what it now Uruguay) origin. All were registered in British records as Spanish to avoid them appearing as Argentines.[50]

But even more important, were the British immigrants, the majority of Scottish origin, who adapted to the gaucho customs, from the way they saddled and mounted their horses, to the way in which they handled the livestock. Many gaucho words have remained and are still linked to various places in the *camp*, like "rincón", "corral", "gaucho", "paso libre", "estancia", "cerro", "tordillo", "zaino", "colorado", "recado" etc. All these words are still in use today.[51]

The Islands in those days had no roads or fences, only corrals in the settlements of Puerto Louis or Soledad and Stanley. Little by little, following the Patagonian model, farms and outposts began to appear.

---

[48] Armstrong, Patrick, *Darwin's Desolate Islands*, Chippenham, London, 1992, p. 52.
[49] Solari Yrigoyen, Hipólito; Ibid, p. 14 onwards.
[50] Solari Yrigoyen, Hipólito; Ibid, p. 21 onwards.
[51] Munro, Richard; *Place names of the Falkland Islands*, Shackleton Scholarship Fund, London, 1998.

Sheep in their corrals at Port Louis.

The British Occupation

Communications were either by horse or by boat from one island to another or even within the same island. The only means of communication was a personal journey, through sending messages or correspondence. The gauchos who remained lost all contact with the continent. Not only were the gauchos isolated but the Scottish contract workers did not leave for years either, and sometimes stayed for life. This system remained practically unchanged throughout the whole period.

The origin of the cattle dated back to the original livestock imported by Bougainville in 1764. By 1833, there had already been many *criollo* cattle introduced from the Pampas, having become a strong local breed of various colours as described by Darwin.[52]

The horses did not reproduce like the cattle. The reasons are unknown because in Patagonia the wild herds always reproduced easily. Perhaps the dampness and distemper effected a natural control.

The English naval officers, in various reports to the Admiralty blamed gaucho customs and the way they rode the horses, as well as the use of spurs for the short active life (only three or four years) of the horses.[53] The truth of the matter was that the *gauchos* treated their horses well, but the hardship of the climate exacerbated their preference for new horses. Even in the Pampas a gaucho is always proud of riding young horses, sometimes even untamed.

---

[52] Spruce, Joan; *Corrals and Gauchos*, Falklands Conservation, 1992, p. 6.
[53] Spruce Joan; ibid, p. 7.

The British Occupation

It is also likely, even though the *gauchos* are known for the way they care for their horses, that they probably slaughtered the mares to eat the meat. The *"pampas indians"* had always enjoyed eating the mares and it was a custom adopted by some gauchos. Other horses were slaughtered for their hides and horsehair in an environment where natural resources were scarce.

The British associated the *gauchos* with indians, with the mixed Spanish blood indians, but avoided calling them Argentines. The truth is that many *gauchos*, after the British occupation, were brought from Montevideo and Punta Arenas, but there were also Argentines including foremen who came from the Patagonian settlements. Many of the *Oriental gauchos* (from Uruguay) were either black or mulatto. Amongst these was Juan Arcie, well known for his skills, who was drowned while driving cattle in 1864.

A few Spanish from Gibraltar also settled in the Islands. Among them was Andrés Pitaluga, who arrived in 1841 and was a gaucho foreman in Puerto Louis. After working in various places on the Islands his family established a farm in San Salvador which they still have. [54]

There were also English *gauchos*. Among them was Avery Mitchel, who was employed as a workman and Head Horseman in Port Louis. Another European gaucho was Louis Dufrais, one of the few Frenchmen to stay.

The *gauchos* lived freely on the Islands, moving from

---

[54] Spruce, Joan; ibid, p. 11.

Sheep shearing.

The British Occupation

farm to farm, according to the work required, in the same way as they did the on the Pampas, but in a much more rigorous climate and unable to escape the authorities. Some were hanged for actual or presumed crimes. The facts here are mixed with myths. No foreman was ever prosecuted for hanging or whipping a Gaucho.

From 1840 on East Falkland, the Lafone settlement in Lafonia (the south of the island) flourished, with the building of a salting house. A Norwegian ship, the *"Napoléon"*, brought the Lafone family from Montevideo together with more than 100 others and gauchos from Montevideo and Punta Arenas. Lorenzo Fernandez was the *gaucho* foreman. In general the gauchos were brought without their women, so that their numbers remained limited. However, there were numerous exceptions. Several gaucho families lived in the Hope Place salting house.[55] They came to the Falklands with the expectation of making some money and then returning to the pampas. Most never went back.

Murders and hangings continued for years. The desperation of some gauchos who could never return home can only be imagined. In 1874, Roberto Gonzalez murdered one James Miller in Darwin. The next day he was found hanged. In those days, the law was in the hands of the foremen, and for many years Governors simply turned a blind eye.

West Falkland has been inhabited and divided into farms since 1870.

---

[55] Spruce, Joan; ibid, p. 15.

There were some gauchos who integrated into the British community. Thus many British surnames appear amongst the gauchos. The registers also show several marriages like those of Andrés Pitaluga and Miss Charmosa and Agustine Fleuret and Richard Atkins.

Life on the Islands was difficult, as much for the gauchos as for the Scottish, Irish and English immigrants. Vegetables could only be grown with difficulty, trees were slow to grow and wheat would not thrive. All the provisions and other basic necessities were imported from Montevideo or Punta Arenas, or traded with visiting ships. There was never a problem with milk, because there had always been dairy cattle on the Islands.

There were appreciably different lifestyles on the Islands. The gauchos lived in thatched huts known as *"rancias"*[56]. In general these were built out of dry peat with tussac grass roofs. The main houses were sometimes of stone and others were of imported materials, like wood and sheet metal. In Stanley they also used the remains of the many wrecked ships. The best houses were well appointed with imported furniture. The furnishings of the gauchos were limited to their saddles, their cots, a table and a bench. They had no running water or bathrooms.

There was never a shortage of food. The abundance of livestock made meat available at all times. The *yerba mate* for the gauchos and the tea for the English was always available in the stores in Stanley and Darwin, as were sugar and other luxury articles, but at high prices.

---

[56] Derived from the Spanish "rancho" or "ranchería".

The British Occupation

The gauchos had only a few personal possessions, including the tack for their horses, a lasso, their *bolas* and their knives.

The *bolas* or *boleadoras* were known as "balloes" by the Scottish shepherds. The knife was used to eat, for work, to brand the cattle, to butcher cattle, to work the hides and for self-defence. *Gauchos* never carried firearms, which were only used by foremen and the English.

The game of *taba* was introduced by the *gauchos*, and was played by generations of Falkland Islanders, who have adopted it as their own.[57]

Gaucho clothing was used by many Scottish sheep farmers and survived until 1982.[58]

British Naval officials who visited the Islands and whose ships had to remain for repairs, enjoyed outings to the *camp* with *gauchos*, as reported in the chronicles of times of Darwin, FitzRoy and thereafter.

Since these times Spanish and British surnames have been mixed up amongst the *gauchos*, for instance James Pitaluga[59] in Port Howard, Casimiro Pinas in Salvador, the Despreux in Estancia, the Charmosas in Smylie's Village and James Campbell in Corral.

New Spanish names appeared in the maps of the

---

[57] Spruce, Joan; ibid, p. 21.
[58] On a journey to Saunders Island in 1995, I encountered an old gaucho of Scottish origin dressed in gaucho style. In later journeys I did not find anyone dressed as a gaucho.
[59] The Pitaluga family originally came from the British colony of Gibraltar.

Islands: *"dos lomas", "cerritos", "corral", "rodeo", "tranquilidad", "campito", "campo verde", "cantera", "point frío", "terramota", "laguna", "legua", "torcida point", "pioja", "cómodo ditch", "ganada grande", "chata creek", "l'antioja", "horqueta", "boca", "isla", "rincón del toro", "galpón", "piedra sola", "laguna seca", "rincón de la yeguada", "cerro Montevideo"* (named no doubt by an Uruguayan), *"ruana rincón", "campina pond", "manada"*.[60]

Many terms appeared to be derived from a confused mixture of English, Spanish and the typical language of the *gauchos* (not *lunfardo*[61] the Buenos Aires slang).

In the spoken language there were many words referring to horses and livestock. To this day one can hear: *"alazán", "colorado", "negro", "pestaña blanca", "picazo", "mala cara", "gateado", "sarco", "bozal", "cabresta", "bastos", "cinch", "cojinilla", "sobrepuesto", "meletas", "tientas", "manares"*.[62]

From the archaeological point of view the *gauchos* only left traces in the stone and peat corrals that can be seen from afar as soon as one approaches the Islands from the air. It is symptomatic that practically the only constructions left by the *gauchos* were for the cattle and not for themselves.

The corrals were made of earth, stone or peat depending on the materials available in the area, but were always round and almost 2m high. This clearly indicates the characteristics of wild cattle and wild

---

[60] Spruce, Joan; ibid, p. 31
[61] While Gaucho slang included many indian words, *lunfardo* was heavily influenced by Italian.
[62] Spruce, Joan; ibid, p. 32

The British Occupation

horses. Some corrals are still in excellent condition, such as those in Darwin that are made out of stone, or those on Saunders Island. Some earth corrals in Puerto Louis can only be barely discerned. The corrals were situated in places where it was relatively easy to round up the cattle or near the settlements. We must bear in mind that there was no wood on the islands and it was therefore impossible to build wooden corrals.

Several years later wood was systematically imported from Staten Island whilst it was not occupied by Argentina, and later from Punta Arenas.

The Catholics

The catholic settlement on the islands occurred during the first French occupation and the foundation of Port Louis and was witness to the different phases of the islands' development.

Amongst the French founders of Port Louis in 1764 was Father José Pernetty, a Benedictine priest who accompanied the members of the expedition to satisfy their spiritual needs.

When the Islands were handed over to Spain in 1767, two French priests stayed on with the settlers. In less than two years the Spanish built the first chapel on the Islands, called *Nuestra Señora de la Soledad*, with a modest 10 feet high tower.

In 1774 the bell tower was completed to call the 80 inhabitants to participate in the religious services. In 1780 the church was renovated and a pulpit was added as well as a christening font, necessary for the many births taking place on the Islands.

The *gaucho* never made a public display of his religious faith but was undoubtedly a firm believer and the small chapel was an important spiritual support for those living in those desolate regions.[63]

In 1790 Father Pius de Aguiar wrote to the Bishop of Buenos Aires to say that the church was too small as it could only hold half of the 200 people who lived there. As a result of the petition, and thanks to the funds sent from the capital of the Vice-Royalty, a new church was built of bricks and stone and was consecrated on 4 November 1801.

The last Spanish parish priest was Father Juan Canosa, who left the Islands in 1811 when Viceroy Elío from Montevideo ordered the withdrawal of the Spanish forces from the Islands as a result of the growing independence movement in the River Plate.

When the English ordered the transfer of the capital from Port Louis to Stanley, 75% of the population were Anglicans and had their own chaplain. The Catholics, in those days gauchos, the descendents of the French settlers and some Irish immigrants, had no spiritual support.

In 1850, Tomás Havers, a devout Catholic, rented a house in Stanley where he offered religious services on Sundays and religious instruction during the week.

---

[63] Of the current Islanders, very few attend Mass on Sundays despite there being three churches, one Catholic, one Anglican and one Protestant.

The British Occupation

Havers wrote to Cardinal Wiserman –Archbishop of Westminster– and to Cardinal Bernalo in Rome, requesting English speaking Catholic priests.

A few years later in 1857, Father Kirwan was sent to the Islands. The lack of official support and the scarcity of resources delayed the construction of a chapel, which was finally built in 1873 and replaced by another in 1885. The first Mass was celebrated there on 28 February 1886.[64]

Finally, a church was built in 1899, thanks to the efforts of the Catholic community –a beautiful wooden chapel– the Saint Mary, which is still today offering spiritual comfort to the Catholic Islanders, including Irish, Spanish, Uruguayans, a few Argentines as well as the crews of visiting Spanish and Polish fishing boats.

The old chapel was made available as a parochial residence and the Catholic community currently consists of a parish priest, two nuns and almost 200 worshippers.

The Anglican Mission and the History of Christ Church Cathedral[65]

In 1841 Commander Alan Gardiner resigned his commission in the Royal Navy and emigrated with his family to Port Louis.

Gardiner's objective was to establish a mission on the

---

[64] Etchebarne Bullrich, Conrado; "Historia de la Iglesia Católica", *La Prensa*, Buenos Aires, 24 July 1994, p. 7

[65] Murphy, Gervase; *Christ Church Cathedral*, Lance Bidewell, London, 1991.

Falklands to civilize the *Yagan* Indians in Tierra del Fuego. To do this he required an operational base, for which he chose Keppel Island, which was known to have a good harbour located northeast of West Falkland.

After a fund raising trip to London in 1844, he founded the Patagonian Missionary Society, which in 1868 changed its name to the South American Missionary Society.

That same year James Moody, the brother of Governor Moody, was appointed as the first Anglican chaplain in Stanley.

In September 1850 he left Liverpool on board the *"Ocean Queen"* with his companions: the surgeon Richard Wellis, Joseph Erwin, a volunteer from the Young Christians' Association, John Bryant, a carpenter and John Pearce and John Badcock, both fisherman. They brought with them two 26ft auxiliary boats for short trips.

Unfortunately, and despite the support of the George Despard Society, the mission failed as a consequence of the lack of adequate logistical support and provisions. The entire group either died of hunger or drowned.

George Despard then decided to take over the reins of the mission and travelled with his wife, children, his adoptive son Thomas Bridges and Alan Gardiner Jr.

The mission began with a small hut in Tierra del Fuego. Unfortunately his lack of tact in his relationship with the Indians resulted in the massacre of 8 missionaries and the return of Gardiner to England in 1861.

The British Occupation

Thomas Bridges, who was only 18, but had made the effort to learn the indiam language, decided to stay on. The Reverend Stirling arrived on Keppel Island the following year to take charge of the mission, and despite the previous failures, a house made of tree-trunks was built in Ushuaia Bay in the Beagle Channel in 1869. It was there that Thomas Bridges, having been left in charge of the mission, conducted the first baptisms in Tierra del Fuego in 1871.

Stirling, in recognition of his success, was appointed Anglican Bishop of the Falkland Islands. He was ordained in Westminster in 1869 and took charge of the church in Stanley in 1872.

Bishop Stirling was succeeded by the Reverend Lowther Brandon, who was in charge of the Diocese for almost 30 years, looking after the spirituality of the Anglican settlers.

The original Anglican Church, Holy Trinity of Stanley, had been destroyed by a mudslide in 1886.

It was then that the decision was taken to build the Christ Church Cathedral, a splendid stone church on Stanley Bay that was consecrated in 1892.

Ships and Shipwrecks[66]

The main reason for the British occupation of the Islands was their strategic location for world trade at the

---

[66] Southby Tailyour, Ewen; *Falkland Islands Shores,* Conway Maritime Ltd, London 1985.

beginning of the 19th century, a situation that remained until the beginning of the 20th century.

Every year thousands of ships were forced to round Cape Horn to reach the Pacific ports. After the independence of the American colonies all the American ports of the Pacific –until then closed to Great Britain– became free ports. Great Britain, which was the main naval power, took *de facto* commercial possession of most of the American ports.

If we add to that the *"Race to the Pacific"*, which began in 1848 with the American occupation of California, we can understand the magnitude of the maritime traffic.

The only alternative port to the Falkland Islands was Punta Arenas in the Magellan Straits. A city that had been much influenced by the British.

In the age of sail the passage from the Atlantic to the Pacific was not easy. There were only two alternatives; the classic Spanish route through the Magellan Straits, with the difficulty of navigating in the channels against almost constant, strong headwinds and with a very difficult passage into the Pacific, or to go around Cape Horn in the most dangerous seas in world, in ships that were not designed to be able to sail so close to the wind.

Poncet, Sally & Jerome; *Southern Ocean Cruising*, Australian Geographic Magazine, 1991.
Miller, David; *The Wreck of the Isabella*, Leo Cooper, London, 1995.
Dodge, Bertha, *Marooned*, Syracuse University Press, New York, 1986.
Cameron, Jane; *The Falklands and the Dwarf*, Picton Publishing Limited, London 1995.
Moir, Geoffrey; *The History of the Falklands*, ChrisPrint, Croydon, 1995.
Smith, John; *Condemned at Stanley*, Picton Publishing, UK, 1985.

The British Occupation

It is not surprising that having been either dismasted or forced back by impossible weather, many ships' captains were driven back to the Falkland Islands by the currents and winds. In Patagonia there are practically no harbours and the constant offshore winds made it difficult for large merchant ships loaded with cargo to moor safely.

This explains why Stanley Bay has one of the most impressive collections of hulks and remains of wooden sailing ships. Most of these ships were built in either Great Britain, which was the principal naval power of the time, or in the USA and Canada, both of whom took part in the race to join the coasts of the Atlantic and Pacific before the time of the Panama Canal or trans-continental railways.

These enormous wooden ships are well preserved in the damp, windy and cold climate of the Islands. More than 300 ships have foundered in the waters of the Falkland Islands. Many more have disappeared in the breakers around the exposed coasts to the south of the archipelago. Some of these hulks are the only existing remnants of these types of ships. Brigantines, barques, clippers, frigates and all kinds of cargo sailing ships can be found on its coasts.

In the second half of the 19th century Stanley Bay was one of the busiest ports in the South Atlantic. Gold fever in California and the desire for quick wealth were the main reasons that led to unscrupulous privateers putting to sea in vessels unsuitable for the southern seas and weather conditions. Some carrying immigrants and others with only cargo formed part of the group of wrecked ships between the Falklands and Cape Horn. The discovery of gold in Australia increased the number of ships that passed through Falklands' waters even more.

Since 1890 the replacement of sailing ships with steamships limited the number of ships that had to stop in Stanley. The opening of the Panama Canal in the first decade of the 1900s almost completely stopped all the traffic through the Islands.

Among the best-known shipwrecks on the Falklands' coast is that of the *"Philomel"*, which rests on the beach in Stanley Bay. It was a fishing boat, measuring 75ft in length and with a 19ft beam, built in Great Britain in 1945 and was used for inter-island transport. It caught fire and sank in July 1971.

Another well-known sunken vessel is the *"Capricorn"*. It was a Welsh ship, built in 1859. In February 1882 it was heading for the Pacific ports with a full cargo of coal when it ran into heavy weather at Cape Horn. In the middle of the storm, for reasons unknown, the entire cargo caught fire. The captain sank the ship in shallow water off the coast of Staten Island to put out the fire and then used the pumps to re-float the vessel and sail it to Stanley. But the damage caused by the storm and the fire was irreparable and the ship was abandoned at Stanley. For many years it was used as a store and later as accommodation for troops during the Second World War.

Perhaps one of the most characteristic shipwrecks was the *"Jhelum"*. She was a British ship of 428 tons, 123ft long and a beam of 23ft, built in Liverpool in 1849. She made her final voyage in 1870, bound from El Callao to Dunqerque. But, overloaded, she got into

The British Occupation

difficulties rounding the Horn. After nearly sinking and suffering innumerable problems, she reached Stanley in August 1870 where she was abandoned after the crew refused to sail again in a ship in such a poor state of repair. Her hull still lies at the end of the jetty in front of Sullivan House in Stanley.

Another such ship is the *"Margaret"*. She can be seen almost beneath the official dock. The *"Margaret"* was a Canadian clipper of 615 tons built in Halifax in 1836. She arrived in Stanley in 1850. Her original voyage was from Liverpool to Valparaiso with a cargo of coal but, overloaded, she was unable to withstand the pounding of the seas in Drake Passage and returned, practically destroyed, to Stanley from where she never sailed again.

One of the best-preserved wrecks is that of the *"Charles Cooper"*. She remains in front of the Falkland Islands Company jetty. She was a wooden North American ship on passage from Philadelphia to San Francisco with a cargo of coal. As a result of damage to the hull she arrived in Stanley in 1866. She was acquired by a museum in New York but has yet to be moved there.

This brief resúme of the some of the shipwrecks that can be found in the islands gives one an idea of the intense traffic of commercial ships that existed in the second half of the 19th century in this part of the world. At the same time it shows the difficulties in navigating these waters and how Stanley had become a repair port with ample work for carpenters, plumbers, caulkers, sail makers and other tradesmen involved in ship repairs. All this disappeared with the introduction of steamships at the end of the century and with the opening of the Panama Canal a few years later.

131

Aerial view of Stanley.

The *Camp*[67]

Apart from maritime life in Stanley, the political disputes, official journeys and Governors, the real life of the Islands, in the barely two centuries in which the Islands had been inhabited, is in the *Camp*,[68] which is how the Islanders describe everything outside Stanley.

With an economic system based on a monopolistic company, the "Falkland Islands Company", owner of the majority of the land and all the businesses on the Islands, and a few other absentee landlords, the *camp* was left in the hands of foremen who were in charge of the upkeep, breeding and shearing of the flocks of sheep that sustained the Island's economy.

In the best colonial style the farms were administered by a vertical structure with the ultimate decision making taking place in London. The criteria were minimum expenditure and maximum production. Almost 700 Falkland Islanders (today less than 400) inhabited the Falklands' *camp*.

The homes of the foremen were comfortable and similar to the main houses of the Patagonian *estancias*, tidy, decorated and practically without trees, a few

---

[67] Smith, John; *Those Were The Days*, Falkland Islands Trust, Bluntisham, 1989.
Wilkinson, Rosemary; *Diary of a Farmer's Wife*, Lyons Lithographic, Hampshire, 1992.
[68] An English word derived from the Spanish word campo.
[69] Take 2 onions and 4 potatoes. Fry the onion and potatoes in butter with salt and pepper. Then simmer in half a litre of milk for 30 minutes. The secret was not to let the soup boil.

chickens, dogs, pigs and a small vegetable garden completed the rural habitat. The situation of the workmen was more austere, with no bathrooms or hot water. They had one meal a day, usually mutton, and a few luxuries such as biscuits, tea, *yerba mate**, all of which was meticulously deducted from their daily wage.

During the early years most of the workmen were Uruguayan, Chilean and even Argentine gauchos. Later the Scots and Irish gradually replaced them. But they all adapted to the local customs, not too different from those of Patagonia. The foremen were generally English. Many mariners from the ships that put in or were wrecked on the coast also became part of the Falklands' community.

These families formed the basis of Falkland Island society. Today many Falkland Islanders are proud to say that their families have lived on the Islands for 5 or 6 generations.

The sheep required much care and attention. It was necessary to build fences and corrals, to shear, castrate and butcher the livestock. The cutting, collecting and drying of peat was also very time-consuming. Peat was, and still is, used as the principal fuel for heating and cooking.

The people lived in absolute isolation on the farms, especially on the more remote islands. The only means of communication was the local ship that brought provisions and collected the wool two or three times a

---

(*) The mate is a tea originated from Paraguay and is widely drink in Chile, Argentina, Paraguay, Uruguay and southern Brazil.

year. Many workmen only left their farms four or five times in their lives to visit Stanley. Most of them did not leave the Islands at all. Education was restricted to that which could be taught at home and sometimes by itinerant rural teachers who occasionally passed through the farms. Those who lived in Stanley or Darwin considered themselves privileged as they had primary schools.

Only the wealthy minority could afford to send their children to continue their studies in Great Britain. There was a great distinction between the Islanders who did not have a British passport and the expatriates. Only the latter had passports and the right to an annual trip to Britain. Their respective salaries were also very different.

The 3.5 million acres of the archipelago was divided into 30 farms, including those in the hands of the Falkland Islands Company (FIC), and had a stock of 600,000 head of wool-bearing sheep. These had replaced the 100,000 head of cattle that remained after the Spanish and Argentine period.

This system remained practically unchanged until the events of 1982.

One of the greatest difficulties for the rural population, as in Patagonia, was the chronic lack of women. The few women there left the Islands at the first available opportunity, either with a sailor, a soldier or a merchant.

Those who remained had an even more isolated life than their husbands, as they did not even participate in the general work of the settlement. This does not mean that they were not extremely busy, keeping the fire going in the house, looking after the vegetable garden and the chickens, caring for their children (many were born and many died), looking for penguin eggs to supplement the diet or picking small, edible fruit.

There are more than 70 varieties of shrubs on the Islands, many of them are edible although some are toxic.

From the time of the old mariners of the 17th and 18th centuries, the qualities of the scurvy grass *(Oxalis enneaphylla)* were well known. It was so named because of its efficaciousness in combating scurvy. A delicious beverage with vitamin C, so necessary for the seamen and the inhabitants of these desolate lands, was produced from the stems of this fleshy, dark green plant. M. Pernetty, one of the French pioneers on the Island, called it *"vinagrette"* and it was known by this name for many years. It reproduces easily and is identifiable by its typical white flower.

Another plant widely used by the inhabitants is the "diddle-dee" *(Empetrum rubrum)*. It is one of the most common plants on the Islands. It is invasive and dominating in the hard *camp*. It also has fleshy leaves and stems and can be recognised by its deep red colour. Although the fruit is not sweet it has a characteristic flavour and is ideal for making marmalade, sweets and pies, which break the monotony of the Island diet.

The "tussac" grass *(Parodiochloa flabellata)* is a grass with thick, fleshy leaves and stems that grow to a height of 2m and are found especially on raised coasts and cliffs fertilized by seabird guano. The stem is edible and there is

The British Occupation

no doubt that it supplemented the diet of the rural workers on their journeys across the Falklands *camp*. Its height and softness also makes clumps of it ideal for resting in, protected from the wind. Another of its characteristics is that it stays green throughout the year.

The "Teaberry" (Myrteloa nummularia) derives its name from its leaves, which were made into tea by the early inhabitants. With a distinctive, sweet flavour it is found in damp areas of deep peat.

The "Sea Cabbage" *(Senecio candicans)* is a fleshy lettuce, found on the coasts, that grows to a height of 80cm, has a characteristic yellow flower and is also known for providing protection from scurvy.

The most abundant grass and the principle nutrient for the sheep is "Whitegrass" *(Cortaderia pilosa)*. It is the commonest grass on the Islands but its appearance varies with the soil in which it grows. When it is young and tender it is excellent animal feed. When it is old and dry it is useless. The farmers have regularly burn the grass in spring so that new tender shoots will grow to feed the sheep.

Another characteristic grass is the "Cinammon Grass" *(Hierochloe redolens)*. It has long, thin, flat, fibrous green leaves and the flowers and seeds have a distinctive aroma. It is found in undergrazed areas and is a very nutritious grass.

The Islanders' diet was also based on fish, caught in the many bays and streams on the Islands. Penguin eggs supplemented the otherwise monotonous diet that was occasionally varied with stews of Upland Geese from the highlands. The Upland Goose is tame and herbivorous with tender meat and a very pleasant flavour. Ducks, of which there were plenty on the Islands, were also part of the diet.

Amongst the animals most disliked, was the local fox, or *Warrah*, which was exterminated by the English colonists. The Patagonian Fox was re-introduced on Weddel Island by its eccentric owner, Mr Hamilton. This animal caused many problems for lambing ewes and is still not under control. The European Rabbit was also successfully introduced and is easily hunted in the area around Port Louis.

But the main domestic pests on the Islands are the unwanted rodents. Rats and mice invaded the Islands from shipwrecks and the ships that put in to harbour. This is why the main domesticated animal on the Island is the cat, kept by every householder.

Social Life

It cannot be said that social life in Stanley was lively, but the English brought with them many of the customs that were taken to other far-flung corners of the Empire. A small, elegant upper class, formed by the Governor, his wife, the Protestant minister and his family, the General Manager of the Falkland Islands Company and the captains and senior officers of visiting ships were part of the elite of the Islands.

The organizing of balls was a regular event, originally held in the Government Stores, later in Gilbert Cottage and, since the end of the century, in the Town Hall. They regularly held one or two balls a month. Some of them were grand balls on the occasion of the Queen's Birthday, the May Ball, the Battle Day Ball and the Fancy Dress Ball.

Other social events were parades and exercises by the small Falkland Islands Defence Force in the presence of the Governor and senior officials.

But the most popular parties were no doubt the Christmas Sport Dances, which coincided with the horseraces, being the only occasion when the great majority of those who lived in the *camp* would travel to Stanley. Displays of *gaucho* skills and the horseraces have always been the most popular events in Stanley.

In the 19th century, football and rowing races were introduced in Stanley Bay. The latter sport was later abandoned.

However pubs were and remain the principle form of recreation in Stanley. Beer and Scotch combined with a good game of darts was, and remains, the popular form of entertainment in the evenings.

Among the ladies and families bridge was always popular to liven up the long winter evenings. It is still relatively popular on the Islands.

In 1927 the introduction of radio communication produced a significant change to Island customs. Listening to the radio replaced homemade musical entertainment. Communications between the farms and with Stanley became easier.

Conrado Etchebarne Bullrich

The 1919 Celebrations

This is still remembered today as one of the most important occasions on the Islands until the events of 1982.

The Battle of the Falklands, which took place near the Islands, brought the reality of the First World War close to home for Islanders.

On the morning of 8 December 1914 an observer of the Falkland Island Defence Force saw the German Fleet approaching. The British ship *HMS Glasgow* fired a warning shot to alert *HMS Canopus* to the danger. That is how the battle, which ensured British primacy in the South Atlantic for the rest of the war, started. The British squadron was composed of *HMS Invincible, HMS Inflexible, HMS Kent, HMS Caernavon, HMS Cornwall* and *HMS Bristol.* The German Fleet was formed by the *Gneisenau*, the *Nürnberg*, the *Scharnhorst*, the *Leipzig* and the *Dresden*, together with the transport ships the *Bäden* and the *St. Isabel.* After a bloody battle and a long and hard chase, the whole of the German fleet was sunk with thousands killed.

In the winter of 1919 the moment for the British to celebrate victory had come. On Sunday 16 July a day of thanksgiving was declared. The Governor, Sir William Douglas Young, presided over a solemn ceremony that included the placing of a commemorative plaque in memory of the British servicemen who died in the Battle. There was also an impressive parade of British forces along Ross Road, followed by a concert in the Town Hall. *"Rule Britannia"* was sung for Britain, *"La*

Entrance to the Port Louis farm.

Marseillaise" for France and *"La Brabaconne"* for Belgium. There was then a childrens' party and finally a public firework display. The parties included a formal dinner and ball. The celebrations continued for more than a week, with boat races and other events. From then on "Battle Day" has been celebrated in the Falkland Islands. An impressive monument overlooking Stanley Bay commemorates the battle.

Island Cooking

Island cooking is not limited to scarce local products. In Stanley the possibility of trading with visiting ships meant that the Globe Store was able to stock a wide range of products and rich local culinary arts developed.

We should start with soups, indispensable in this cold, desolate and windy climate. Every family had its own favourite recipe, handed down from generation to generation. Among the most popular were potato and onion soup (especially Mrs. Morrison's recipe),[69] mushroom soup, carrot soup and *criolla* marrowbone soup.

In a port there is no lack of fish. The trout from the San Carlos River are particularly famous. For many years the record was held by Terry Spruce, General Manager of the Falkland Islands Company, with a fish weighing 21lbs. The fish were traditionally cooked over an open fire on the banks of the river. Other recipes included Baked Mullet, Fish Pie, Mushroom Mullet, and Oven-Baked Trout and, of course, fried fish.

The British Occupation

Every farm had chickens and ducks and there were many different recipes. The best known were Roast Goose, Goose in wine and Teal Duck, Casserole and Chicken-in-a-Jug and the ubiquitous barbecued chicken.

There were always eggs too. Apart from breakfasts one could choose from Baked Cheese Eggs, Egg and Ham Casserole or the traditional Egg Curry for those whose stomachs could stand it.

Economic and ingenious recipes for meat were also created. Roast Chops and Onions, Mutton Chop Cutlets, Garlic Mutton Chops, Breakfast Chops and traditional Christmas Lamb and pasties. Rice with meatballs was always popular with the children. All these were accompanied with the locally-made pickle.

Puddings, biscuits and cakes cheered up the Falkland Islanders' afternoons. They had to use their creativity to make up for unavailable ingredients. Caramel Tart, Butter pudding and Chocolate Pudding were made for special occasions, as well as the local specialty Penguin Egg Pavlova, Lemon Tart and the everyday tart or Teaberry Tart and Teaberry Cake, Teaberry Rolls and Teaberry Rum Cake.

Biscuits were also popular, including oatmeal biscuits, brown biscuits and cream crackers. All these were homemade on Falkland farms.

V

THE ARGENTINE CLAIM

Anglo-Argentine Relations

The evolution of the Argentine claim from the beginning of the British occupation must be analysed in the light of the development of Anglo-Argentine relations, including those before the Conflict.

Commercial and economic interests versus deeply rooted emotions were and remain the principal ingredients of this story. Of all the European powers, the United Kingdom was undoubtedly the one that had the greatest impact on the economic and political life in the Provinces of the River Plate, which would later form the Argentine Republic. At the same time England had been the foreign country that caused most mixed feelings among Argentines. Perhaps this is because Great Britain has been the foreign state that has had the longest and most successful relationship with the River Plate and the only country that invaded Buenos Aires in early 19th century and with which Argentina fought a war in the 20th century.

The origin of the Anglo-Argentine relationship goes back to the Spanish colonial period. The relationship became more important with the collapse of the Spanish Empire and had its moment of glory after the institutional organisation of the Argentine Republic. In this period (1860-1930) Argentina had become an informal member of the British Empire. It was unthinkable then that there could be any dispute over the Falkland Islands. After the decline of both countries, as a result of the crisis of the 1930s, and the deterioration of the bilateral relationship, the old dispute over the Islands resurfaced.

Great Britain and the Birth of Argentina

At the beginning of the 18th century, the need of the emerging British Empire for economic expansion led to a direct confrontation with the Spanish Empire and pressure for the opening up of the economies of the British colonies on the American continent.

As a result of the Treaty of Utrecht[70], Great Britain was able to achieve a monopoly of the slave trade in Spanish America through the British South Sea Company. Thus, with a "black base"*, the British began their legal and illegal commercial activities in Buenos Aires. Particularly smuggling, which not only enriched the English merchants, but also provided the main source of growth for Buenos Aires at a time when nearly all legal trading through the port was prohibited.

---

[70] The same Treaty through which Britain obtained Gibraltar.
(*) Slave market.

The Argentina Claim

This flourishing illegal trade eroded the links between the River Plate and the capital of the Vice-Royalty. Lima was more than 3,000 miles away, over difficult roads wich included several deserts, rain froests and the Andes intself. From there one still had to cross two oceans to reach Spain. There is no doubt that a direct journey to London was much shorter and more profitable. Through the 18th century and despite the deterioration of the Anglo-Spanish relationship, British trade in Buenos Aires continued to grow.

This commercial influence was even greater after the creation of the Vice-Royalty of the River Plate in 1776 and specifically after the passing of the *"Free Trade Regulations Act"* in 1778. From the point of view of the English merchants, Buenos Aires was nearer than any port in the Pacific or Indian Oceans.

In the first years of the 19th century, as a result of the Napoleonic Wars, Spanish trade with its colonies was totally paralysed. Great Britain was thus presented with the opportunity of conquering the River Plate. In 1797 Trinidad Island had already been occupied, followed a few years later by the Dutch Cape Colony. In 1806 and 1807 the British attempted to invade Buenos Aires and Montevideo. Both were military failures but served to generate a sense of self-esteem amongst the *"porteños"* which proved invaluable for the success of the May Revolution in 1810.

In 1782 Lord Shelbourne said, *"We prefer trade to dominion"*[71], his vision became a reality in the River Plate.

---

[71] "We prefer trade to dominion", Anthony McFarlane; *The British in the Americas*, Longman, New York, 1994, p. 305.

In 1825 Great Britain was the first power to recognise the independence of the United Provinces of the River Plate by signing a treaty of friendship and trade.

However, this did not prevent them from taking the Falkland Islands by force a few years later in 1833. The relationship with Argentina worsened for almost thirty years. Besides the episode of the Falkland Island there were also the Anglo-French blockades of the River Plate in the 1840s and the local civil wars.

It was only after 1860, when Argentina was able to organise itself institutionally and when the British were firmly convinced that *"Trade was much better than dominion"*, that the Falkland Islands problem was forgotten and a prosperous relationship was established between the two countries. Argentina and Great Britain had complimentary economies and both were interested in avoiding North American penetration of the Southern Cone.

After the *"Conquest of the Desert"* led by General Roca in the second half of the 19th century and the opening up of British markets to the production of the pampas, the Argentine economy grew rapidly, based on trade with Great Britain. In only a few years British investment created a network of railways throughout the country, built ports, cold storage facilities and new banks specialising in foreign trade.

This relationship was mutually beneficial. By 1920 Argentina had one of the highest incomes per capita in the world and had become one of the most promising countries of the 20th century. Immigrants and assets

The Argentina Claim

flooded in in equal measure. Great Britain had become the centre of world trade and its people had acquired an enviable quality of life, not least thanks to the inexpensive produce of the Argentine pampas. By 1913 Argentina was the destination of 42% of British exports to Latin America and provided 58% of imports from the continent.[72]

British influence was especially important among the Buenos Aires elite. The British way of life was adopted among the wealthy *porteños*. Football, rugby, tennis, yachting, polo and horse racing established firm roots among the Argentines.

However the crisis of the 1930s would put an end to this almost idyllic situation. The feeling of loyalty for the *"informal empire"*, a long tradition of responsibility and hundreds of millions of pounds in investments did not stop Great Britain from sacrificing its interests in Argentina in favour of the Empire. The Ottawa Conference of 1932 left Argentina out of the British world. The Roca-Runciman Pact was not only unable to reverse this, but accentuated the anti-British feelings of an increasingly influential group of Argentine nationalists. For the first time in almost 100 years the Falkland Islands became an issue again.

The Second World War brought about the end of the British Empire and the rise to power of General Juan Domingo Perón in Argentina. In 1945 Perón fought with equal passion against the so-called *agro-ganadera* (landowning cattle farmers) oligarchy and British

---

[72] Cairns P.J. and Hopkins; *British Imperialism 1688-1914*, Longman, New York, 1994, p. 288.

interests, both of which had been responsible for building the country. He was successful in his enterprise and Argentina entered a dark period that lasted nearly fifty years.

While the Anglo-Argentine economic relationship deteriorated the Falklands issue grew in importance. After Perón there was not a government that did not pursue the matter.

Links with the Islands

Apart from the diplomatic claims and the different elements of the Anglo-Argentine relationship, there existed an intense relationship between the River Plate and the Islands. The gaucho culture of the River Plate area was maintained intact on the Islands thanks to the continuing influence of the region. Despite English efforts to *"Anglicise"* the Islands, they never lost their links with the continent.

After the British occupation of the Islands in 1833 a dozen or so *gauchos* remained, as did all the cattle and all the horses introduced by Vernet, the Spanish and Bougainville before him. Pigs, chickens and other domesticated birds also remained.

The commercial relationship with Buenos Aires was interrupted for a time, but already by 1845 the Britons Whitington, Culey and Governor Richard Clement Moody had imported 900 sheep from the River Plate region with the intention of replacing cattle rearing with sheep farming for wool. In the short term there were

The Argentina Claim

great difficulties in adaptation and after only a year the number of wool-bearing sheep had dropped to only 180.[73]

At the beginning of the 1850s Samuel Lafone, a Uruguayan resident, father of Dr. Samuel Lafone Quevedo,[74] had acquired the southern half of East Falkland and populated it with sheep also brought from the shores of the River Plate. The Falkland Islands Company had simultaneously imported 200 Cheviot sheep from Scotland. From this cross-breeding the Falklands flocks developed, and in only a few years, spread throughout the Islands.

The other channel of contact between the Islands and the Continent in those years, were the journeys of Luis Piedra Buena. Piedra Buena set sail in the whaling ship *"John Davison"*, commanded by Captain W H Smiley, who, as well as seal hunting undertook commercial transactions and smuggling between the Islands, the Patagonian Coasts and Punta Arenas. He also delivered provisions to the British missionaries in Tierra del Fuego. On various voyages the ship was under the command of Piedra Buena himself, who in 1859 took command of the *"Nancy"*, later renamed the *"Espora"*.

Piedra Buena did a great deal of business between the Islands and the continent, not always successfully.

He also delivered cattle from the Falklands to Pavón Island, on the continent. Cattle that adapted very well but on their return soon became wild.

---

[73] Pereira Lahitte, Carlos T de; *Contribución al conocimiento de las vinculaciones entre las Islas Malvinas y el territorio continental argentino*, p. 19.
[74] Argentine Ethnographer, Director of the Museo de La Plata.

Other voyages between the Islands and the continent were made by Ernesto Roquard, a Frenchman living in Patagonia, who also took Falklands cattle to Patagonia.

After 1880, and at the end of the Desert Campaign, links between Patagonia and the Islands increased dramatically.

In 1884, Patagonia was divided into five new regional governments.[75] Among the instructions given to the new Governor of Santa Cruz was a requirement to colonise the territory with immigrants and cattle from the Falkland Islands.

Consequently, in 1885, the "Patagonian Sheep Farming Company, Estancia Cóndor" owned by H P Wood & Co., was founded on 200,000 hectares of land granted by the Government and with 30,000 sheep brought from the Falkland Islands.

The Governor of Santa Cruz, Carlos María Moyano travelled to the Falkland Islands in 1885 to promote new investments, and to buy 5000 sheep from Mr. Felton. Moyano's business ventures were approved by decree by President Roca.[76]

Among the original Falkland Islander colonists of Santa Cruz, were Herbert Felton, William Haliday, John Rudd, George MacGeorge and George Felton. They all obtained land granted by government in exchange for committing themselves to populate it. Later, other Falkland Islanders like John Scott, William Rudd, John

---

[75] Law 1532.
[76] Decrees of 28 May and 11 July 1885.

The Argentina Claim

Blake, John Hamilton, Donald Patterson, Robert Blake and Henry Jamieson also settled in Santa Cruz. The Buenos Aires newspapers made regular reference to this Falkland Islands colonisation.[77]

There were personal relationships alongside the economic links. Moyano had married a Falkland Islander, Ethel Turner, daughter of James Turner and Rose Claire.

During these years the naval transport ship *"Villarino"* made numerous journeys to the Islands in support of Governor Moyano's business transactions.

It is important to remember that during the greater part of the 19th century, the ecclesiastical authorities in Buenos Aires exercised jurisdiction over the Catholics on the archipelago.

This was as a result of a group of Irish immigrants on the Falkland Islands requesting the Catholic archbishop of Westminster to send priests to the Islands. The response indicated that the request had been passed to Buenos Aires, as the ecclesiastic authorities there were responsible for the Islands. The Irish priest Antonio Domingo Fahy was designated to provide for the spiritual needs of the Islanders. Father Lorenzo Kirwan, who accompanied Fahy, was responsible for the founding of the Catholic Church Stella Maris, later called St Mary's. Another priest who was active on the Islands, was Dean Patrick Dillon, later appointed Canon of Buenos Aires Cathedral, who years later became a Senator for the Province of Buenos Aires and was a

---

[77] Editorial, *La Prensa*, 18 February 1887.

founder of the Irish/Argentine weekly newspaper, *"The Southern Cross"*. In addition to all these links, there was of course the Anglican Mission on Keppel Island and its missionaries in Tierra del Fuego, as described in previous chapters.

Diplomatic Negotiations

Argentina had maintained its claim since 1833, but not always by applying the same degree of pressure. The British, for their part, safe in the security of their naval and military superiority, had always refused to recognise any Argentine claim. It was only in 1964, in the context of the global move towards decolonisation, and withdrawal of the old colonial powers, that Argentina decided to present its claim to the United Nations. The Argentine request was inspired by UN Resolution 1514(15) of 1960, which expressly stated *"the need to put and end ... to all colonisation in all its forms and dimensions"*. The objective of the United Nations decolonisation policy was to return full self-determination to peoples subjected to colonialism, but also in accordance with the UN Charter, respecting national unity and territorial integrity.

Argentina submitted the issue to the C24 Committee*. Subcommittee III, in charge of this issue, determined in its conclusions and recommendations that Resolution 1514 was applicable to the Falkland Islands, took note of

---

(*) A special committee in charge of examining the application of the Declaration regarding the granting of independence to colonial countries and peoples.

the existence of a sovereignty dispute between the governments of the United Kingdom and Argentina and recommended that both parties negotiate a peaceful solution to the problem.

The subcommittee said that the solution had to take the interests of the population into account. This was the intermediate position between that of the United Kingdom which maintained the need to take into account the desires of the Islanders, and that of Argentina which considered that the desires of a population artificially implanted by a colonial power, should not be taken into account.

The report was then approved by the full Committee and presented to the 20th General Assembly where it was approved on 24 November 1965 with 87 votes in favour, none against and 13 abstentions, among them Great Britain, various of its ex-colonies and the United States.

At that time there was no communication between the Islands and the continent, a policy which had been maintained since Peron's first government, and designed to pressure the British into negotiating.

With the approval of the Resolution, the British UN representative announced that his government would obey the decision and privately advised the Argentine representatives that communication between the Islands and Argentina should be resumed to enable both peoples to establish links, but that the United Kingdom would not cede sovereignty without the Islanders consent.

Conversations between the two foreign ministers, Miguel Angel Zabala Ortiz and Michael Stewart began in

1966. Already in 1968, during the government of General Onganía, Foreign Minister Nicanor Costa Mendez had agreed with his British counterpart a memorandum of understanding that accepted a transfer of sovereignty once Great Britain could be satisfied that the interests of the Islanders could be safeguarded, in compliance with UN Resolution 2065.

However, the Labour Government of Harold Wilson backtracked as a result of strong parliamentary pressure from the Falkland Islands Company lobby.

The disappointment of Foreign Minister Costa Mendez, until then a confirmed anglophile, would sew the seeds of Galtieri's unfortunate venture 14 years later.

Between 1966 and 1969, Argentina successfully obtained new and similar resolutions in the UN. The lack of contact with the Islands and the prohibition on travel provoked various incidents that at the time filled the pages of the newspapers.

Argentines and Flags in the Islands

Alongside the official claims, negotiations, UN Resolutions and the growing frustration of Argentine diplomats, various Argentines took private initiatives, some diplomatic, others adventurous, and some almost criminal.

In 1957, the Radical politician Hipolito Solari Yrigoyen, made a good will journey to the Islands with his wife. They arrived in the Islands from Montevideo in the *"Darwin"* that used to trade between the Islands and

The Argentina Claim

Uruguay, for many years the only link from the Islands to the outside world. They were well received and took the opportunity to meet the Governor and the main local farmers. The Falklands then was a community isolated from the world, and the inhabitants –the kelpers– lived in a situation of abandonment and decline. The population had not grown since the beginning of the century and those who could, left the Islands. However, the Falklands Islands Company, the owner of most of the land and controller of all commerce, was making money and did not want to change the *status quo*.[78]

One of the few cases of authorised immigration from Argentina to the Islands is that of Reynaldo Ernesto Reid. Reid, a Patagonian resident, took advantage of his British passport and travelled to the Islands in 1960 to settle. He married an Island girl, and had many children. This case was important then, because it concerns an individual who was able to express his ideas and, for years was critical of the existing colonial situation on the Islands. In those days few voices were raised against the Falkland Islands Company and the Governor.

Other visitors were the law student Federico Miré in 1962, who remarked on the cordial reception he received and César Greslebin, the *Gente* magazine journalist.

A romantic episode that acquired great notoriety in its time, was the flight from Rio Gallegos on 8 September 1964 by Miguel L. Fitzgerald, an Argentine of Irish descent. Fitzgerald landed in his single-engine plane, the *"Don Luis Vernet"* on the Stanley racecourse,

---

[78] Solari Yrigoyen, Hipólito; *Malvinas, lo que no cuentan los ingleses*, El Ateneo, Buenos Aires, 1998.

with the sole purpose of raising an Argentine flag and delivering a statement to the Governor. He returned without incident to Rio Gallegos. His success had wide repercussion in the media and merited a complaint by the British Ambassador in the United Nations.

The second flight was less romantic and more akin to an act of terrorism. On 28 September 1966, Dardo Cabo, and his Cóndor group of 17 youths, hijacked a scheduled Aerolineas Argentinas airliner en route from Buenos Aires to Rio Gallegos and forced it to land on the Stanley racecourse. They raised several Argentine flags, which continued to fly for 36 hours, handed a statement to the Governor and then gave themselves up. They were repatriated to Argentina on the *"Bahía Buen Suceso"* and were then tried and sentenced by the Federal Judge in Ushuaia. One of the passengers on the airliner was Héctor Ricardo García, the editor of the newspaper *Crónica* who apparently also had links with the Condor group. This incident received wide media coverage and raised the Falklands issue in the British press.

On 27 November 1968 Fitzgerald made his second flight to the Islands. On this occasion he did not go alone but was accompanied by Héctor Ricardo García, editor of *Crónica*, and another journalist Juan Carlos Nava. They were unable to land on the racecourse and instead put down on a road where they became stuck in the peat. They had to return to the continent on the British ship *"Endurance"*, which was also carrying the British Foreign Secretary Lord Chalfont.

Communications with the Islands

In 1970, Luis María de Pablo Pardo, the then Argentine Foreign Minister, initiated conversations with the British which were intended to renew communications with the Islands.

These negotiations culminated in 1971 with a joint declaration, which included articles safeguarding the respective sovereignty claims and allowing direct, regular air flights between the Islands and Argentina. To enable the latter, Argentina cooperated with the construction of the airport in Stanley. An agreement was also reached for the supply of Argentine oil and gas to the Islands and travel to Argentina for Islanders in need of medical attention or to complete their education*. Also agreed was an exemption from military service** for Islanders who could then visit Argentina without fear of problems with the authorities.

The opening of communications was a notable success for Argentine diplomacy, due mainly to the enthusiasm and efficiency of Colonel Luis González Balcarce[79].

(*) As there was only primary school education on the Islands.
(**) Then obligatory for young Argentines.
[79] Colonel Luis Gonzalez Balcarce was instructed by the Argentine Foreign Office in the early 70s to follow and solve all the personal problems of the Islanders. He made several trips to the Islands were he was very successful and made many friends. Later, he opposed the 1982 war and the change of name of Stanley. He still works in the Foreign Office and returned to the Islands 18 years after the war where he was received by many old friends.

LADE (Lineas Aereas del Estado) established a regular weekly flight between Comodoro Rivadavia and Stanley. Initially using sea planes then, thanks to the airport set up in Stanley, with turboprop aircraft and finally from 1975 –when the British improved the runway– with Fokker 28 aircraft. The Islanders made great use of this connection that replaced the bi-annual ship from Montevideo. Many Islanders completed their secondary education in Buenos Aires, others attended Argentine hospitals, and many women had their children in Buenos Aires. Some made friendships that are maintained to this day. A few even spent their honeymoon in Bariloche.[80]

In turn many Argentines visited the Islands as tourists. The arrival of the Argentine ship *"Libertad"*, with 350 tourists, and the voyage of the Argentine Navy yacht, the *"Fortuna"* in 1972 were widely reported. In March 1974 a group of sailing enthusiasts, with the support of the Argentine Navy and the CUBA club sailed three yachts to Stanley. They competed in several races in Stanley Bay and the boats were then donated to the Islanders. One of the yachts was named "El mar nos une"* as a friendly gesture. The boats were much used until the war of 1982.[81]

Fuel and gas were sold on the Islands by the Argentine utility companies, *YPF* and *Gas del Estado*. Maritime transport started to carry cargo from Buenos Aires and Ushuaia to the Islands and vice versa. The quality of life on the Islands improved.

---

[80] As was the case with Terry Spruce, General Manager of the Falkland Islands Company, and his wife Joan.
(*) "The Sea Unites Us".
[81] Saguier Fonrouge, Carlos; *Mis recuerdos de las Islas Malvinas*, Revista Timoneles, Buenos Aires, October 1999, p. 36.

The Argentina Claim

Private businessmen like the Patagonian cattle farmers, Guillermo Bain and Conrado Visser, conducted business with the Islands.

Some Argentines even moved there. Among them was María Villanueva, originally from Santa Fé, who arrived on the Islands in 1972 from Comodoro Rivadavia. María, after her divorce from her first husband, an Anglo-Argentine who had inherited some property on the Islands, married the well known British naturalist, Ian Strange and lives on the Islands to this day.

The decade of the 70's was a sad period for Argentina. The end of General Lanusse's military government of 1973 was a period of economical and political turmoil. The Peronist government, firstly headed by Campora, followed by Perón himself and finally Isabelita, produced some of the worst governments in living memory.

Argentina entered an inflationary spiral and a period of economic and social stagnation. It experienced an increase in guerilla activity and repression that resulted in the military coup of March 1976. Argentina then was not an easy country to sell.

However, negotiations between the two sides continued with apparent progress –or at least it appeared so to the Argentine negotiators– tempered with frustration resulting from British reluctance to agree to any kind of commitment.

In 1973, Argentina was successful in persuading the General Assembly of the United Nations to pass Resolution 3160 (XXVIII) that hardened the terms of Resolution 2065 and expressed its grave concerns at the lack of progress.

In 1974, the British Conservative Prime Minister Edward Heath, suggested the possibility of shared sovereignty or a condominium. This was unwisely rejected by the Argentines.

Argentina had become a member of the Non-Aligned movement and felt it had the strong support of the United Nations.

From 1975, faced with Argentina's deteriorating internal situation, the British decided to take unilateral steps to consolidate the *status quo*. To this end, the Shackleton Mission was sent to look at the options for the independent economic development of the islands. Argentina, then under Isabelita Peron's government, withdrew its Ambassador in London, provoking reciprocal action by the British in Buenos Aires. The situation worsened to the point where an Argentine Naval ship fired warning shots at a British scientific research ship, 78 miles from the Islands.

After the military coup of March 1976[82], the relationship with Great Britain improved and the two sides began to explore solutions to put an end to the dispute. Among these was the *"lease-back"* alternative, which in practice meant British recognition of Argentine sovereignty and the simultaneous leasing of the Islands to Great Britain for an extended period.

In 1979, Margaret Thatcher became British Prime Minister and, for a while, continued the conciliatory policies of her predecessors. The Secretary of State at

---

[82] Which took place with the support of the US and its NATO partners, all of which recognised the new government.

the Foreign Office, Nicholas Ridley, tried to promote the lease-back solution. Very poor management of the issue in London, Buenos Aires and the Islands, and the leaking of the proposal to the public, generated fierce opposition, firstly in the Islands and then in the British Parliament.

In a memorable Parliamentary debate in the House of Lords in December 1981, the difficult Falklands problem was aired with great frankness. In the debate Lord Morris and Lord Shackleton emphasized the need for economic development of the Islands and pointed out the possibilities offered by fishing and oil exploitation. Lord McNair highlighted the importance of encouraging adequate immigration.[83] Lord Buxton of Alsa expressed his concern over the Foreign Office's apparent disinterest in the Islands.* Viscount Montgomery of Alamein[84] realistically made it clear that any solution for the future of the Islands must take Argentina into account. *"We must work together, the British, the Argentines and the Islanders"*, Montgomery said firmly. Sadly neither the Argentines nor the British were disposed to walk the path of understanding.

In Argentina the failure of this solution generated wide disillusionment. Foreign Minister Camilion transmitted this to Lord Carrington, his British counterpart, who did not respond to his letters. The Anglo-Argentine

---

[83] "Encouragement of immigration of the right sort" – meaning white Anglo-Saxon.
(*) This view was shared by the Argentine Military Junta.
[84] After 1982, Lord Montgomery was a key participant in meetings of the ABC, organised jointly with CARI and which formed the basis for the re-establishment of diplomatic commercial and cultural relations between Argentina and Great Britain after the war.

relationship entered a profound crisis. After General Galtieri became Argentine President and Dr. Costa Mendez took over as Foreign Minister, Argentina began to harden its position in response to the British freezing of the negotiations. Despite this, an agreement was reached in New York for the renewal of communications and a joint statement was issued on 1 March 1982. The joint statement was ignored by the Argentine Military Government thereby disenfranchising the Argentine negotiators.

There then began a chain of events, which led both sides to war on 2 April 1982.

VI

THE WAR OF 1982

> *"The hard drinking General Galtieri took a rash gamble: to distract public attention, he ordered the armed forces to seize the British Falkland Islands..."*
>
> The Economist [85]

Great Britain

In 1981 Great Britain was in a state of decline. Margaret Thatcher's Conservative Government was in difficulty and the United Kingdom, affected by the policies of the 1970s had fallen behind countries such as France, Italy or Japan. Thatcher's tough economic policies were not showing results and the political outlook was not encouraging.

---

[85] "Pocket Latin America", *The Economist*, London, 1994, p. 128.

View of Rose West. Mount Two Sisters.

The War of 1982

As recently as 1945 Great Britain was still one of the three super-powers, together with the United States and the Soviet Union, with bases and troops stationed all over the world and a navy that could muster more than a thousand ships.[86] But, as the exercise of power relies on economic strength and the Second World War had ruined Great Britain, the situation had changed. At the end of the war Great Britain still accounted for nearly 9% of the world economy, but by 1980 this had fallen to 4% and was smaller than the shares of France, Germany, Japan and even Italy.

This declining situation made it very difficult to maintain the biggest Empire in the world. To do it without the good will of the USA was impossible. The authorising of colonial independence was not just a moral gesture but was also an economic necessity.[87] Once the decision had been taken, its execution was carried out with great skill, avoiding both suffering and war for the colonial peoples and humiliation for Great Britain. The Empire lost its colonies, but not its pride.

To dismantle the Empire the same procedures were used in successive colonies that had obtained their independence. The rules of the game were drawn up in London and the process ended with a Royal visit, the lowering of the Union Jack and the transfer of power to a democratic parliament. That this system was not applicable in many primitive societies was irrelevant, because by the time they collapsed*, the United Kingdom had already withdrawn elegantly.

---

[86] Strong, Roy; *The Story of Britain,* Hutchinson, London, 1996, p. 528.
[87] Strong, Roy; ibid, p. 528.
(*) In Africa they all collapsed.

167

In 1946 it was announced that the withdrawal from India would take place on 1 January 1948. The conflict between the Hindu and Moslem communities forced Lord Mountbatten, the Royal representative to partition the sub-continent into India, Pakistan and Ceylon (Sri Lanka) and to bring forward the date of independence to 15 August 1947. Great Britain withdrew with grace but could not avoid successive wars between India and Pakistan in a conflict that remains unresolved.

In 1948 independence was granted to Burma, the first former colony to opt not to become a member of the Commonwealth, the institution that replaced the monarchy and was designed to maintain the unity amongst the ex-colonies.

In the same year, 1948, Great Britain pulled out of Palestine. It was not easy. Already in 1917 it had promised the Jewish authorities that a Jewish state would be created but, despite the promotion of immigration and the terrible persecution they had suffered in Europe, Jews formed only 30% of the population of Palestine. Great Britain withdrew in May 1948, leaving the problem in the hands of the United Nations. Various Arab/Israeli wars have been fought since then and the conflict continues.

These tensions weakened Great Britain's position in the rest of the Arab world. In 1954 she withdrew from Sudan and Egypt, but retained control of the Suez Canal, whose owner was a French company. Then Great Britain and France, in a short-lived diplomatic manoeuvre, persuaded Israel to attack Egypt in order to give them the excuse of intervening and recovering the Canal. Lack of support from the United States obliged Great Britain and France to stop the war without having

Argentine trenches with view to the San Carlos port.

achieved their objectives and to accept a cease-fire imposed by the United Nations. Great Britain had ceased to be a great power. However, she retained formidable regional influence.

The Suez Crisis accelerated the British abandonment of Africa. The withdrawal began in the colonies with the least British settlers. Ghana achieved independence in 1957, Nigeria in 1960, Sierra Leone in 1961 and Gambia in 1965. Kenya suffered a difficult pullout in 1963, because of the power of the established British settlers. Tanzania (which was in fact the ex-German colony of Tanganyika) became independent in 1964 and Uganda in 1962. Zambia and Malawi had been abandoned in 1954.

The most difficult one was Rhodesia (Zinbawe) where there was an important British colonial presence that did not want to hand power to the African majority. Thus, Ian Smith, with British consent, issued a unilateral declaration of independence in 1965. This situation remained until 1980 when Great Britain finally withdrew. In the 1970s the Rhodesian situation impacted negatively on the Falklands problem. Great Britain did not want to set negative precedents.

By the time Harold Wilson became Prime Minister in 1964, Great Britain was neither a world power nor a colonial power. It retained its seat and its right of veto in the United Nations Security Council and had been a nuclear power since 1957. The last colonies were released; in 1967 Great Britain withdrew from Malaysia and Aden, and from Singapore in 1971.

The once enormous Empire was reduced to a few

The War of 1982

Islands[88], Hong Kong, Gibraltar and the Falkland Islands. These last three were subject to sovereignty disputes from bordering countries: China, Spain and Argentina. Everything seemed to indicate that the first to be resolved would be the Falkland Islands. In 1965 the United Nations had adopted Resolution 2065, insisting that both parties seek a solution to the dispute and in 1971 an agreement on links between the Islands and Argentina. Both these events seemed to suggest that the Islands would be returned to Argentina in a reasonable period of time.

Argentina

However, Argentina in the 1970s was a country moving backwards. In 1973, after many years in exile, Juan Domingo Perón was elected President of the Republic for a third time. It was the same Colonel Perón who had instigated the nationalist *coup d'etat* of 1943, had flirted with the axis powers of until almost the day of their defeat and who had confronted the United States and Great Britain from 1945 onwards. He was elected on a Presidential ticket shared with his third wife, "Isabelita"* and based his government on Minister López Rega, an obscure, esoteric personality with links with the Arab world. Perón began to apply a third world, nationalist and slightly anti-North American foreign policy. The consequences were dismal. Argentina entered

---

[88] Anguilla, Bermuda, The British Virgin Islands, St Helena, Ascension, Tristán Da Cunha, Turks and Caicos, South Georgia, South Sandwich, British Indian Ocean Territory, British Antarctic Territory and the Sovereign Base Areas at Akroriti and Dhekelia in Cyprus.

(*) María Estela Martinez de Perón.

British helicopters patrolling.

The War of 1982

into a period of political and economic chaos and, when Perón died in 1974, his widow "Isabelita" took over and López Rega's power grew enormously. With the complicity of the United States, a new Military Junta took control in early 1976.

The Military Junta became an appendix of the cold war between the North Americans and the Soviets. They collaborated with the Americans in Central America and undertook an internal war –best described as a witch-hunt– in Argentina with the purpose of annihilating and physically eliminating terrorism. Many innocent people also died and many were driven into exile. Politically, Argentina was no longer amongst the third world countries nor was it among the western democracies. It was in fact isolated. The economic situation continued to worsen, as the military only intensified the interventionist Peronist policies.

The Junta's policies toward its neighbours in Latin America were no better. They nearly went to war with Chile in 1978 as a result of not respecting the arbitration that had granted the islands to south of the Beagle Channel to Chile. An arms race with Chile ensued and the dispute remains to this day.

The Argentine Foreign Ministry

On 22 December 1981 Nicanor Costa Méndez became Foreign Minister. The President and Commander in Chief was General Leopoldo Galtieri, whom Costa Méndez had only met the day before his appointment.

In this first meeting they had talked extensively about the problem with Chile and Galtieri had said "we cannot accept the Papal proposal (over the Beagle Channel dispute) in the terms that have been expressed"[89]. Costa Méndez not only agreed but also wanted to denounce the Arbitrage Agreement of 1902[90]. Both shared a belligerent stance, similar to that of the Chilean dictator, General Augusto Pinochet Ugarte. The consequences of opening this second front would be paid during the Falklands Conflict.

Not one word was mentioned at the time regarding the Falklands. Galtieri did however tell Costa Méndez that he was the President's Foreign Minister and the not Junta's. This helps us to understand the difficulties he had with the other members of the Military Junta. The consequences of this would also have to be paid during the course of the Conflict.

Costa Méndez had been Foreign Minister to President Onganía during the 1960s. Since then he had remained resentful of Great Britain for the lack of any progress in the negotiations over the Falkland Islands in agreement with United Nations Resolution 2065 of 1965.

On 22 December 1981 he met his predecessor Oscar Camilión with whom he had a long talk about the Falklands. Camilión expressed his scepticism about the future and success of the negotiations with Great Britain. He told Costa Méndez about the meeting he had

---

[89] Costa Méndez, Nicanor; *Malvinas, esta es la historia*, Sudamericana, Buenos Aires, 1993, p. 15. Galtieri is referring to the Beagle Channel dispute with Chile and the Pope's proposal for solving the problem.
[90] Costa Méndez, Nicanor; ibid, p. 21.

had with Lord Carrington, the British Foreign Secretary, at the United Nations in September. He said that he had the impression that the issue was a low priority for the United Kingdom and that the British had no interest in finding a mutually acceptable solution. In contrast, for Costa Méndez, the resolution of the southern conflicts was Argentina's primary foreign policy goal.[91]

The next meeting was with Under-Secretary for Foreign Affairs Enrique Ríos and Ambassador Sans. The subject was the instructions that had to be given to the Argentine representatives at the United Nations for their meeting with their British counterparts scheduled for 26 February 1982. In Costa Méndez' view, nothing had changed since 1966[92], and this time he aimed at achieving better results. He was not aware of the loss of power and prestige that Argentina had suffered during the fateful 70s. Even less did he realise the abyss towards which the country was edging.

Costa Méndez thought that Argentina had already been excessively patient on the matter. In an article, published in *"La Prensa"* on 17 January 1982, the well-known journalist Iglesias Rouco –who had important connections with the armed forces– suggested that the Americans were beginning to support the Argentine cause and that Argentine possession of the Island would facilitate a diplomatic settlement of the dispute. A second article made reference to a supposed plan by Costa Méndez to recover the Islands.[93]

---

[91] Costa Méndez, Nicanor; ibid, p. 22.
[92] Costa Méndez, Nicanor; ibid, p. 22.
[93] Costa Méndez, Nicanor; ibid, p. 76. Costa Méndez confirmed the veracity of Iglesias Rouco's statements.

At the end of February 1982 Iglesias Rouco published an article in La Prensa which asked the question *"Why don't we occupy the Falkland Islands?"*. This article was probably written with Costa Méndez' full knowledge and was designed to put pressure on the British negotiators. On 16 February Galtieri informed Costa Méndez of a plan to defend Argentine interests in the South Atlantic.

The British intelligence services did not see what was happening in Buenos Aires. Or perhaps they did, and left events to follow their course. It was either a trap for Costa Méndez or simply the British service's incompetence.

The British negotiators —who were studying a proposal sent by Ambassador Ross on 27 January— did not show signs of being aware of what was happening. The proposal from Ross was not realistic. In the first place it sought straightforward British recognition of Argentine sovereignty. The rest of the proposal consisted of ways to achieve it. In other words, they were not seeking negotiations, only results. The British negotiators were also far removed from reality and showed no interest in negotiations at all. The meetings of 26 and 27 February failed. The British did not even have the grace to respond to the Ross proposal. However a joint statement was released which made reference to the need to find a solution to the sovereignty dispute.

Following Galtieri's instructions, Costa Méndez issued a much firmer statement on 2 March. It disavowed the previous joint declaration and said that Argentina considered itself free to *"choose the process that best serves our interests"*.[94] On 4 March he held an unfriendly

---

[94] Costa Méndez, Nicanor; ibid, p. 90.

meeting with Williams, the British Ambassador, during which both parties exchanged protests.

On 6 March, Thomas Enders, the Secretary for Inter-American Affairs for the United States, arrived in Buenos Aires. He spoke of El Salvador and Nicaragua, where the Military Junta had cooperated with the US, and of the Falkland Islands. Costa Méndez assured him that Argentina would not go to war with Chile! *"So, there will be no war?"* asked Enders. Costa Méndez' responded by assuring Enders that there would be no war with Chile. The naiveté of the Americans was remarkable. Did they not suspect anything? Or did they just allow events to take their course?

On 5 March the navy told Costa Méndez that operation *"Alfa"* was going to be launched. The operation was a repetition, only this time in the South Georgia Islands, of the action taken by the navy years earlier on Thule Island in the South Sandwich archipelago. The operation would be carried out during the activities of Mr. Davidoff in the South Georgies.[95] This was clearly an anomalous situation that reflected the chaotic way in which Argentina was governed. It was not the Foreign Minister who informed the navy, but the navy who informed the Foreign Minister. Admiral Anaya, who ran the navy without any government control, had already decided that it was the appropriate moment to re-take the Falkland Islands by force in the face of British intransigence. It is not clear whether the original decision was to take action in April, or whether they

---

[95] Constantino Davidoff was an Argentine scrap-metal merchant who had obtained permission from the British to dismantle the whaling station on the South Georgia Islands.

took advantage of the situation created by Davidoff and acted on it.

On 10 March, Anaya held a meeting with his friend and counsellor, former Foreign Minister Bonifacio Del Carril, with whom he had met on several earlier occasions to discuss the Chilean situation. Anaya informed him that they would take the Falklands within a month and that they did not anticipate any British reaction.[96] Del Carril, who represented the Argentine "establishment"*, did not raise any objections.

On 20 March the naval transport ship *"Bahía Buen Suceso"* disembarked workmen and equipment on the South Georgias. They did not put any troops ashore, but the Argentine flag was hoisted. After several days of fruitless negotiations between the two sides, both helping to magnify the incident rather than minimizing it (for instance the Governor of the Falkland Islands, Sir Rex Hunt, informed London that the Georgias had been occupied militarily).[97] Despite North-American last minute pressure to avoid the inevitable, Argentine –in a bloodless operation (with the exception of the death of Captain Giachino)[98]– re-took the Falkland Islands on 2 April 1982.

---

[96] Del Carril, Bonifacio; "Cómo se perdió la paz en 1982", *La Nación*, 4-4-89, Buenos Aires.

(*) It must be said that the Argentine business community sapported the Military Junta as well as the foreign multinationals (including American and British ones) did.

[97] Connor, Ken; *The Secret Story of the SAS*, Weidenfeld & Nicholson, London, 1998, p. 240.

Hunt, Rex; *My Falkland Days*, David & Charles, London, 1988.

[98] Kasanzew, Nicolás; *Malvinas a sangre y fuego*, Abril, Buenos Aires, 1982.

After the deed was done, almost the entire Argentine political class supported the action, future President Alfonsín and many senior politicians travelled to the Islands to support the Military Junta's venture.

The British Reaction

Great Britain had not reacted –in any preventative way– to all the indications from Argentina in the months of January, February and March of 1982. Then, from 2 April 1982 onwards they acted with absolute conviction that they would not stop until they had obtained Argentine surrender. Many questions were asked, and are still being asked, about the lack of any British reaction in the period from January to March and the overwhelming response after 2 April. "Was it the incompetence of British diplomacy and their intelligence service?" The resignation of Lord Carrington would seem to indicate that it was. Other sources have more conspiratorial views of the events.

British policy between 1979 and 1990 revolved around Margaret Thatcher. She was an unrivalled Prime Minister who, against all the odds, modernised Great Britain. It was the first time since 1830 that a British Government had decided on the reduction of the State and the expansion of the private sector.

Before Margaret Thatcher, post-war Britain had lost an Empire and had not found a role for itself. It was not easy to accept that what had once been the British Empire was now only a middle-ranking European power. When the European Economic Community was formed in 1957, Great Britain stayed out, giving priority to the Commonwealth and its relationship with the United States. Harold Macmillan had wanted Great Britain to become a member, but in 1963 Charles de Gaulle vetoed British membership on the grounds that Great Britain was an American satellite state and that such status was not compatible with the goals of the Community.

The truth is that the relationship between Great Britain and the United States had deteriorated somewhat since the Suez Crisis. When John Kennedy, of Irish Catholic origin, was elected to the American Presidency in 1961, very little help with the emerging Northern Ireland problems was forthcoming.

During the reign of Henry VIII, England had incorporated Wales in 1536. With the Act of Union in 1707, which incorporated Scotland[99], Great Britain was born. The Scots and Welsh integrated with relative ease.[100]

The situation with Ireland was different. For centuries it had been occupied by the English. Its Catholic inhabitants were denied political and economic rights. A Protestant minority, imported from England and Scotland and sustained by military force, owned all the land on the island. The subjugated Irish were never able to recover from the butchery of Oliver Cromwell which killed nearly half the population and resulted in

---

[99] Scotland recently re-established its own government in 1998.
[100] It was not easy for all the Welsh. Proof of this is the Welsh immigration to Patagonia in the middle of the 19th century. These immigrants, from the leading power in the world, decided to move to the Patagonian desert in search of opportunities that the British Empire denied them.

The War of 1982

the disappearance of the upper class altogether. The Irish worked the land for the landowners, but had no rights and could be dismissed at the whim of the owner with no claim to compensation for having improved his land. They were left to make the best of it in a situation of abject poverty and squalid living conditions. Irish unification was declared in 1801, the Irish parliament was closed and the United Kingdom was born. In 1845, and as a consequence of repressive policies, the failure of several crops and a people whose staple diet was the potato, a terrible famine struck Ireland and reduced the population by half. To this day Ireland still has not recovered the population it had in 1845.

Irish nationalism was taking hold and had strong support from Irish immigrants in America. In 1875 Prime Minister Gladstone had sought a solution to the Irish problem, but without success. Only in 1903 were the Irish allowed to own property in their own country. But they still did not have the right to their own government. The oligarchic House of Lords vetoed any change to the *status quo*. We must remember that universal suffrage was only introduced in Great Britain in 1928. But by 1911 the Lords had lost there right of veto and, in 1920 Great Britain recognised the inevitable and signed the Ireland Act. Irish independence of was approved in 1949.

Great Britain remained in control of Northern Ireland, with its Protestant majority but a significant Catholic minority. The inequality of the situation led to a civil war that was still unresolved in 1982.

As with the Rhodesia situation in the 70s, Great Britain could not create a precedent with the Falkland

Islands that would complicate an already difficult situation in Northern Ireland.

The relationship with Europe had improved considerably and, in 1973, thanks to the fight put up by Prime Minister Edward Heath, Great Britain was admitted to the European Community. As a result of the developing Cold War, the relationship with the United States had been consolidated. At the beginning of 1982, the conservative government of Ronald Reagan had a strong ally in the Conservative Prime Minister Margaret Thatcher. Both situations, the excellent relationship with Europe and the equally close relationship with the United States went unnoticed by the incompetent diplomats of the Argentine Military Junta.

Margaret Thatcher's only weakness was on the internal front and what better than a war to unite a people. Galtieri's venture of 2 April 1982 was just what Margaret Thatcher needed. If it was planned or if there was a conspiracy beforehand, the Argentine Military Junta could not have handled things worse.

The United States

The Argentine Military Junta and Foreign Minister Costa Méndez misinterpreted the North American position regarding Argentina and under-estimated the traditional Anglo-American relationship.

On 30 March 1982, Ambassador Schlaudemann visited Costa Méndez and confirmed his offer to mediate in the conflict sparked by the South Georgias affair. The

Argentine Minister rejected the offer and said that now the problem involved the Falklands as well and any mediation should include these Islands. Schlaudemann expressed his surprise and as the situation exceeded his instructions, the meeting ended without agreement.[101]

It is hard to believe that the Americans had no previous knowledge of the intentions of the Military Junta. The range of contacts between the Argentine and American military was intense at every level. US information services were widely deployed throughout Argentina.

It was not until 1 April that the Americans acknowled-ged the imminent invasion and Ambassador Schlaudemann then requested an urgent meeting with General Galtieri who saw him at 6pm. The American naval chief for the South Atlantic and the US military attaché accompanied the Ambassador to the meeting with Galtieri, where they clearly expressed the need to avoid the use of force. They did not apply much pressure and thereby reinforced the Junta's misconception of the American position.

President Reagan telephoned Galtieri at 9pm that night. Galtieri only took the call at 10.15pm. Reagan pleaded for a conflict to be avoided and offered to send Vice-President Bush to mediate. Galtieri replied by saying that the operation had already been launched and the best he could offer was to delay the transfer of sovereignty for a year.[102]

---

[101] Costa Méndez, Nicanor; ibid, p. 171.

[102] General Vernon Walters, who was in charge of Latin American operations at the CIA, informed Galtierii of the likely british response, to which Galtieri turned a deaf ear. "Los dictadores eran el mal menor", Interview with Vernon Walters, *Clarín*, 5-9-99.

The dialogue between the United States and Great Britain was much more fluent. They agreed to an urgent meeting of the Security Council. The meeting convened at 10.35 pm (Argentine time) that same day. Argentina was already losing the diplomatic battle. That night the Security Council issued a declaration requesting that both sides should avoid the use of force.

Security Council Resolution 502

In the early hours of 2 April the almost bloodless* reoccupation of the archipelago began. At 6pm that same evening Great Britain broke off diplomatic relations with Argentina, but avoided issuing a formal declaration of war.

Costa Méndez, who travelled immediately to New York to attend the Security Council session, thought it probable that there would be an unfavourable majority of the United States, Japan, France, Ireland and Guyana voting with Great Britain and only Panama voting with Argentina. But he also reckoned on being able to count on the vetoes of China and the Soviet Union.

He could not have been more mistaken. Neither the Chinese nor the Russians were prepared to support the Argentine anti-Communist dictatorship, nor were they willing to provoke the western powers in an area under their control. There were no vetoes. He was also wrong in his estimation of the favourable votes. Ireland supported Argentina and no pressure was applied on

---

(*) Only one Argentine casualty and no British.

The War of 1982

Japan, which had (and still has) an unresolved dispute with Russia over the Kuril Islands (known by the Japanese as the Northern Territories), very similar to the Falkland Islands dispute.[103] Spain, under pressure from Britain, surprised Argentina with a declaration disavowing the use of force. The Non-Aligned Movement also failed to support Argentina. Only the day before, Nicaragua, with the support of the non-aligned movement, had criticised Argentine involvement in Central America. Uganda, Togo, and Zaire supported Great Britain. Jordan, after a personal call from Margaret Thatcher to King Hussein, did likewise.

Eventually, and with a large majority, Resolution 502 was approved. It read " The Security Council, recalling the declaration formulated by the President of the Council in the 2345th session of the Security Council, held on 1 April 1982, which called on the Governments of Argentina and the United Kingdom of Great Britain and Northern Ireland to abstain from the use or threat of force in the region of the Falkland Islands, deeply concerned at reports of an invasion by Argentine armed forces on 2 April 1982, declaring that there exists a breakdown of peace in the Region of the Falkland Islands;

1) Demands an immediate cessation of all hostilities;

2) Demands the immediate withdrawal of all Argentine forces from the Falkland Islands;

3) Exhorts both the governments of Argentina and the United Kingdom to seek a diplomatic solution to

---

[103] Etchebarne Bullrich, Conrado; "Las malvinas japonesas", *La Nación*, Buenos Aires, 6-8-95.

their differences and to fully respect the goals and principals of the Charter of the United Nations".

The diplomatic defeat had been complete. The Resolution did not even mention the earlier Resolution on decolonisation, or the Falklands specific Resolution 2065. The arrogance and misjudgment of the Military Junta and Foreign Minister Costa Méndez led to this result.

All that remained was to await the British reaction.

The Conflict from the British Perspective [104]

For Margaret Thatcher, the British Prime Minister, this was the opportunity to become a real national leader.

In her view, Great Britain had been in retreat since the Suez fiasco of 1956.[105] The conflict over the Falkland Islands was an opportunity to reverse that trend and reaffirm British honour.

In her earlier analysis prior to the conflict, she accepted that some kind of arrangement with Argentina should be reached concerning the sovereignty dispute. The *"leaseback"* option always seemed to be the most acceptable solution[106] if and when the Islanders accepted it.

---

[104] This chapter is based on the version published by Mrs. Thatcher in her book *The Downing Street Years*, Harper Collins, London, 1993.
[105] Thatcher, Margaret; ibid, p. 173.
[106] Thatcher, Margaret; ibid, p. 175.

But the Islanders had not accepted it and Thatcher was not prepared to impose it on them. Consequently, her government rejected the possibility of achieving a *"leaseback"* settlement. *"If we had been skillful, we could have continued talking with the Argentines, but the diplomacy was becoming ever more difficult... The possibility certainly existed that the Argentines would opt for a military alternative, as since 1976 they had maintained an active military presence on the Sandwich Islands."* [107]

In Thatcher's analysis, the Argentine military, frustrated by the stalled negotiations and arrogantly sure of their supposed importance to the United States in the continental fight against communist guerrillas, thought that they could get away with it.

It all began with the unauthorised landing of a group of Argentine scrap metal merchants on South Georgia on 20 December. The situation was then aggravated by the failed New York talks in February 1982. On 3 March the Prime Minister received a telegram from the British Embassy in Buenos Aires setting out the need to draw up contingency plans. On 20 March the Argentine scrap merchants raised the Argentine flag on the Georgias and the British Government sent the *"Endurance"* from the Falklands to South Georgia, but with instructions not to make contact with the Argentines. Thatcher maintains that at this time she did not foresee the conflict.

On Sunday 28 March, according to Thatcher's version, invasion was thought to be an imminent possibility and she had a conversation with Lord Peter

---

[107] Thatcher, Margaret; ibid, p. 176.

Carrington, who had already spoken to the Alexander Haig, the American Secretary of State, to ask for American intervention to stop the Argentines. On 30 March, as a means of pressure, it was decided to send a nuclear submarine to the South Atlantic. Although it would take 15 days to arrive it was still considered a deterrent.[108] On 31 March confirmation was received from the intelligence services that the Argentine fleet had been seen sailing towards the Falklands. While the Defence Secretary, John Nott, was of the opinion that recovering the Islands by force was not an option, the Royal Navy reported that it could have a fleet, including the aircraft carriers *"Hermes"* and *"Invincible"*, ready to sail in 48 hours. The same day President Reagan was asked to put pressure on Galtieri to halt the invasion. A little later, reports were received that the US Ambassador to the United Nations was having dinner that night at the Argentine Ambassador's Residence in New York. The signals being received by the Argentines could not have been more contradictory. After a conversation between the Queen and Mrs. Thatcher, it was agreed that Prince Andrew would participate in the invasion on the *"Invincible"* as a further sign of the British government's seriousness about sending a Task Force, and of the Crown's approval of Britain's last colonial war of the century.

On 2 April, Thatcher received a report from the Foreign Office pointing out the potential risks to British residents in Argentina, the difficulty of obtaining United Nations support, the shaky support of the EEC and the

---

[108] It was considered that just announcing the sending of the submarine would act as a deterrent.

The War of 1982

United States as well as the risk of creating an international public image of Great Britain as a colonial power. All these potential difficulties were successfully overcome.

The British expatriates in Argentina were never molested, so this problem never materialised.

Within the European Community, French President François Mitterand gave Britain his unconditional support.[109]

Simultaneously, the British Ambassador to the United Nations, Anthony Parsons, who acted with much more skill than his Argentine counterparts, persuaded China and Russia that this was not a Cold War issue but that it fell within the western powers' area of influence. On 3 April he duly managed to get Resolution 502, which called for the Argentine withdrawal from the Islands, quickly agreed. King Hussein of Jordan, a country with a seat in the Security Council, received a personal telephone call from Thatcher and assured her of his support.

The same day Thatcher achieved another resounding success. This time in the House of Commons, where she appealed to the patriotism of the British island *"race"*. From then on British tabloid newspapers adopted a racist and militaristic line. From the outset Thatcher felt that the Argentines would not withdraw and, as she was not prepared to make concessions, preparations for battle began.[110]

---

[109] France is the only other country, besides Britain, with a colony in South America (French Guyana).

[110] Thatcher, Margaret; ibid, p. 184.

In their calls to NATO allies, the British emphasized that this was not just a matter concerning Argentina, but that it was important to show the Russians the consequences of any attack on a NATO country. The effectiveness of the argument worked.

In Thatcher's interpretation of events, Alexander Haig's frenzied diplomatic intervention in flying from London to Buenos Aires and Washington, only helped her plans, giving time for the fleet to advance and slowing down any action by the United Nations.[111]

The European Economic Community and the countries of the Commonwealth imposed a trade embargo on Argentina. Ireland was the only country to oppose this measure and Italy applied the embargo for only one month.

On the American continent, Thatcher rapidly obtained the support of Canada, the Caribbean states, Guyana and Chile. The latter was thanks to her personal contacts with the dictator Pinochet.[112] Chile's geographical location made it of key importance to the conflict. Not only the possibility of providing support for covert operations but also by distracting Argentine troops through an active Chilean presence on the borders and re-transmitting intelligence reports.

---

[111] Thatcher, Margaret; ibid, p. 188.
[112] Thatcher's loyalty to Pinochet some 20 years after the end of the war is noteworthy. When Pinochet was arrested in London in 1998 as a consequence of a Spanish extradition request for his violation of human rights, Thatcher publicly expressed her solidarity with the ex-dictator and called for his release. There is no doubt that Chilean collaboration (including a possible second front against Argentina) was an important contributory factor to the success of the British military campaign.

The War of 1982

Alexander Haig's negotiations continued, but Thatcher's position remained firm: the future of the Islands was to be decided in accordance with the wishes of the Islanders. Her only concession was that she would accept a withdrawal of Argentine troops and would reinstall British administration, but without either a Governor or soldiers. This alternative, especially the part concerning the wishes of the Islanders was completely unacceptable to the Argentines. Thatcher also emphasized that British title over the South Georgia Islands was indisputable as opposed to the Falklands.

From 14 April the US began to support the British position more openly. They allowed the use of the military base on Ascension Island and assured Britain of their usual military support in times of peace. The British aircraft carriers arrived at Ascension Island on 16 April. The same day the Americans were informed that South Georgia would be recovered by force. Haig and Francis Pym made their final effort to find a diplomatic solution on 24 April. Their efforts were boycotted by Thatcher.[113]

The recovery of South Georgia and the establishment of a 200-mile exclusion zone around the Falklands was announced on 26 April. The re-taking of South Georgia did not pose many problems for the British with the exception of the loss of a helicopter on a glacier, due to bad weather conditions. There were no British casualties. The Argentine submarine *"Santa Fé"* was sunk and the Argentine garrison, under the command of Captain Astiz, surrendered almost without a fight. There was a

---

[113] Thatcher, Margaret; ibid, p. 208.

confusing episode when an Argentine NCO was killed after the surrender on board the *"Santa Fé"*.[114]

On 30 April Reagan informed Thatcher that Haig's mission had ended and that the United States would provide military assistance.

Thatcher's main concern was the apparent resurgence of the United Nations and the peace proposals of the Peruvian Secretary General Perez de Cuellar. Ambassador Tony Parsons warned Thatcher that the United Nations must be avoided, as they would probably order a freeze of military actions, thus allowing Perez de Cuellar to mediate.[115]

At 1.30pm on 2 May Thatcher decided to change the rules of the engagement of the British nuclear submarines. A few hours later the nuclear submarine *"Conqueror"* sank the Argentine cruiser *"General Belgrano"* outside the exclusion zone, causing the death of 321 sailors.[116]

This act of war ended the peace plans of Perez de Cuellar. Diplomatic efforts were at an end and the British concentrated on the military recovery of the Islands.

Another of Margaret Thatcher's great diplomatic successes in May 1982 was to avoid the postponement of the Pope's visit to Britain. The visit took place normally, despite the war in the South Atlantic.

---

[114] Barker, Nick; *Beyond Endurance*, Leo Cooper, London, 1997.
[115] Thatcher, Margaret; ibid, p. 211.
[116] For some people this action was a war crime because it took place outside the exclusion zone and outside the war zone.

The British military cemetery at San Carlos.

The diplomatic achievements of Margaret Thatcher's government opened the way for the military victory.

The Islanders' view of the War

Until 1982 the Islanders had lived in a colonial situation of isolation. They had practically no political rights, they did not have the rights to British citizenship and were not even owners of their land. The Falkland Islands Company was the principal landowner and had a complete commercial monopoly. The situation had improved a little since the communications agreement with Argentina in 1971, the establishment of flights from Comodoro Rivadavia and the sale of YPF* products on the Islands.

The Islanders had been brought up to fear the Argentines and were apprehensive of the fact that some lived on the Islands (the representatives of LADE**, YPF and a some Spanish language teachers). They were aware of the Argentine claim and had the impression that the Foreign Office was attempting to reach a settlement with the Argentines.

The invasion of 2 April was a surprise but at the beginning was accepted with resignation as an inevitable fact. On one occasion a prominent Islander said to me *"We thought that was it. The anxiety over the dispute was over, and a new future lay ahead".* At 8pm on 1 April the Governor informed the population that the invasion was

---

(*) Yacimientos Petrolíferos fiscales was the state owned ail corporation.
(**) Líneas Aéreas del Estado, was the state owned military airline.

The War of 1982

imminent. The local radio journalist, Mike Smallwood, asked the population to remain calm and announced that his music programme would continue.[117]

The night of 1 April was magnificent southern, no wind, no clouds and thousands of stars in the sky, absolutely calm. It all seemed unreal for the Islanders. At 4.30 in the morning, the Governor went on local radio and informed the population that the invasion was about to happen and, a little later, at 6am the landings began and shots could be heard and explosions could be seen from a distance. The Islands surrendered at 10am and a few minutes later the Argentine national hymn was played on the local radio and the Argentine flag was raised at Government House.

The Islanders have not complained of having been mistreated. Although they did not like the idea of being submitted to a military government. Some precise details, like the issue of documents, having to drive on the right side of the road and the presence of troops caused much anxiety and nervousness among the population. However, they tried to maintain their usual lifestyle as much as possible.

Through Communiqués 3 and 4, the population was informed that their way of life would be maintained, there was religious freedom, respect for private property, freedom to work, freedom to enter and leave the Islands, public services would function normally and, that temporarily, all pubs and clubs would be closed.

The situation was very different in Darwin where the

---

[117] "Don't panic folks, we will now continue with *record requests...*" Quoted by Smith, John; ibid, p. 20.

Argentine garrison commander, suspicious that Islanders had been passing information to the British forces, decided to imprison the whole community (almost 100 people) in the village Community Hall.[118] They were held there for nearly 30 days.

Once military action started, the Islanders could only hope for the British victory. With one or two isolated exceptions there was no resistance to the Argentine occupation.*

The Military Campaign

After British Vulcan aircraft bombed the airstrip in Stanley at the beginning of May and the sinking of the cruiser General Belgrano on 2 May, Argentina counter-attacked with its Air Force and Navy planes and went after the British fleet which was approaching the islands.

On 3 May the British sank an Argentine patrol boat north of the Islands and on 4 May the Argentines fired four advanced technology *Exocet* missiles and sank the British frigate, the *"Sheffield"*. The action was now firmly in the hands of the military rather than the diplomats.

On 7 May the British extended the exclusion for Argentine ships to the whole of the South Atlantic beyond Argentina's 12-mile territorial limit. The Argentine fleet returned to port, from whence it did not

---

[118] I visited the Hall in 1994 and it is extraordinary that 100 people, including women and children, had been locked up there for more than 30 days.

(*) One islander was expelled: Mr William Luxton.

Mount Pleasant military base.

leave for the rest of the war. On 9 May the fishing boat the *"Narwal"* was sunk, on 10 May the transport ship the *"Isla de los Estados"* and on the 16th the transport *"Río Carcarañá"*, after which the Argentine troops on the Falklands were dependent exclusively on supplies flown in by the Hercules aircraft. From then on British Harrier jets became a daily presence in the skies over Stanley.

Simultaneously groups of British Commandos began the first attacks.[119] On 15 April, they had successfully destroyed all the Pucará aircraft stationed at Pebble Island, a few days later they destroyed the aircraft stationed at Darwin and they then attempted an attack on the aero-naval base of Río Grande in Tierra del Fuego. This operation failed, but the Commandos were able to escape thanks to Chilean logistical support.

The air battle intensified and in the week of 20 May, Argentine aircraft scored some important successes. On 21 May they sank the frigate *"Ardent"*, on the 24th the frigate *"Antelope"*, on the 25th the destroyer *"Coventry"* and the transport ship, the *"Atlantic Conveyor"*. Back in Buenos Aires, these successes created the impression that negotiations could be forced. This impression lasted only a short time.

On 21 May the British landed without ground force opposition at Port San Carlos and San Carlos in the north west of East Falkland. The Argentine Air Force attacks on the *"Task Force"* ships were constant. Despite the courage of the pilots, the lack of battle practice and the poor preparation of their bombs rendered their attacks less effective.

---

[119] Connor, Ken; *The Secret History of the SAS*, Weidenfeld & Nicolson, London, 1998.

The War of 1982

The British divided their forces. One part headed towards the south to take Darwin, where an important Argentine garrison was positioned. On 29 May, after a hard battle lasting 12 hours that cost the lives of many Argentine soldiers, and the English Lieutenant Colonel Jones who led the attack, the British took Darwin. At the same time the rest of the British troops headed to the north of East Falkland. On 29 May they took Teal Inlet and on 1 June, the strategically important Mount Kent, the highest peak on the Islands from where they could see Stanley. Between 4 and 8 June troops disembarked in Bluff Cove. On 8 June the Argentines reacted and sank the troop carriers the *"Sir Galahad"* and the *"Sir Tristan"*.

Argentina lost many aircraft in the last week of May and the first week of June.[120]

The British, having achieved naval superiority from 7 May and air superiority from 8 June, decided to launch their assault on Stanley.

The Argentine forces, commanded by General Menéndez, the military Governor of the Islands, had structured their defences on fixed positions around Stanley. The best troops were to the east of the town in the area close to the airport, where they expected the British to land. To the south, all the beaches were mined and the defences to the west were some 50km from Stanley on Mounts Harriet, Two Sisters and Longdon. A second line of defence was on Mounts William and Tumbledown and Wireless Ridge, all with direct views over Stanley and within range of the artillery stationed there.

---

[120] Burden, Rodney; *The Air War*, ed. Arms & Armour Press, Dorset, 1986.

The Argentine troops, with the exception of the NCOs and officers who were professional soldiers, were comprised of young and inexpert conscripts. The strategy was based on antiquated concepts dating from the First and Second World Wars. Morale was very low, due to poor leadership, logistical errors (supplies remained in Stanley instead of being distributed to the troops) and a poor relationship between the officers, NCOs and soldiers.

The British troops, all fully professional, were trained and armed to NATO criteria and were prepared for combat with Soviet forces in the context of the Cold War that existed in those years. The importance of intelligence work in the campaign is also notable, particularly the interrogation of captured Argentines.[121]

British troops of 42 Commando, transported to Mount Challenger by helicopter, launched the first attack on Mount Harriet, which fell on 11 June after several hours of fighting. On 12 May they took the important position of Two Sisters. The Parachute Regiment attacked Mount Longdon from the north and, after a fierce battle, took the position. Perhaps the fiercest battle was fought by the Scots Guards when they took Tumbledown. Simultaneously, the Gurkhas advanced on Mount William, which was taken without resistance as the Argentine forces fled. The British advanced easily and on the morning of 14 June they had taken the barracks at Moody Brook and Sapper Hill at the gates of

---

[109] West, Nigel; *The Secret War for the Falklands*, Little Brown & Company, London, 1997.
[121] Bransby, Guy; *Her Majesty's Interrogator*, Leo Cooper, London, 1996.

The War of 1982

Stanley. After several hours of negotiations, at 9 pm on the evening of 14 June, General Menéndez surrendered the whole of the archipelago, including West Falkland, which had seen no fighting, to the British forces.

The military action resulted in 255 British dead and 777 wounded.[122] There were 700 Argentines killed and more than 1000 wounded. Nearly all those killed died in combat. The overall figure includes the 321 killed on the *"General Belgrano"*.[123] The behaviour of troops on both sides was, in general, in accordance with the Geneva Convention,[124] although there were accusations that some Argentine soldiers were killed after they had surrendered.[125] The Argentine Air Force lost 36 officers, 14 NCOs and 5 soldiers and were notable for their bravery during many dangerous missions against the British aeronaval forces. In contrast, of the 56 officers, including the Captain on the "General Belgrano", all but three survived. Of the NCOs and sailors, the 218 who died represented a third of the total crew.[126] The Argentine Navy also lost 22 men in other ships and 2 naval pilots. The Royal Navy lost 87 men, of whom 13 were officers.[127] Of the total of 255 British fallen, 28 were officers, 141 died in air attacks (31 in attacks by the naval airforce) and only 64 died in combat with the defending Argentine troops. Some 37

---

[122] Hastings, Max & Jenkins, Simon; *The Battle for the Falklands*, Chaucer Press, London, 1983.

[123] Bonzo, Hector; *1039 tripulantes*, Sudamericana, Buenos Aires, 1992.
Woodward, Admiral Sandy; *One Hundred Days*, Harper Collins, London, 1992.

[124] Landaburu, Coronel Carlos Augusto; *La guerra de las Malvinas*, Biblioteca del Oficial, Buenos Aires, 1989.

[125] Bramley, Vincent; *Excursion to Hell*, Pan Books, London, 1992.

[126] Middlebrook, Martin; *The Fight for the Malvinas*, Viking, Suffolk, 1989, p. 115.

[127] Middlebrook, Martin; *Task Force*, Penguin, London, 1985, p. 383.

combatants died in accidents. The land-based Argentine troops lost 261 from the Army and 37 from the Marine Corps. At the end of the war the British captured a total of 12,978 Argentines. [128]

The British *"Task Force"* lost 6 ships, had 10 ships seriously damaged, lost 12 Harrier aircraft and two dozen or more helicopters. The Argentines lost 5 ships and more than 100 aircraft –31 Skyhawks, 26 Mirages, 23 Pucarás, 1 Canberra, 1 C130 and 18 helicopters.

The economic cost of the war was also high. It is estimated that it cost each sideover $ 5,000 million. [129]

The war demonstrated Britain's overwhelming military superiority, but also highlighted the strategic, tactical, logistic and leadership errors of the Argentine Military Junta. But all these pale into insignificance alongside the shameful diplomatic process. It is probable that the British were never at any time disposed to negotiate, but were helped in their strategy by the ineptitude of Argentine diplomacy. In contrast, the bravery with which some of the Argentine forces fought, especially the Air Force and the naval aviators, was remarkable.

It was a total defeat, both in the diplomatic and military fields. It also had important domestic political consequences in Argentina because, the following year the Military Junta had no choice but to call for free elections and hand over the government to a democratically elected President.

---

[128] Middlebrook, Martin; *Task Force*, Penguin, London, 1985, p. 384.
[129] Sources: MOD, Britain; International Institute for Defence Studies, John Llewellyn, Global Chief Economist, Lehman Brothers, Reuters. *La Nación*, Buenos Aires, 16-4-99.

VII

THE SEDUCTION POLICY

The Immediate Post-War Period

The war had political consequences in Argentina, the United Kingdom and on the Falkland Islands themselves.

In Great Britain it assured a Conservative Government for almost two decades, firstly with the successive governments of Margaret Thatcher and then of her heir John Major. Great Britain consolidated its economic position with an aggressive policy of free enterprise and strengthened its bonds with the United States, generating a new reality which has come to be accepted, even by the Labour Party, led by Tony Blair, at the end of the 90s. From a military point of view, the war meant a victory for the Royal Navy, which maintained its reputation as one of the finest navies in the world.

In Argentina, the defeat (not the war) led to the fall of General Galtieri, who was replaced by General Bignone as President.

In an effort that has gone largely unrecognised,

The Falklands journalist Patrick Watts interviewing the daughter of former Foreign Minister Di Tella.

Bignone, in a little over a year successfully moved the country towards democracy and sent the military back to their barracks. From an economic standpoint financial reconstruction began after the enormous amount of resources squandered on the war. The recovery from the economic embargoes imposed by the Commonwealth and the European Community also began.

In terms of foreign relations, Bignone was successful in restoring the relationships with the United States and the European Community. There was great progress achieved in passing successive United Nations resolutions ratifying Resolution 2065 of 1965 and making clear that the military actions had not altered the natural justice of the conflict and the need for the parties to negotiate a solution to the sovereignty dispute.

During Galtieri's term, the United Nations issued Security Council Resolution 502 calling for the immediate withdrawal of Argentine troops and Resolution 505, which through the good offices of the Peruvian Secretary General, Javier Pérez de Cuellar, appealed for an immediate cease-fire. This Resolution, boycotted by the British, was not adequately utilized by Argentina.

With the war over, and with Bignone as President, the new Foreign Minister Juan Aguirre Lanari promoted new resolutions in the 38th and 39th sessions of the General Assembly, designed to start sovereignty discussions. He obtained important support from the United States, who prior to the war had always abstained, but now supported his efforts to get sovereignty negotiations off the ground.

United Nations Resolution 37-9 (1982), that ratified Resolutions 1514 (1960), 2065 (1965) and 3160 (1973), re-affirmed the need for both parties to take the interests of the population of the Islands into account and called on both sides to renew negotiations to find the quickest possible solution to the sovereignty dispute. The Resolution was carried by 90 votes in favour, 12 against [130] and 52 abstentions. The same Resolution reiterated that the Secretary General should act as mediator.[131] The Organisation of American States[132] and the Non-Aligned Movement[133] formally supported the Resolution.

The United Kingdom informed the UN that it would not comply with this Resolution. Speaking in the House of Commons, on 23 November 1982, the British Prime Minister Margaret Thatcher stated that "the negotiations on sovereignty of the Falkland Islands are completely out of the question".[134]

In November 1983, the United Nations passed Resolution 38-12, which took into account the cessation of hostilities and the lack of progress in the negotiations and reiterated the Resolution of the previous year. The Resolution was passed by 90 votes in favour to 10 against.

---

[130] Those voting against were: Antigua & Barbuda, Belize, Dominica, Fiji, The Gambia, Malawi, New Zealand, Oman, Papua New Guinea, the Solomon Islands, Sri Lanka and the United Kingdom.
[131] CARI, *Malvinas, Georgias y Sandwich del Sur*, CARI, Buenos Aires, 1991, Tomo IV, p. 427.
[132] 8th plenary session of 20 November 1982.
[133] 7th Conference of Heads of State, New Delhi, 1-12 March, 1983.
[134] Document AA-AC of the United Nations 109-752. Item 27.

The Falklands artist, James Peck with one of his works exhibited in Buenos Aires.

The Foreign Policy of President Alfonsín

At the end of 1983, Raul Alfonsín became President of Argentina. The new President appointed Dante Caputo as his Foreign Minister. Both arrived with ideas of the Social Democrats from the 1960's and did not realise that the Cold War was coming to an end.

They therefore decided to increase Argentina's participation in the Non-Aligned Bloc and to adopt a foreign policy contrary to the interests of the United States. They wasted an excellent opportunity, because Argentina's re-entry in the democratic world had been well received among all the western powers.

In 1984, a meeting was organised in Berne between representatives of the United Kingdom with the aim of normalising such meetings and restarting the negotiations on sovereignty of the disputed islands. The meeting was a complete failure. In addition to British intransigence, there was the fact that Argentine negotiators did not appreciate the incompatibility of a third war policy with progress in the negotiations with the United Kingdom. The direct consequence of this failure was the ending of the honeymoon between Alfonsín and the European countries that had supported the return of Democracy to Argentina. This was especially true of the British conservatives, led by Thatcher, who lost confidence in the social democrat Alfonsín and Caputo. During the rest of Alfonsín's presidency there were no further advances in the relationship between the Untied Kingdom and Argentina.

The economic crisis, into which Argentina had fallen during President Alfonsín's term, including hyperinflation, weakened Argentina's position internationally. This was reflected in the lack of interest shown by the British to negotiate.

The Radical Party's only successes were in the United Nations. On 6 November 1984, the General Assembly of the United Nations approved Resolution 39-6, by 89 votes in favour, 9 against and 54 abstentions.

President Alfonsín's diplomacy had obtained less votes than that of General Bignone. Important countries like Australia, Belgium, Canada, Egypt, France, Germany, Greece, Israel, Italy and Portugal all abstained. The Argentine diplomats did not realise that, despite the approval of the Resolution, they were losing ground.

The following year, the United Nations approved Resolution 40-21, which did not mention the sovereignty dispute, nor the preceding Resolutions. Nonetheless, it received 4 votes against (including the United Kingdom) and 47 abstentions (Including countries like, Germany, Portugal, New Zealand, Egypt, Israel and Ireland). In 1986 and 1987, there were similar Resolutions.

During the radical government, relations with Great Britain not only did not improve but actually worsened. Due to the boom in fishing in the South Atlantic, the United Kingdom tried to promote, through the auspices of the FA, the internationalisation the regulation of fishing in the region

Argentina attempted to anticipate whatever measures the United Kingdom might adopt by signing bilateral fishing agreements with Bulgaria and the Soviet Union, which implied the recognition by these countries of Argentine sovereignty over Falklands waters. The British reacted by unilaterally establishing a 150 mile protection zone around the Islands, within which only fishing boats licensed by the British government of the Islands are allowed to operate.

Alfonsín's government was disconcerted. They tried unsuccessfully to obtain American support in order to make the British review the decision. The United Kingdom not only refused to agree, but the in 1988, announced an important military exercise, *"Fire Focus"* around the Islands. Diplomacy failed again with Argentina's inability to obtain a meeting of the Security Council to discuss the issue. They were only able to inform the Security Council of what had happened.

By the middle of 1989, Argentina's situation could not get worse. The country was mired in the hyperinflationary struggle, and with a government that had lost its way, was forced to anticipate the handing over of power to the Peronist Carlos Menem. If we add this to the fall of the Berlin Wall, and the end of the Cold War with the victory of the United States, we can see the absurdity of the third world policies and of the confrontation pursued by Argentina.

Change of Policy

President Menem, who in his electoral campaign had said *"it doesn't matter how much blood we spill, we are going to recover the Falklands"*, appointed Domingo

Tony and Joan Spruce, and their fond memories of their honeymoon in Bariloche in the 70s.

Cavallo as his Foreign Minister. Cavallo introduced a 180° turn in Argentine Foreign Policy.[135]

It was decided to "de-Falklandise Argentine Foreign Policy", abandon the Non-Aligned Movement and rebuild the relationships with the United States and the European Community. For this it was essential to rebuild relations with the United Kingdom.

Through the good offices of Brazil a meeting was held in New York, where it was agreed to meet formally in Madrid. Thus it was on 19 October 1989, that Argentina and the United Kingdom signed the Madrid Agreement in which it was agreed to install a sovereignty "umbrella".[136] They agreed to try to rebuild the bilateral relationship without affecting the sovereignty claims over the Islands. Both countries declared a cessation of hostilities and abstention from the use of force to resolve the dispute. A working group was created to discuss the problems of fishing and the lifting of the exclusion zone to allow mercantile trade. They also agreed that there would be no claims for damages resulting from the war. There are those who believe that although the hostilities ended on 14 June 1982, the state of war only ceased with the Madrid agreement.[137]

In February 1990, there was a new Madrid agreement, which reiterated the sovereignty umbrella and

---

[135] Etchebarne Bullrich, Conrado; "Conducta mafiosa de los kelpers le impide a argentinos comprar tierras", *Ambito Financiero*, Buenos Aires, 20-7-99.

[136] Actually, a fiction which denies certain circumstances, and assumes that the sovereignty claim remains protected.

[137] Fraga, Contralmirante Jorge; *Malvinas, Evolución de la cuestión desde la guerra*, Revista Militar, June 1995, p. 77.

agreed to the re-establishment of diplomatic relations, to suspend the exclusion zone (although new limits were established for Argentine ships and aircraft approaching the Islands), a series of measures concerning military communications with the purpose of avoiding incidents and agreement to allow visits to the Argentine cemetery by the next of kin of Argentine servicemen killed during the war.

In order to give priority to the bilateral relationship, the promotion of annual Resolutions in the General Assembly was suspended. There was also a fear that the quality of the Resolutions would diminish, by becoming increasingly bland as result of the difficulties in obtaining votes despite having abandoned their third world policies.

This change in policy was accentuated when Guido Di Tella became Foreign Minister.

The entire Foreign Policy of the previous Radical government (which had been very similar to that of the previous Peronist governments) was discarded, with the exception of the two fundamental successes of Alfonsín's administration: Mercosur and the improvement of relations with Chile.

The main priority of Argentine foreign policy became its reintegration into the western, developed world. This required strengthening internal democracy and establishing the best possible relationship with the United States. An unfortunate, descriptive and metaphorical expression by the Foreign Minister "carnal relations" became the catch phrase for the new bilateral relationship. The improvement did not reach the desired level of excellence as a result of Argentina's failure to comply on the question of patents, which was required by American pharmaceutical laboratories. An excellent relationship was forged with Europe. This was also not easy because of European intransigence in maintaining the Common Agricultural Policy that discriminated against Argentine products. In the case of Great Britain there was also great success in re-establishing an excellent bilateral relationship in terms of trade, culture and sport; but no success in advancing the sovereignty dispute, due to continued British obstinacy. Minister Di Tella's best efforts to find a solution to this aspect of the relationship were insufficient.

In the United Nations, Argentina voted systematically in accord with the United States and Great Britain and participated in important UN peace missions in the Gulf War, in Cyprus and in former Yugoslavia. Further distancing itself from the so-called "Third World" countries.

However, and a little incongruously, Argentina maintained its pressure on the UN's C24 Committee on de-Colonisation where, through the years, Argentina had reiterated its claim and obtained favourable Resolutions which insisted that both parties renew sovereignty negotiations. From that time onwards, the Committee's sessions were attended by some of the most notable Argentine diplomats, including the then Ambassador to the United Nations and the Foreign Minister himself. The British delegation consisted of two members of the Legislative Council of the Falkland Islands.[138] The

---

[138] The author attended the Committee's sessions in 1998 and 1999 and was witness to the support of the Committee for Argentina.

Committee's meetings, in particular the more recent ones, have served as a forum where Argentines and Islanders can exchange ideas.

Policy Towards the Islands

From very early on in his term of office, and subsequently with great perseverance, Foreign Minister Di Tella has recognised the need to break down the dispute into its component parts. On one side is the sovereignty dispute, which has remained frozen since the Madrid Agreements. And on the other, the need to re-establish normal relations between the Islands and the continent, to allow mutual visits, to avoid incidents and to reach agreement on crucial issues like fishing and oil.

To advance his policies Di Tella held more than 50 meetings with successive British Foreign Secretaries.[139]

On the Islands there is a population of approximately 2000 people who live well, thanks to the income derived mainly from fishing licensing (wool production, the traditional resource is now running in deficit). There is also a British military base staffed with close to 2000 servicemen and women, to assure the British presence on the Islands.

The Islands are governed by a Governor (a Foreign Office official) appointed by the queen and a Legislative Council, which is elected by the inhabitants. The

---

[139] He met more times with British Foreign Secretaries than did all his predecessors put together.

Islanders, who suffered during the 1982 conflict, have undergone anti-Argentine indoctrination for many generations. This still exists today and had led to Islanders rejecting any kind of link with Argentina whilst the sovereignty claim persists. They did however accept the need to reach agreements that were in their interests –on fishing and oil.

There were also various agreements, in line with the Madrid Agreements, on a variety of military issues: to avoid incidents, on security, rescues, navigation and air traffic control. These agreements were crowned by the successful visit to Britain of General Balza, the Argentine Army Chief, in 1996. At the same time Argentina had reduced its military expenditure to less than 1% of GDP, whilst the comparative figure in the United Kingdom was still close to Cold War levels at 4%.[140]

Two years later, the official visit of President Menem and his daughter Zulemita to London was finally agreed. This visit was also a highly successful mark of the normalisation of the bilateral relationship (with the exception of the Falklands dispute). A few months later the Prince of Wales paid a reciprocal visit to Argentina and the Falkland Islands.

Progress in the bilateral relationship during the decade of Menem's Presidency was enormous. From a situation of no commerce between the two countries, bilateral trade reached record levels of $1,000 million in 1998. Additionally, many British companies invested a total of more than $1,000 million in Argentina. Notable

---

[140] In recent years this has been reduced. It is now estimated to be between 2.5 and 3% of GDP.

examples are: British Gas, Shell, Eagle Star, HSBC, National Grid, Glaxo, Reckitt & Colman, GNK, Unilever, Ladbroke, Cadbury, Lloyds Bank, Inchcape, Monument Oil & Gas, Sun Alliance, Pillsbury, Rover, Smithkline Beecham, Pilkington and Portia Clark Chapman among others.

Fishing

Fishing for the *"Illex"* squid, the predominant species in the region, needed an agreement. The squid is born in the St. George Gulf on the Argentine continental shelf and migrates southeast during its growth period, arriving in the waters around the Falklands where it feeds and remains for a year, after which it dies. As the squid is found outside Falklands waters is was impossible for the British to impose unilateral controls on catches. The fishing agreements that were put in place during Di Tella's term of office could not refer to sharing the Islands' fish stocks without deciding which resources belonged to the Islands, which to the continent and how over-fishing and stock depredation could be controlled.[141]

The Fisheries Commission was established in 1990. There have already been twenty formal meetings that have established a *modus vivendi*, which allows for short-term agreements for the conservation of fish stocks. Argentina considers a long-term agreement unacceptable until there is progress on the sovereignty dispute.[142]

---

[141] Fraga, Contralmirante Jorge; "Malvinas, evolución de la cuestión desde la guerra", *Revista militar*, June 1995, p. 69 onwards.
[142] Etchebarne Bullrich, Conrado; *The Falklands, Britain and Argentina*, Oxford, 1997.

Another concern of the Islanders is illegal fishing by third countries, especially Taiwan and Korea. Poaching also affects Argentine waters and short-term agreements have been reached to deal with the problem. All these agreements have been approved under the terms of sovereignty "umbrella" established by the Madrid Agreement of 1989.

Oil

Something similar happened with oil. There are indications of the existence of hydrocarbons –oil and gas– in Falklands waters. In theory, the British could exploit these resources without Argentine cooperation. But, in practice, the costs would be enormous and would require huge investments in an area subject to a territorial claim.

After many years of disagreement, including unilateral British decisions that changed the *status quo*, an agreement on oil and gas was reached in New York on 27 September 1995, by Di Tella and Malcolm Rifkind, the British Foreign Secretary. The agreement consisted of a joint declaration to cooperate in the exploration and exploitation of oil in the offshore waters of the Falkland Islands. The declaration did not include waters around The South Georgia and South Sandwich Islands. A special cooperation area was also established in waters that belong partially to the Islands' continental shelf and partially to Argentina's continental territorial platform.

As a result of opposition to the agreement in the Argentine Congress there has been no advance in exploitation in the special cooperation area.

Great Britain issued exploration licences for the northern zone of the Falklands continental platform but, so far, the results have been negative. As the presence of hydrocarbons has been confirmed, it is probable that, with improved oil prices and better technology, the issue will re-surface.

Opposition Criticism

Di Tella's change of policy on the Falkland Islands, particularly his recognition of the important role the Islanders have in any solution of the dispute, received strong criticism not only from the opposition but also from his own party.

Amongst the Peronists, important critics were Senator Eduardo Menem and the previous Argentine Ambassador to London, Mario Cámpora. In the opposition, one of the constant critics has been Ambassador Lucio García del Solar.

Nevertheless, towards the end of Di Tella's term his critics have shown more moderation and many have decided to support his policies.[143] In the case of Garcia del Solar, after having criticised the oil and fishing agreements, he accepted that, *"The Foreign Minister's idea of winning over the islanders is basically constructive and useful if it had been done more subtly and discreetly".*[144]

---

[143] The Deputies Raimundi (FREPASO), Maurette (Peronist), and Stubrin (Radical) accompanied the Argentine delegation to the United Nations in 1998 and 1999.
[144] García del Solar, Lucio; *La contribución de las Naciones Unidas a las negociaciones entre la Argentina y el Reino Unido,* Buenos Aires, 22-6-95.

There appears to be a general agreement amongst the various Argentine political factions that the government should work with the Islanders on the question of peaceful coexistence, whilst putting pressure on Great Britain to negotiate on the sovereignty dispute.

It seems that the new Foreign Minister Adalberto Rodriguez Giavarini, appointed by President Fernando De la Rua, will follow Di Tella's policies though not its forms.

Argentine Visits

At the end of the war the British decided to stop all contacts between the Islands and Argentina. Not only was all air and sea links with Argentina prohibited, but also anyone travelling on an Argentine passport was banned from entering the Islands. No business or commerce of any kind was allowed with Argentines, nor were they allowed to acquire either goods or land on the Islands.

From the beginning of his term of office, Foreign Minister Di Tella allowed the links between the Islands and Chile to overfly or pass through Argentine waters, a gesture of good will that was not reciprocated by the colonial British administration. Thanks to this policy a link was established between Punta Arenas and Stanley. Firstly with twin-engine Otters of Aerovías DAP and then with Boeing 737s of Lan Chile. This connection allowed many Islanders to cross to the continent and many of them visited Argentina.[145] Only in 1999, as a result of the

---

[145] Good will visits were made by, among others, Graham Bound, Janet Robertson, Terry Betts, Kevin Kilmartin, Fred Clark, Stuart Wallace, Ian Strange and James Peck.

The Seduction Policy

deterioration of Anglo-Chilean relations after the arrest of General Pinochet in London, did the British accept a monthly direct flight from Río Gallegos and the admission of Argentines travelling on Argentine passports.[146]

British Policy

For many years Britain had no clear policy on their intentions for the future of the Islands. In the 60s and 70s, with growing global decolonisation movement, they imagined that the Islands would have to be ceded to Argentina and did everything possible to delay the eventuality.

At the end of the war in 1982, the Conservative governments of Thatcher and Major began to think in terms of the Islands remaining British permanently, maybe as a colony, an overseas territory or an associated state. They therefore began the policy of fortifying the Islands, which ensured dominion over the waters and continental platform of the Islands and was intended to legitimise their possession of the Islands. From 1986, the Islanders were also authorised to be democratically responsible for domestic affairs. Simultaneously, they attempted to ensure the economic viability of the Islands. For this they built an international airport in the Mount Pleasant military base that allowed direct air links from London. They built a first class secondary school for the education of the new generations of

---

[146] For many years the Islanders admitted Argentines travelling on other passports.

Alastair Forsyth, co-author of the Bullrich-Forsyth proposal, tasting Tussac grass.

The Seduction Policy

Islanders, built a sophisticated hospital and expropriated the land belonging to the Falkland Island Company to put land-ownership in the hands of the Islanders. Their final measure was to grant all Islanders British nationality which, until then they did not enjoy.[147]

Throughout this time they maintained a complete freeze on any links between the Islands and Argentina. They prohibited visits by Argentines, business with Argentines, trade with Argentina, flights from Argentina and the purchase on the Islands of goods of Argentine origin. Meanwhile, they tried to establish a special relationship with Chile, based on Punta Arenas. Firstly they set up flights with the local company DAP, subsidised by the Islands' government, and then with Lan Chile, similarly subsidised. At the same time they tried to minimise the number of Spanish speakers on the Islands. To do this they substituted temporary immigrants from the British colony of St. Helena for the traditional Chilean work force. These immigrants, either black or mulatto, were not given permanent residence to maintain the basically Anglo-Saxon population on the Islands.

The new Labour Government of Tony Blair and his Foreign Secretary, Robin Cook, found that policies on their Falkland Islands colony were completely opposed to those that the Labour Party had traditionally followed. Argentina was hopeful that there would be a change of policy. It was not to be.

---

[147] The inhabitants of the other British colonies in the South Atlantic were not given British citizenship on strictly racial grounds: the majority were either black or mulatto.

Shortly after assuming power, the Labour Government issued a document on British policy towards the Islands.[148] This document re-named the colonies as *Overseas Territories*.* The British colonies that had survived the dissolution of the Empire (a period that formally came to an end with the return of Hong Kong to China in 1997) were: Anguilla, Bermuda, the British Virgin Islands, the Cayman Islands, the Falkland Islands, Gibraltar, Montserrat, Pitcairn, St. Helena, Ascension, Tristan da Cunha, the Turks & Caicos Islands, the British Antarctic Territory (as it was classified under the Antarctic Treaty), the South Georgia Islands, the South Sandwich Islands, the British Indian Ocean Islands and the sovereign bases of Akrotiri and Dhekelia on Cyprus.

Part of the basis of the document was that the colonies (Overseas Territories) maintain their links with Great Britain if they so desired. Thus Great Britain changed its traditional claim over the Falkland Islands based on its interpretation of the historical facts (certainly a weak position) for the principle of self-determination of the people. It also affirmed its support of the independence of those territories whose populations wished to remain within the Commonwealth.

The White Paper restated the strategic interest in the military defence of the territories and made special mention of the base at Mount Pleasant.

A new element in the document compared to previous policies is the decision to implement the defence of human rights in the territories and the fight

---

[148] The White Paper of 6 April 1999.
(*) Overseas Territories is a translation of the French euplhemism for colonies: territories d'outre mer.

against discrimination in particular. Also preservation of the environment and the fight against drugs (including money laundering).

Nothing is said about resolving the sovereignty disputes that exist over the Falkland Islands and Gibraltar, but the paper makes clear the policy of retaining the *status quo*, defending the territories and that any change will require the agreement of the inhabitants.

A New Game [149]

For many years Argentina was considered the *"naughty boy"* of the Falkland Islands conflict. It was said that Argentina had neither the patience nor the perseverance needed to make progress along the difficult and laborious road of negotiations. After all, Argentina was the country that had strayed to the edge of the law, that had been governed by a Military Junta, that had invaded the Falklands in 1982 and that had suffered hyperinflation of its own making.

But in the last ten years things have changed considerably. Not only is Argentina now a stable, democratic country, with a solid currency and a growing economy, it has also reintegrated with the western democracies and re-established positive relations with the United States and the European Union.

Relations with Great Britain, as we have seen, have also been improved on all levels.[150] One must recognise

---

[149] Etchebarne Bullrich, Conrado; "A Useless Unilateral Cold War Policy", *Buenos Aires Herald*, 30-9-96.
[150] Etchebarne Bullrich, Conrado; "Une nueva relación argentino-británica", *La Prensa*, Buenos Aires, 16-9-94.

the efforts of Di Tella together with those of the Foreign Office, of the British Embassy in Buenos Aires and of many businessmen. Also the efforts of CARI[151], which through the ABC conferences, was the first to prepare the ground for the re-establishment of Anglo-Argentine relations.

Argentina has also lifted all the restrictions on Falkland Islanders visiting and conducting business there. Neither has it imposed restrictions on its citizens wishing to visit or do business with the Islands.

It would seem that over the last few years (as was the case when the conflict began), it is the British who are playing the role of *"naughty boy"*. For 18 years the British Government impeded all contact between the Islands and Argentina; it would not authorize flights in either direction, would not allow Argentines to visit[152] and prohibited all forms of interchange. One must also add the indoctrination that the local population receives and the erroneous information they have about the history of the Islands.[153]

It is a dangerous game, which when played by others on a different stage was known as the Cold War. The South Atlantic Wall is almost a caricature of the Berlin Wall or the Iron Curtain.

---

[151] Consejo Argentino de las relaciones Internacionales (Argentine Council for International Relations)
[152] The visits of next of kin of soldiers buried in the Darwin cemetery were organised in a "Soviet style". The relatives were permanently supervised by the military, the visits only lasted 24 hours, and they were not allowed to leave the cemetery, the air base of their place of accommodation.
[153] Repeated constantly ranging from oil prospects, to speeches of the Councillors in the United Nations.

Typical Falklands cat, necessary on the Islands to control the large rodent population.

The conflict entered a period of *"Cold War"* from which, thankfully, it seems to be emerging.[154]

The solid support of Mercosur and the change of Chile's position [155] –after overcoming all the border disputes– has changed the balance of power in the South Atlantic. Additionally, the South African experience, where democracy has replaced the apartheid regime that for many years had Great Britain's support, completes the picture that creates favourable conditions for Great Britain to begin to seriously look for solutions to the sovereignty dispute.

The Re-establishment of Communications with the Islands

The policy of "getting closer" [156] has had results. In the middle of 1999 the Islanders, under pressure from the Foreign Office, and as a result of the deterioration of Anglo-Chilean relations due to the detention of General Pinochet in London, accepted the need to have links with Argentina, including direct flights and Argentine visits. An agreement was finally reached on 14 July after 17 years without any regular communication between the Islands and Argentina.

The agreement was the climax of Di Tella's policy of seduction.

---

[154] Etchebarne Bullrich, Conrado; "Two hopes, a couple of misunderstandings", *Buenos Aires Herald*, 19-3-99.
[155] Etchebarne Bullrich, Conrado; "Un cambio favorable", *La Nación*, 5-10-96.
[156] Called "seduction" by the media and known by the Islanders as the "charm offensive".

The Seduction Policy

The first point in the agreement was to allow Argentines to visit the Islands. In contrast to what happened in the 1970s, now Argentines can present their own passports for travel to the Islands.

The second was the re-establishment of the weekly Lan Chile flights from Punta Arenas to Mount Pleasant, with one monthly stop in Rio Gallegos.

The last was the formulation of a basis for controlling illegal fishing in Falklands waters.

This agreement was reached under the terms of the *"umbrella"* established in 1980, which still remains in force with both parties unshakable in their sovereignty claims.

There can be no doubt that the lack of both communications and visits of Argentines to the Islands were two of the factors that made it difficult to improve mutual trust, an essential requirement to enable advances in other areas. These agreements are only the first step in what is needed for a successful re-establishment of links between the Islands and the continent.

However, not all the reactions were positive. As much in the Islands as in Argentina there were many who expressed their opposition to the agreement, but -reflecting the change in attitude- it was supported by the great majority on both sides.[157]

---

[157] *Menem's Visit Made a Difference*, Penguin News, 4-6-99. Betts, Terry; *Well Done Councillors*, Penguin News, 2-7-99.

Americanos del Sur

During the 18 years since the war, official contacts between the Islands and the Argentine government were practically non-existent.

This opened the way for non-profit organisations like CARI[158] and Americanos del Sur to take an active role in bringing the Islanders and Argentines closer together.

CARI organised a series of conferences known as ABC[159], which were held alternately in London, Buenos Aires, Oxford and Salta. These conferences analysed the Anglo-Argentine relationship including the sovereignty dispute over the Falkland Islands. Senior figures on all sides attended including representatives of the Islands. The conferences were a success and helped in the re-establishment of Anglo-Argentine relations including allowing contact between Foreign Minister Di Tella and Senator Eduardo Menem with some of the Island Councillors like Lewis Clifton and Sharon Halford.

Americanos del Sur is a non profit civil association founded in 1989 with the purpose of promoting peace and friendship among the peoples of South America. Suggested as a consequence of the publication of the book "Americanos del Sur en el Siglo XXI"[160] (South

---

[158] Consejo Argentino de las Relaciones Internacionales (Argentine Council for International Relations).

[159] Argentine British Conference. The author had the opportunity to attend several of these conferences.

[160] Etchebarne Bullrich, Conrado; *Americanos del Sur en el Siglo XXI*, ed. Emecé, Buenos Aires, 1989. Commentaries on the book were published in *El Cronista Comercial*, 9-12-90, *La Prensa*.

Americans in the 21st Century). More than 300 articles were published subsequently to promote its ideals.

Americanos del Sur began to become involved with the Falkland Islands in 1994, supporting a visit there by the author and his wife, which included stopovers in London and Ascension Island.[161]

The same year a documentary film *"The Argentine Camp"*[162] was produced and directed by the author with the aim of showing the Islanders the way of life in the Argentine countryside and the successful way in which immigrants of different nationalities have been integrated into the community. Copies of the film were sent to every family on the Islands. Never before has the Islanders received non-political information on Argentina.

In January 1995, Americanos del Sur supported a new journey to the Islands by the author, this time with his family.[163] The visit was another success and allowed many inhabitants of the isolated Islands to have contact with and get to know an Argentine family. There were also trips to Japan to study the conflict with Russia over the Kuril Islands* and the tremendous similarities

---

[161] A very fruitful journey. We were the first married Argentine couple to travel to the Islands since the war (even though we travelled on Irish passports). A detailed description of our stay on the Islands was published in La Prensa, 24-6-94.

[162] Cacigavisión 1994. "Los malvinenses verán el campo argentino por dentro", *La Nación*, 11-2-95; "Conrado plays Santa, but the family has to do the licking", Penguin News, 7-1-95.

[163] Etchebarne Bullrich, Conrado; "Más que una vacación, un homenaje", *Gente magazine*, 13-4-95. Etchebarne Bullrich, Conrado; "Las Malvinas por dentro", *La Nación*, 12-3-95.

(*) Known as the Northern territories by the Japanese.

between the two disputes[164]. Also to Thailand to study the different disputes over the sea south of China which are disputed by Thailand, Vietnam, China, Taiwan and the Philipines.[165] Historical studies on other colonial links with Argentina were also undertaken.[166]

In January 1996 a new journey was made with the grandchildren of Foreign Minister Di Tella.[167] These were all factors that contributed to the thawing of relations, on a human level, between the Islanders and Argentina.

Further journeys were made to the Islands, London and Oxford[168] in 1997 and 1998 with the aim of spreading the ideals of the association. In May 1998, with the sponsorship of Americanos del Sur, *"The Bullrich-Forsyth Proposal: A Way Forward"*[169] paper was published in the Penguin News and received an interesting reception. The same proposal was made public in Buenos Aires in October 1998, thanks to CARI.[170]

In February 1999, a journey by the author and Carlos

---

[164] Etchebarne Bullrich, Conrado; "Las Malvinas japonesas", *La Nación*, 6.8.95. The Japanese organisation JASCAA co-sponsored the journey.
[165] Etchebarne Bullrich, Conrado; "Las islas Malvinas no son un caso aislado", *La Avispa*, May 1996.
[166] Etchebarne Bullrich, Conrado; "Las colonias de la reina del Plata", *La Nación*, 24-8-97. Etchebarne Bullrich, Conrado; "Cuando Hawaii tuvo bandera argentina", *La Nación*, 14-9-97.
[167] "Invasión de los pequeños Di Tella", *La Nación*, 4-2-96; "Little Di Tella's Success", *Buenos Aires Herald*, 4-2-96.
[168] The author participated in seminars held by the Centre for International Studies, St. Anthony's College, Oxford, May 1997.
[169] See Annex I.
[170] "Debate por Malvinas en el CARI", *Clarín*, 10-10-98; "The Way Forward for Malvinas Solution", Buenos Aires Herald, 20-10-98; "Islanders tell Bullrich Forsyth; we've already got what we want", Penguin News, 22-5-98.

The Seduction Policy

Appel, an agricultural engineer was supported with the purpose of promoting the possibility of establishing agricultural links between the Islands and the continent, including possible technical interchanges and Argentine investment in agricultural exploitation on the Islands. It has not been possible to carry these ideas forward due to the strong opposition of this sector on the Islands[171], but the door remains open. With only two exceptions the British have, for nearly a century and a half, effectively blocked all Argentine efforts to buy land in the Islands.[172] Nevertheless, once again the possibility is there.

The activities of CARI and Americanos del Sur shows once more how non governmental organisations can play an important role in defusing conflicts and re-establishing friendship and contact between countries and peoples.

At the end of 1999 Americanos del Sur took an active role in the organisation of a regatta from Buenos Aires –Mar del Plata– Stanley within the spirit of improving friendly relations between the Islanders and Argentines.[173]

---

[171] "En Malvinas no quieren propietarios argentinos", *Clarín*, 5-2-99; "Malvinas, otro argentino fracasa en comprar tierras", *Ambito Financiero*, 5-2-99; "South American Dreamers", Telegraph Travel, London, 13-3-99; "El adelantado del canciller", *Noticias Magazine*, 13-2-99; "Conducta mafiosa de los kelpers les impide a argentinos comprar tierras", *Ambito Financiero*, 20-7-99; *Weddel Island is still for sale*, Penguin News, Stanley, 5-2-99.

[172] Charlie Rowe, an Argentine of Scottish origin, inherited "The Globe" and stayed on the Islands. As a result of the war in 1982 he was obliged to sell (*La Nación*, 5-9-96, "El dueño argentino de las Malvinas", by Germán Sopeña); and John Hamilton, an Argentine of Falklands descent who lived Buenos Aires, but who owned Weddel Island and also had to sell after the 1982 war.

[173] Etchebarne Bullrich, Conrado; "Nuevas ideas", Revista *Bienvenido a Bordo*, September 1999.

Ian Strange, the naturalist, conservationist, writer, and the designer of the famous Island stamps, demonstrates his working method based on directly copying nature.

VIII

THE ISLANDS TODAY

The Kelpers

The dispute continues, but the islanders are not the same. They are now wealthy and cultured. Fishing, oil, tourism and education offer them a promising future, provided they reach an agreement on the difficult sovereignty issue.[174]

"Kelpers", was the name given to the Islanders by officials of the Crown and especially by British managers and administrators of the Falkland Islands Company.[175] The word originates from *"kelp"*, an enormous algae with metre long stems which surrounds the Falkland Islands coastline and is abundant on the seabed. It was and still is a great danger for coastal navigation, as the propellers

---

[174] Etchebarne Bullrich, Conrado; "Doce años después", *La Prensa*, 24-7-94.
[175] The word *kelper* was not used in Argentina. The story told by Harold Foulkes in his book *Los Kelpers*, Corregidor, Buenos Aires, 1983, p. 21, is illustrative: "The first time I heard the word Kelper in reference to those born on the Falkland Islands, was in London, at midday on 10 December 1964, from John Ferguson, columnist on Latin American affairs for The Observer."

of small vessels can easily become tangled in the long stems. *"Kelper"* had a certain pejorative connotation, especially during those years when the Islands were left to their own devices and exploited by the Falkland Islands Company. The *kelpers* of those days were simple folk without much education who were dedicated to looking after the sheep.

That was not the denomination given in Argentina. For many years they were referred to as *"malvinenses"* or *"malvineros"*, which had no negative implications. Nevertheless, during the years immediately before and after the war of 1982, the majority of the Argentine press, used the word *"kelper"* to refer to the Islanders precisely because of its negative connotation. It was a period when feelings were running high. Over the last four or five years, perhaps as a consequence of Di Tella's actions and also due to the passage of time, most of the Argentine media has begun to treat the Islanders with more respect.

The reality is that the Islanders today have little in common with the kelpers of yesterday. The majority of the Islanders now live in Stanley with all the conveniences of modern life. They live in attractive house with views overlooking the bay. They all have electricity, telephones and running water and each household has one or two cars.[176] Most people are, in one form or another, public employees. Salary levels are high and per capita income is in excess of $40,000 per annum. This figure, that could sound like an exaggeration, is a calculated by dividing the total island income,

---

[176] Not counting the military, there are more than 1,000 vehicles, 4x4s (the majority), cars, motorcycles and quads.

The Islands Today

which is inflated by the revenue derived from fishing licences, by the comparatively small number of inhabitants.

To this we must add the support in kind received from the British government. This includes the building of roads, the international airport at Mount Pleasant and the fantastic secondary school and modern hospital, all built after the war.

The level of education and culture of the Islanders has also changed. Today nearly every child finishes secondary education and a high proportion then travel to the United Kingdom to undertake university studies. Through the local radio (FIBS) and the weekly newspapers (The Penguin News and the Teaberry Express) and also through local and satellite television the Islanders are well informed about events in Argentina and the rest of the world.

The Islanders today are friendly and sociable.[177] Only a very few accord with stereotype of ignorant, aggresive, taciturn and isolated Islanders. They have constructed a sophisticated little society that includes students, writers, naturalists, researchers, business people, government employees, landowners, farmers, farmhands, teachers and sailors.[178] All this diversity in a population of only 2000 people. To be a small society so distant from the

---

[177] This is the impression I have received from all the Islanders I have met and the great majority of visitors to the Islands in the last few years would agree. Among others, the description by Mollie Ridout in her book *The Real Live Falklands*, London 1992, is interesting.

[178] The census of 1996 shows 205 professionals of whom 45 work in healthcare, 47 in teaching, 21 accountants, 4 lawyers, 18 engineers, 6 clerics, 13 pilots and naval officials. There were 380 employees, 95 salespersons and 230 rural workers. There were only 3 people looking for work.

rest of the world every person has to form a part of an integrated community. Everyone knows that it is impossible to go unnoticed in such an environment.[179]

I do not think there exist many communities of this size with such a diversity of interests.

No doubt part of the prosperity and cosmopolitan flavour of the Islands today is due to the sovereignty dispute and the efforts of, first, the Argentines, and then the British, to win the hearts and minds of the Islanders. In the 1970s Argentina introduced petrol and gas to the Islands along with a postal service and flights to the continent. After the war the British continued with this policy a making the Islanders lives easier, despite the high costs involved.

The fishing agreements signed with Argentina -under the protection of the *"sovereignty umbrella"*[180]- allowed the development of this new industry in such a form that they are no longer dependent on subsidies from London. This in turn has given the Islanders much more security.

The Falkland Islanders staunchly defend their interests. In London there is the *Falkland House*, which in effect functions as the Islanders' embassy to the British government. They are also concerned to organise an efficient lobby in parliament. Parliamentarians and officials are regularly invited to the Islands with the object of promoting their view of the conflict. The

---

[179] Wigglesworth, Angela; *Falkland People*, Peter Owen, London 1992.
[180] A result of the Madrid Agreement of 1989 that allowed for practical advances to be made without affecting the rights of the parties in the sovereignty dispute.

Islanders mowing the lawn.

Falkland Islands Association, also based in London, publishes a newsletter and maintains contacts with various interest groups. Within the Parliament there is the *Falkland Islands Parliamentary Group*, which has lost a few members since the overwhelming victory of the Labour Party which allowed Tony Blair to become Prime Minister. The modern *kelpers* also carry out diplomatic missions in multilateral organisations and as petitioners attend the sessions of the Decolonisation Committee of the United Nations, as well as the Commonwealth gatherings. Certainly a formidable performance for such a small community.

Evolution and demographic composition

There are different versions regarding the exact population of the Islands. The sources a different. If we guide ourselves by the official[181] information on the evolution of the population of the Islands since the beginning of British occupation, it can be divided in three stages. The first is of growth and consolidation of the colony which was practically maintained until the opening of the Panama Canal, an event that brought about the reduction of number of merchant ships that travelled the South Atlantic to cross to the Pacific Ocean. Let us recall that the objective of the British occupation of the Islands was to offer an alternative harbour port) to the ships which were travelling to Orient by the Cape Horn route.

---

[181] Census Report 1996, Falkland Islands Government.

The Islands Today

Year	Inhabitants
1851	287
1861	541
1871	811
1881	1,510
1891	1,789
1901	2,043
1911	2,272

The second stage lasted until the war in 1982. The colony was stagnant, with no future, the inhabitants were impoverished and practically incommunicado from the rest of the world. There are signs of a decreasing population on the Islands. There were almost no new immigrants and many Islanders migrated to the United Kingdom and New Zealand. Some migrated to Argentina. The colony was even unable to sustain the growth of the natural vegetation.

Year	Inhabitants
1931	2,392
1946	2,239
1953	2,230
1962	2,172
1972	1,957
1980	1,813

Child running on the beach, in the background a minefield.

The Islands Today

The third stage covers the time after the end of the war to the present. The economic boom brought about by the fishing licences, as well as the expenditure of the British government on security, defence and communications, has resulted in a consistent increase in the local population since 1982.

Year	Inhabitants
1986	1,916
1991	2,091
1996	2,564
2001	3,200 (estimated)

One traditional fact is still evident in the last census on the composition of the population: the shortage of women. Of the total number of inhabitants included in the census, 1,450 are male and 1,117 are female. These numbers include children. But if we take the population ranging between the ages of 25 and 55, we find 810 men and only 558 women. This situation has caused serious problems for a significant sector of the adult male population. Some of the causes are the high levels of dissatisfaction, alcoholism, depression, separations and divorces revealed by the statistics.

Of the total number of the inhabitants, only 1,267 were born on the Islands and those resident for more than ten years, including natives, total only 1,336. These are the genuine Islanders.

Of those born elsewhere, British citizens are the vast

majority: 885. The second in importance are the temporary immigrants from St Helena: 253, according to the census, but over 400 according to other sources [182]. There are 49 residents from other Anglo-Saxon countries (the US, Australia, Canada and New Zealand), and from Latin-American countries there is a total of 70 (Chileans [183], Argentines and Uruguayans). The remaining foreigners are from different countries with a relatively important German community (18 residents).

The official language on the Islands is obviously English. The second most spoken language, and the one taught at schools as the first foreign language, is Spanish. [184]

The Islanders from the "camp"

For many years wool had been the only industry on the Islands. The economy of the Islands was based on sheep breeding, shearing, and raw wool exports through the Falkland Islands Company. After the war, there was a social revolution on the Islands. The lands belonging to the Falkland Islands Company and to some other non-resident landowners (including some Argentines) were expropriated. These lands were re-sold to the Islanders on soft terms. Many of them were employees and foremen of the previous landowners.

---

[182] There is apparently a group of non-declared or illegal immigrants, or perhaps because they work on the military base and live in Mount Pleasant, there is no need for them to register.

[183] According to the 1996 census, the Chilean residents amounted to 42.

[184] During the post-war period, for political reasons, French was taught instead of Spanish.

A Falklands boy playing on the beach.

As a result there is now a rural society composed of small and medium sized landowners. The surface of the land is vast, but as in Patagonia, this does not reflect the magnitude of the operational side, because there is a low animal ratio per acre ratio. In fact many of the new landowners are working at a loss and only survive through subsidies granted by the local government, which is keen to maintain the population in the *"camp"*. Many of these agricultural businesses are on sale. But, due to the lack of interested parties and the prohibition which exists on land sales to Argentines, very few have been successfully sold.[185] One sees farms that have been abandoned because the owners have been unable to find buyers despite low asking prices.

All the farms put together cover an area of 2,700,000 acres, with 1,400.000 acres on East Falkland, 1,000,000 acres on West Falkland and the remainder spread among the small islands. The principal landowner is Falkland Landholdings Ltd., which has taken over the land that belonged to the Falkland Islands Company for more than a century. It owns nearly 500,000 acres including Fitzroy Farm, North Arm, Goose Green and Walker Creek, all these in Lafonia and the south of East Falkland. The rest of the farms are divided between 88 other owners whose properties average 30,000 acres in size with an average of 7,000 sheep on each. The largest have more than 50,000 sheep and the smallest less than 5,000.[186] The latter are a

---

[185] One of the few successful sales involved two British millionaires Sir Harry Solomon and Leonard Licht who, according to an article written by the London correspondent of La Nación, Graciela Iglesias, and published on 10-12-99, bought a 30% share of Falkland Landholdings for US$3 million.

[186] The statistical details of the number of owners, farms, sheep and rural population are drawn from "Falkland Island Farming Statistics", Department of Agriculture, Government of the Falkland Islands. The details of the farms are taken from the map entitled "Falkland Islands Farm and Settlement Boundaries" also published by the Island Government.

A Falkland Islander repairs the pavement.

problem as their production does not earn enough to maintain even one family.

The Islands' rural population has consistently diminished in recent years. Currently less than 350 people live permanently in the *camp*. In 1986 there were 700 people in the rural community. Many rural customs and traditions that were acquired and retained since the days of the *gaucho* were still firmly established in the 1960s and 70s but have subsequently been lost.[187] Rural life in those times was not easy, but the Islanders took great pride in the land which gave a meaning to their lives. The typical rural activities, which were governed by the seasons, gave rise to a rich store of anecdotes and stories of daily life based on the events of a busy community.[188]

Falklands *camp* life has changed. The majority of farms have no workforce and the owners must carry out all the work themselves. Even in the larger farms there is a notorious scarcity of farm labour. Many owners complain about the current bureaucratic difficulties in bringing Chilean and Uruguayan labourers to the Islands as they did in the past. The government favours the introduction of St. Helenians, but their lack of understanding of farm work and rural life has resulted in these new immigrants staying almost exclusively in Stanley or in Mount Pleasant. Some estancias have even been abandoned.

---

[187] Edwards, Roger; *The Other Side of the Falklands*, Drift publica-tions, Hampshire, 1993.
[188] Wilkinson, Rosemary; *Diary of a Farmer's Wife* (More Humorous Tales of Life on a Falkland Islands Farm), Black Sheep Books, Falkland Islands, 1993.

The Islands Today

Modern technology is also now being used. The Agriculture Department on the Islands, particularly since the arrival of its Australian Director, Bob Reid, has undertaken extensive work on modernisation that has promoted the use of new technologies amongst the great majority of rural producers.[189]

Modern motorcycles and quad bikes have replaced the horse in rural work. Electric fences have taken the place of traditional fences. The mobile telephone, the fax, answering machines, personal computers and satellite television have completely changed the old customs. The ease of travel to Stanley in the daily FIGAS flights has overcome the farms' communication problems. The modern Falkland farmer can communicate with the world but also suffers the consequences of globalisation, among these the fall in the price of wool.

Mount Pleasant

Of the 500 civilians[190] who live at the Mount Pleasant military base, 353 are male and 130 are female. The great majority is from either the United Kingdom or St. Helena. In the opinion of David Lang[191] these people cannot be considered as Islanders. Of course, the military personnel, who number nearly 2,000, cannot be considered part of the Island population either.

---

[189] The important work of the Agriculture Department is reflected in its annual reports.
[190] According to the 1996 census there were 483. Census Report, Government of the Falkland Islands.
[191] The Attorney General on the Islands.

Stanley

Stanley has been the capital of the Islands since 1845 when the seat of government was transferred from Puerto Louis. The site was chosen because it had the best harbour for the Royal Navy ships.

Since that time Stanley's inhabitants have always been involved in the administration of the colony and the operation of the port. Since 1982 Stanley has grown in an impressive manner. New houses, newly paved streets, new neighbourhoods and new public buildings are the external signs of the wealth generated by fishing activity and the investment made by the colonial government.

The social life in Stanley and the customs of its inhabitants have changed dramatically. From being a small town where nothing happened, today it is connected to the world. The very existence of the sovereignty dispute has resulted in visits by important officials, parliamentarians, retired Prime Ministers and British Crown Princes. In recent years there have been journalists on the Islands almost constantly.

The majority of Stanley's inhabitants today work, in one form or another, in government offices, in the primary school, the secondary college, in the development corporation, in the government air service company or in the hospital.

Commercial activity is also important because, in addition to the needs of the 2,000 inhabitants, one must

The Islands Today

take into account the things bought by tourists and the occasional cruise liners that visit the Islands.

Several first class hotels [192] and their respective restaurants satisfy the needs of travellers. The shops and foodstores [193], especially those of the Falkland Islands Company, are well stocked. Today in Stanley one can find any product that would normally be used in any modern society. There is even an Internet Café, which allows anyone without a personal computer in their home, or visitors, to get connected to the outside world. One cannot fail to mention pubs [194], the classic places for Islanders to meet, have a few drinks and play a game of darts. Each pub has its regulars and one even has its own football team.

The Islanders are not very religious and few attend mass on Sundays. Nonetheless, there are several options. The Anglicans, who form the majority of the population, have the beautiful Christ Church Cathedral, a delightful stone church with a welcoming interior, overlooking Stanley Bay. The Catholics, mostly of Irish and South American origin, have St Mary's Chapel, a charming wooden building with beautiful stained glass windows. Others include the Tabernacle, the Jehovah's Witnesses and the Baha'i. All have their followers.

---

[192] The principal ones are the "Upland Goose Hotel", the "Malvina House Hotel" and "Emma's Guesthouse" in Stanley. In the camp there is the "Blue Beach Lodge" at San Carlos, the "Pebble Island Hotel on Pebble Island (Isla Borbón), "Sea Lion Lodge" on Sea Lion Island and "Port Howard Lodge" on West Falkland. The service and attention is excellent in them all.

[193] Among others the Beauchene Supermarket, Falkland Farmers, West Store,, Fleetwing, Homecare, Falkland Supplies, Kelper Store, Philomel Store, Reflections, Stanley Co-op, Teresa's, The Gift Shop, The Pink Shop and The Tool Box.

[194] Notably The Globe, The Ship, The Victory, Deano's and The Stanley Arms.

There are several options for weekends and holidays. There is a golf club on the way out of Stanley and a horse racing track. Fishing is free and popular. For the fanatics there is a Darts Club. For those who like swimming there is a heated, indoor public swimming pool in the Community School. There are also groups of bridge players and others who play football.

Little remains of the monotonous and boring life of yesteryear. Modern Stanley is a small capital full of life and activity. If in addition one takes into account the almost non-existent crime rate as well as the everyday contact with the wild beauty of the South Atlantic, it is easy to see why the Falklanders are fanatical about their Islands.

IX

FALKLANDS OR MALVINAS?

"Die Mauer ist weg"[195]

The Players

The dispute continues, in other words this is an open-ended story. Where do we stand? Who are the players in this on-going drama? What are the alternatives? These are the issues on which we will expand in the following lines.

Officially the Falkland Islands dispute is an argument over the sovereignty of an island territory between the United Kingdom of Great Britain and Northern Ireland and the Republic of Argentina. The conflict is recognised as suchin the United Nations and the Islands are officially included among those territories to be de-colonised.

Argentina basically argues that the Islands are hers by inheritance from Spain, the legitimate owner up to the moment of Argentine independence, that they are a

---

[195] "The Wall has Fallen". 10 November 1989 saw the unforeseen fall off the Berlin Wall. Millions of Berliners who crossed the frontier succeeded where the Cold War and diplomacy had failed.

A typical Island horse in the garden of a Stanley home.

part of the national territory based on the principle of territorial integrity and that in 1833 they were taken by force in an illegal act, which was never accepted by Argentina.

For years, the United Kingdom disputed Argentina's historical arguments, then maintained the theory of usucapion on the basis of the length of time the Islands had been under British dominion, and now says it must apply the principle of free determination of the people and that the inhabitants must decide their own future. They also maintain, that if there had been any doubts, the war of 1982 was enough to dissipate them.

Argentina responds by saying that the Islanders are an artificially implanted population, also artificially maintained Anglo-Saxon by strict immigration controls and also *"Anglicised"* in the extreme. Another point made by Argentina is the small population (2,200 people), whose number is no bigger than the number of personnel in the military base at Mount Pleasant. Finally, it says that the war of 1982 did not resolve the underlying question and that the dispute will continue until a resolution is achieved.

The United Nations partially recognise both positions and maintains in Resolution 2065 of 1965 that the dispute must be resolved taking the *interests* of the Islanders into account.

To this overall picture one must add internal British policy. The United Kingdom, with only a few exceptions, peacefully dismantled its Empire for over more than 50 years. There was one constant factor, to always try to control the process. The last case was the British colony of Hong Kong[196]. There is now agreement amongst all British political parties that Great Britain will only alter the *status quo* with the agreement of the Islanders, and with some sence of control of the whole process.

In March 1999 the British Foreign Secretary, Robin Cook, presented a White Paper[197] to the House of Commons on the future of the Dependent Territories, the euphemism used to describe the colonies. This document produced a complete revision of the situation of the colonies and gave the British objectives for its remaining colonies after the handing over of Hong Kong to China. In the first place none of the inhabitants of these territories had expressed any interest in independence, on the contrary they all wished to remain British. It was made clear that the situations of only the Falkland Islands and Gibraltar could be different. It was decided to create a qualitative change in the relationship between the centre and its colonies. This was reflected in their decision to rename them *"Overseas Territories"*[198] in place of the previous *"Dependent Territories"*. It was further decided to offer British Citizenship to the inhabitants of the territories.[199] Finally it expressed the United Kingdom's readiness to defend the aforementioned colonies. In both the Falkland Islands and Gibraltar, important navy air bases ensure their defence. It also established the respect for human rights, the control of drug trafficking and

---

[196] Dimbleby, Jonathan; *The Last Governor, Chris Patten and the Handover of Hong Kong*, ed. Warner Books, London, 1997.

[197] "White Paper on United Kingdom Overseas Territories: Partnership for Progress", 17-3-99.

[198] Terminology copied from the French "territoires d'outremer".

[199] Until then only those territories where the majority of the population were white, like the Falkland Islands and Gibraltar, had this right. The policy was not implemented. St. Helenians still do not have British citizenship: the only reason is that they are not white.

money laundering in the territories. It is evident therefore that the United Kingdom's intention is to preserve these territories for as long as possible.

In the constitutional reform of 1994, Argentina incorporated a clause that ratified its sovereignty claim over the Islands as an integral part of its territory and established the permanent objective of the recovery of the Islands and the full exercise of sovereignty, respecting the Islanders' way of life.[200]

Although the different Argentine political parties at the end of the 20th century have different views on the question of international relations, they all agree on the need to comply with the constitutional requirement to recover full sovereignty of the Falkland Islands in accordance with the principles of international law. The only significant exception to this is the former Foreign Minister Di Tella, who has stated that he considers this objective to be impossible to fulfil and that it is wrong for countries to have objectives they cannot achieve. An intermediate solution appears to be the one favoured by Di Tella, who has stated that *"shared sovereignty is one of the alternatives. However, we cannot stand by, expecting the penguins to come to us and lay a golden egg... a transaction must be confirmed by the new authorities"*.[201]

---

[200] Constitution of the Republic of Argentina, first transitional article. *"The Argentine Nation ratifies its legitimate and imprescriptible sovereignty over the Falkland Islands, South Georgia Islands and South Sandwich Islands and the maritime areas and corresponding islands, as part of the national territory. The recovery of the said territories and the full exercise of sovereignty, respecting the way of life of the inhabitants, and conforming with the principle of International Law constitutes a permanent and irrenounceable objective of the Argentine people."*

[201] Centeno, Andrea; "Di Tella: la mejor solución es una transacción por Malvinas", *La Nación*, 28-11-99.

The excellent Falkland Island Community School.

Falklands or Malvinas?

Whether the Argentines like it or not there is another group of players in this: the Islanders themselves. The Island community is made up of 2,200 inhabitants of whom 1,800 live in Stanley (among them 360 are children of school age), 400 in Mount Pleasant and 400 in the rural areas. About 200 British expatriates on temporary contracts are included in these figures. Also included are the non-permanent residents from St. Helena (about 300) and the civilians who work for the armed forces (about 300). These figures do not include the military forces in the base at Mount Pleasant (approximately 1,600). About 150 Islanders live outside the Islands.[202]

In short, there are only 1,600 genuine Islanders. If one then discounts the minors, there are only 1,200 adults who represent 25% of the total number of people, including the military who live on the Islands.[203]

These 1200 people are represented by 8 Councillors elected by direct vote in an incomplete single list system. These are the people to whom the United Kingdom has promised to respect their wishes, to whom the Argentine Constitution guarantees their way of life and those whom the United Nations maintain their interests must be taken into account when the future of the Islands is decided.

The Constitution of the Islands is an Act sanctioned by the Queen of England who reserves the right to modify or revoke it.[204] The official name for the territory

---

[202] Source: 1996 census extrapolated to 1999 and cross-checked with the author's own information and other sources. The rural population confirmed by the Department of Agriculture.

[203] The numbers regarding the British forces on the islands differ according to the source. But is can be estimated that over the last years it has fluctuated between 400 and a maximum of 2400.

[204] Acts 444 of 1985 and 864 of 1997.

is "Colony of the Falkland Islands". The Constitution establishes in its first article the people's right to self-determination as in the UN Charter. However, important powers remain in the hands of the Governor, who is appointed by the Queen, including the judicial system.

The fact is that at the end of the 20th century the right to self-determination of the people has grown at the cost of the right of territorial integrity of nations. We have seen in the libanisation of significant regions of Europe and Asia since the fall of the Berlin Wall. Taking aside the juridical positions adopted by the different parties to the conflict, there are three main players: The United Kingdom of Great Britain and Northern Ireland, the Argentine Republic and the Falkland Islanders. We will now analyse the maximum and minimum possibilities and the different alternatives for each of these players.

Interested Third Parties

As well as the principal players in this drama, there are interested third parties that affect the position and the possibilities for the Islanders, Argentines and the British.

Because of its geographical proximity, Chile is one of the most important such countries. For many years Chile wanted to have its own direct access to the Atlantic. This has been an eagerly pursued policy since the founding of Punta Arenas in 1841. Punta Arenas is located on the Magellan Straits to the east of the Andes. Various treaties have been signed with Argentina since 1881, which have

The Islanders' diplomatic representation in London.

granted Chile the Atlantic end of the Straits and the Atlantic islands situated south and east of the Beagle Channel: Picton, Neuva and Lenox.

Years of territorial difficulties with Argentina led Chile, and especially the Chilean Navy, to establish with the United Kingdom a relationship of mutual support in the South Atlantic. Chile also reclaimed an Antarctic sector that included a good portion of waters and lands located east of the Cape Horn meridian line and clearly in the Southern Atlantic.[205]

Chile is a fundamental factor for the solution of the dispute. The Falklands has no possibility of medium or long term sustainability without the active cooperation of Chile.

In recent years, and particularly since the resolution of the border dispute over the *Hielos Continentales*[206] at the beginning of 1999, Chile has changed its traditional posture and now supports Argentina. Chile also has concerns about the independence movement on Easter Island.[207] Another reason for Chile to draw closer to Argentina is its interest in Mercosur. These new strategic interests suggest that Chilean support for Argentina will continue.

There is also no doubt that the United States participated in the dispute. Firstly it was they who

---

[205] Etchebarne Bullrich, Conrado; *Americanos del Sur en el Siglo XXI*, Emecé Editores, Buenos Aires, p. 113 onwards.
[206] Called the *campo de heilos sur* by the Chileans. (Trans. note: southern ice fields).
[207] Which, according to some sources, may have the support of French Polynesia.

instigated the pirate attack by the frigate *"Lexington"* in 1833 that left the Islands in a state of anarchy that allowed the later British occupation. In the 1982 war they were also principal players: from the equivocal signals they sent to Galtieri and the efforts of General Haig to avoid the British re-taking of the Islands by force, to their ultimate logistical support of both supplies and information that facilitated the rapid success of the Task Force, once they could see the inevitability of war.

The whole of the American continent is part of the United States' area of influence. The British presence in the Falkland Islands is only possible with the consent and approval of the North Americans. Without US support the British would not be able to remain there for a single day, as happened in Suez almost 50 years ago. But for the time being there is no evidence that the United States is prepared to change its position. The United Kingdom was the Americans principal ally during the Cold War and continues to be so. There can be no doubt that the Americans would not risk their relationship with Great Britain over the Falklands. Particularly if one takes into account that the relationship between the United States and Argentina was never close. Throughout the second half of the 19th century until the middle of the 20th century Argentina had a traditional policy of avoiding US influence in South America at all costs. In the history of Pan-American Conferences, Argentina was always against Yankee initiatives. During the Chaco War between Bolivia and Paraguay, Argentina sided with the Paraguayans who defeated the Bolivians despite American support. From 1943, Juan Domingo Perón, through his flirtations with the Axis powers and his *"third position"*, did everything possible to distance himself from the Americans. That

The Director of the Teaberry Express, Juanita Brock.

policy was continued by the subsequent military and Radical governments.

Only in 1989 did Argentina accept North American leadership. Nevertheless, today Argentina is still looked upon with distrust by the United States. Only US interest in preserving its relationship with Latin American countries is likely to moderate its pro-British position on the Falklands issue. This will only happen if Argentina retains the unanimous support of the Southern Cone countries, including Chile.

The United Kingdom

As we have seen in previous chapters, over a period of 50 years Great Britain arranged an organised withdrawal from the Empire, starting with India and ending with Hong Kong.

The withdrawal left a handful of small colonies, including the Falkland Islands and Gibraltar, in British hands.

The colonies are no longer one of the important priorities of either domestic or foreign British policies. Nor are they important to the political parties.

Great Britain's priorities are clear:

1) To maintain an excellent economic, political and military relationship with the United States and with its partners in the European Union.

2) To maintain its position as an important military, economic and technological power.

3) To maintain groupings of ex-colonies in the British Community of Nations, over which Great Britain expects to retain an appreciable degree of economic, political and military influence.

None of the remaining colonies is indispensable to any of these objectives. They can help in a minor way to maintain a military presence in Europe, as in the case of Gibraltar, or serve as an excuse to justify the maintenance of an important fleet or ensure the strategic control of an ocean or access to the Antarctic as would be the case of the Falkland Islands.

The relationship with Spain should be more important than the retention of Gibraltar, but only as long as both objectives do not clash. It is evident that for Spain, the relationship with Great Britain, the European Union and NATO have a higher priority than the recovery of Gibraltar. Consequently, this is an outstanding dispute but it is not in Great Britain's interests to resolve it quickly. There is no doubt that any modification to Gibraltar's *status quo* will affect the future of the Falkland Islands.

As for the Falkland Islands, the United Kingdom basically has four alternatives.

The first, and the one that has been adopted as the official policy, is to maintain the current *status quo* at all costs. This means retaining the Falklands as a colony, ensuring its defence with an important military base, preventing the multi-lateralisation of the conflict and maintaining the best possible relationship with Argentina by adopting the concept of the *"umbrella"*, which allows for the indefinite postponement of the resolution of the conflict. And finally, the British posture that it is the

Islanders who have the last word on the future of the Islands.

This alternative has various advantages and risks. The first advantage is that it avoids an unpleasant debate in Parliament. Reducing the size of the Empire has never been popular and the last remaining colonies are defended the most. The war in 1982 is also fresh in their memory. Assuring the control of the Falklands allows the South Atlantic to be a British ocean, especially as they also control the islands of St. Helena, Ascension, Tristan da Cunha, Gough, the South Georgias and South Sandwich. At the same time, Great Britain –despite being a signatory of the Antarctic Treaty– maintains its sovereignty claim over an important sector of Antarctica into which significant investments have been channeled to strengthen their presence. The Falkland Islands are the principal point of access to Antarctica for the British. Their strategic importance in a globalised world and the future possibility of exploiting hydrocarbons and minerals on the islands and in the surrounding waters, must be taken into account.

The risks include the possibility that the dispute will drag on and eventually involve the whole of South America, a region in which the British have a special interest. The conflict could erupt at any moment and the results could be very different from those of 1982. Without taking things that far, an unfavourable relationship with Argentina and South America could have negative economic consequences without mentioning the costs of maintaining the defence of the Islands. It could also have a political and public image cost for the United Kingdom.

Less likely, but perhaps an alternative that might

actually occur, is the possibility that the Islanders might assume full self-determination and take decisions contrary to the interests of the United Kingdom. Such decisions could range from a *"Rhodesia-style"* unilateral declaration of independence with the complicity of some politicians in Britain, complicating the relationship between the United Kingdom and Argentina to the association of countries with interests contrary to those of Great Britain. We must remember that not only China, but also Korea and Taiwan are the principal Asian countries that fish in Falklands waters.

Another alternative for the British would be to force pseudo-independence on the Islands, to achieve the recognition of a group of significant countries and to then present Argentina with a *"fait accompli"* as they did with Belize and Guatemala 20 years ago. Such an outcome would generate an immediate conflict with Argentina with no immediate gain for the United Kingdom. Another negative aspect of the latter, is the fact that for the moment the Islands have no desire for independence and wish to remain a privileged part of Great Britain. It remains, nonetheless, a possibility for the future.

Finally there is the option of negotiating with Argentina some kind of partial handing over of sovereignty. Since the war of 1982 the complete ceding of sovereignty to Argentina has been out of the question. From the British point of view Argentina is not in a position to apply pressure for the restitution of sovereignty. The balance of power is still overwhelmingly on the side of the United Kingdom. Argentina is a country of 35 million people with a GDP of $300 thousand million. The United Kingdom has 60 million people and a GDP of

Falklands or Malvinas?

$ 1,200 thousand million. To maintain the current trend until the end of the 21st century will be enough to narrow the gap.

To this one must also add the British policy of association and alignment with the Commonwealth[208], NATO, the United States and the European Union. The support of Commonwealth countries is important to give legitimacy to the British occupation.[209] The British Commonwealth of Nations is a disparate group of countries that accepts British leadership. The are basically three types of country: the first is Anglo-Saxon and is totally identified with Great Britain –Canada, Australia and New Zealand. The second group is made up of the important ex-colonies like India, Pakistan and South Africa and the third group consists of individually small and unimportant countries and islands who collectively have significant voting power in the United Nations.

The distance and the long term favours Argentina. These are the reasons that might lead Great Britain to a partial negotiation of the sovereignty dispute, whilst its position of superiority allows them to negotiate from a position of strength thereby securing the United

---

[208] A relationship that has been strengthened as a result of the plebiscite of 7 November 1999 in Australia in which a majority of Australians voted to retain the Queen as Head of State.

[209] South Africa, Botswana, Cameroon, Gambia, Ghana, Kenya, Malawi, Mozambique, Namibia, Nigeria, Sierra Leone, Tanzania, Uganda, Zambia, Zimbabwe, Canada, Malta, Cyprus, Bangladesh, India, The Maldives, Pakistan, Sri Lanka, Mauritius, The Seychelles, Lesotho, Singapore, Brunei, Malaysia, Papua New Guinea, The Solomon Islands, Tuvalu, Kiribati, Nauru, Samoa, Fiji, Tonga, Vanuatu, New Zealand, Australia, Dominica, Trinidad & Tobago, Antigua & Barbuda, The Bahamas, Barbados, Belize, Granada, Jamaica, St. Kitts & Nevis, British Guyana, St. Vincent & the Grenadines.

Kingdom's medium and long-term interests. The risks of this alternative are the opposition of the Islanders to any change in the *status quo* and the Opposition parties' use of the issue for internal political purposes. The great advantage would be to remove the main point of friction between the United Kingdom and South America, at the same time safe-guarding their medium and long-term interests.

Argentina

The ultimate Argentine goal is clear: to recover the sovereignty of the Falkland Islands as quickly as possible.

There are clearly only two alternatives. One is to achieve it by force. This alternative is not viable. Not least because of the ethical questions and the illegality of such action under current international law and the Argentine Constitution. This was attempted in 1982 and was a complete failure. And as a direct consequence of that war, the analysis of any other alternative solution was effectively postponed for an entire generation. If this were not enough, the balance of power remains favourable to the United Kingdom as long as they maintain their military alliances remain. This option is therefore invalid and is not an appropriate way of recovering the Islands. It is also precluded by the 1994 Constitution.

Argentina now has the solid political support of the Mercosur countries (Brazil, Uruguay and Paraguay), of its neighbours in the Southern Cone (Chile[210], Bolivia

---

[210] The support of Chile is perhaps one of President Menem's most significant achievements in the context of the Falklands question.

and Peru), and the sympathy of the all the other Hispanic-American countries (Ecuador, Colombia, Venezuela, Panama, Nicaragua, Costa Rica, El Salvador, Honduras, Guatemala, Cuba and Santo Domingo). There is also moral support for the Argentine claim in Italy, Spain and Portugal, but this has not been converted into political support due to the alliances within the European Union.

The second, and only realistic, alternative is to negotiate with the British. To do this it is necessary to prove to them that it is in their own interests to negotiate. For British politicians this is virtually impossible, in current circumstances, without the support of at least a significant part of the population of the Islands. Argentina therefore has no alternative but to negotiate with the Islanders as well.[211]

To get the British to sit at the negotiating table, Argentina must, on the one hand, offer a result that satisfies British interests and, on the other, clearly indicate the consequences and costs the British could suffer if they choose not to negotiate or if a solution is not agreed.

A clear example of this occurred in March 1999, when the Islands lost all links with the continent because of the Chilean government's reprisals against the detention of General Pinochet in London, which resulted

---

[211] This is, in practice, what has happened over the last 5 years. The Islanders have participated in all the negotiations between the United Kingdom and Argentina on the Falkland Islands during this period. They participated in the talks on fishing and oil, those that resulted in the re-establishment of flights and the authorization of Argentine citizens being allowed to visit the Islands on their own passports.

in the cancellation of the weekly LANChile flights from Punta Arenas to Stanley. Argentina, whose interest was to secure permission for its citizens to travel directly to the Islands from the Argentine mainland, asked its Mercosur partners for their support. Brazil and Uruguay duly prevented British flights bound for the Islands from making stopovers on their territory. The only connection the Islands then had with the rest of the world were the Tristar RAF aircraft that communicated London with Stanley, making a stop en route on Ascension Island.

Simultaneously Argentina made the Foreign Office and the Islanders aware that it was not going to press, for the time being, for its ultimate goal; that it would not seek negotiations on the sovereignty issue, nor that all flights should leave from the mainland. They only requested that discrimination against Argentines visitors should cease after 18 years and even accepted the gradual introduction of direct flights.

So it was that the English and the Islanders accepted to negotiate and, after fruitful meetings in London and New York, a satisfactory agreement was reached in which Argentina obtained all that it had proposed for the negotiating round. Argentines were authorised to travel unconditionally to the Islands and direct flights would be gradually introduced.

Now the main difficulty is to determine what are Argentina's minimum objectives on sovereignty, what are the maximum pressures Argentina could apply on London and would be prepared to use, with an acceptable cost/benefit ratio.

It is clear that the recovery of the Islands is

important for Argentina but it is not a priority. The development of the country and the well being of its people are the real priorities. Consequently, if applying pressure to Great Britain would be detrimental to the relationship with the United States and Europe, the costs would then outweigh any possible benefits.

What pressure could Argentina bring to bear? It could continue its constant campaign in the United Nations through General Assembly de-Colonisation Committee Resolutions. It could work on British public opinion, highlighting the costs and the minimal benefits of keeping the Islands. And it could obtain the support of Latin American countries. These kinds of pressures would not seem to have major costs for Argentina, but have proved to be insufficient to bring the British to the negotiating table.

Argentina could concentrate on the fish stocks of the Islands –their main source of income, and incite Argentine and third country fishing boats to fish in Island waters in contravention of the British regulations with the objective of depleting the stock. Something similar was attempted during President Alfonsín's term, with fishing contracts being granted to Russia and Bulgaria– at the height of the Cold War. The results were completely counter-productive. Neither the Russians nor the Bulgarians were prepared to take on the British. As a reprisal, the British extended the controlled fishing zones and closed all the doors on any negotiations with Dr. Alfonsin's government.

Argentina could also increase military pressure by sending more troops to the south, organising naval manoeuvres in waters close to the Falklands or acquiring technology for the development of missiles that could reach the Islands. This alternative was also tried by President Alfonsin's government who, in collaboration with Arab nations, attempted to develop the Condor missile capable of reaching the Falkland Islands from the continental mainland. The objective was not to make war but to increase military pressure on the British, who would be forced to increase their military expenditure, thereby reducing the cost benefit ratio of keeping the Islands. This obviously had a cost for Argentina, a country on the road of development but with only limited resources. Needless to say, the Condor project was a complete fiasco. Not only did it alienate the British, it also worried the Americans who for many years were devoted to controlling missile development around the world. The project only served to distance Argentina from the United States and to deepen British concerns over Argentina's intentions. Soon after President Menem was elected, and as a result of North American pressure, the Condor project was scrapped with the loss of all the money invested in it.

The possibility of renouncing the sovereignty claim has to be included among the options open to Argentina, which is the maximum aspiration of the Islanders. This is what Argentina has done with Bolivia, Uruguay and Paraguay. These were all part of the Argentine Confederation at the moment of independence from Spain. However, this option is not realistic. It is highly unlikely that any Argentine government would adopt it, because despite the fact that the Islanders are pro-British (Britain's main argument), they do not have a legitimate origin as a result of the way in which the United Kingdom took control of the Islands and the artificial way in which they prevented nearly all contact with

A Falklands housewife tending her garden.

Argentina, including by immigration. On the other hand, a European colony in South America at the beginning of the 21st century is unacceptable. The only other exception, the French colony of Guyana is an anachronism which, in due time, will be rectified. The Panama Canal, the only other colony on American continental territory, was returned to the Republic of Panama on 31 December 1999.

No doubt the most realistic alternative for Argentina is a negotiation with the United Kingdom, which should result in *"a draw"*. This option has two main variants and many alternatives. The first would be that the United Kingdom and Argentina jointly approve the independence of the Islands within Mercosur and under the joint protection of both countries. It does not seem likely that a solution on these terms could, for the time being, be accepted in Argentina. The second is the possibility of shared sovereignty. This would clearly require the reform of the national constitution and extremely cautious negotiations as to how sovereignty could be shared. Lastly, there is always the possibility of postponing the dispute and solving precise issues and the administration of the Islands. The disadvantage of this option is that the passage of time benefits those who are in favour of occupying the Islands and exercising "de facto" sovereignty over the disputed territory, and at the some time it will help Malvins on both sides makinj even more difficult a peaceful solution in the future.

A Stanley Radio commentator.

The Islanders

The Falkland Islanders, the Falklanders, the Kelpers or simply the Islanders hold the key to the future of their Island, as and when they act reasonably.

Their situation is complicated. They do not have the power or the right to decide the future of the Islands by themselves. They must negotiate with both the United Kingdom and Argentina.

The reality is that their wishes and interests are different from those of Argentina and Great Britain. The United Kingdom will protect the Islanders as part of their interests. The current situation whereby the interests of the Islanders and the British coincide will not last forever.

On the other hand an agreement is not possible without Argentina. As long as the Argentine claim remains, there is a Damoclean sword hanging over the Islanders, the transfer of sovereignty, which could come about by a change in the balance of power, or simply a change of heart on behalf of Great Britain. Also, the situation could remain unchanged for two or three generations. But this will be an unnecessarily dangerous gamble.

There are various alternatives for negotiated solutions that could be acceptable to the Islanders. Among them is independence under joint Anglo-Argentine protection within Mercosur (a concept that would be hard to sell in any form in Argentina), a shared sovereignty agreement[212], or incorporation into Argentina as an autonomous state under British protection (an alternative that would be difficult to sell to the Islanders).

The Islanders have the most to gain if a good solution should be found, but the most to lose if not.

It seems that the British, the Argentines and the Islanders must discard their respective maximum alternatives (to continue with the current status or transfer sovereignty directly to Argentina) as they are unacceptable to the other parties.

Thus it is necessary to find a negotiated solution for this long- standing dispute.

The time has come.

---

[212] This proposal originated from ideas put forth by Guillermo Makin and Colin Lewis. Both President Menem and his Foreign Minister Di Tella considered shared sovereignty to be a possible solution for the long dispute.

ANNEX

The Bullrich - Forsyth proposal:
Falklands-Malvinas A way Forward

Basis for settlement of the dispute

between the United Kingdom and Argentina over the Falklands/Malvinas islands

An understanding could be reached between the Argentine and British governments in order to submit this proposal through a referendum to the people of the Falklands Islands and of the Argentine Republic.

In case the proposal is approved by the majority of voters in both places both governments would agree to sign a treaty on the following lines.

Basis for the agreement

1.- Both countries would jointly undertake to guarantee permanently the islands' autonomy, democratic constitution, territorial integrity and marine boundaries; and to consult and act together on defence and foreign affairs matters relating to the islands.

2.- Autonomy would be defined as full responsibility for internal affairs as now, and specifically the right to choose language, law, currency and system of education and to determine immigration end tourist policy.

3.- The islands present Constitution would be maintained except that provision would be made for the Governor to be elected in future by the Islanders.

4.- The Islanders would have the right to British and Argentina citizenship and could hold both passports if they chose to do so.

5.- The treaty would provide for the establishment of a three man tripartite Commission (one man, one vote) to oversee the implementation and functioning of the agreement. The Falkland islands representative would be the future elected Governor of the Islands. The Argentina and British representatives would be appointed by their respective governments.

6.- No Argentine troops would be sent to the Islands. The base at Mount Pleasant would be leased to Britain for a fixed period, to be approved by the tripartite commission, and the islanders would take responsibility for the civilian operation of the airport.

7.- The Commission would oversee the existing joint hydrocarbon and fishery commissions. These would be reconstituted on a tripartite basis.

8.- The Commission would be the forum for coordination between the islands and the two guarantors in matters relating to defence and foreign affairs.

9.- No taxes of any kind would be levied In the

Annex

Islands by Britain or Argentina. However Argentina's right to a 3% royalty on oil or gas produced in Falkland waters would be recognised.

10.- Cost of defence, which should be much reduced, and foreign relations would be borne by Britain and Argentina.

11.- Britain, Argentina and the Islands would jointly declare the Islands a special ecological protected zone.

12.- The islands would have their own flag (which could be the present flag, with the islands badge but without the Union Jack). The liason office of the Commission on the islands would normally fly all three flags.

13.- The official name of the islands would be Falkland Islands in English and Islas Malvinas in Spanish. Place names on the islands would be a matter for the islanders.

14.- The agreement would be understood as settlement of the dispute. With the signature of the treaty claims and counterclaims would lapse. There would be a time limit for the ratification of the treaty by Britain and Argentina and for the modification of the Argentine and Falklands Islands constitutions.

15.- Provision could be made for a referendum to be held in Argentina and the Falkland Islands.

16.- The terms of the agreement would be notified to the United Nations as constituting settlement of the dispute.

BIBLIOGRAPHY

Armstrong, Patrick; *Darwin's desolate islands: a naturalist in the Falklands, 1833 and 1834*, Picton Publishing Limited, Chippenham, 1992.

Arguelles, Amilcar; *Islas Malvinas y Soberanía*, Estudios de la Academia Nacional de Ciencias, Buenos Aires, 1997.

Adkin, Mark; *Goose Green*, Orion, London, 1997.

Andrada, Benigno Héctor; *Guerra Aérea en las Malvinas*, Emecé, Buenos Aires, 1983.

Barnard, Captain Charles H.; *Marooned*, Syracuse University Press, New York, 1986.

Barker, Nick; *Beyond Endurance*, Leo Copper, London, 1997.

Betts, Alexander; *La verdad sobre las Malvinas, mi tierra natal*, Emecé, Buenos Aires, 1987.

Brown, Nan; *Antartic Housewife*, Hutchinson, Australia, 1971.

Berguño, Jorge; *Las 22 vidas de Shackleton*, Editorial Universitaria, Santiago de Chile, 1985.

Braun Menéndez, Armando; *Pequeña historia antártica*, Francisco de Aguirre, Buenos Aires, 1974.

Bain, Kenneth; *St Helena*, Wilton, York, 1993.

Berguño, Jorge; *Las 22 vidas de Shackleton*, Santiago de Chile, 1985.

Blair, Tony; *New Britain*, Marlow-Magnum, London, 1996.

Bridges, Lucas; *El último confín de la tierra*, Marymar, Buenos Aires, 1978.

Burden, Rodney & others; *Falklands, the air war*, Arms & Armour Press, Dorset, 1986.

Bonzo, Héctor; *1093 tripulantes*, Sudamericana, Buenos Aires, 1992.

Brown, Nan; *Antartic Housewife*, Hutchinson, Victoria, Australia, 1971.

Bramley, Vincent; *Excursion to hell*, Pan Books, London, 1992.

Braun Menéndez, Armando; *Fuerte Bulnes*, Francisco de Aguirre, Santiago de Chile, 1968.

Bransby, Guy; *Her Majesty's interrogator*, Leo Copper, London, 1996.

Casellas, Albert; *Antártida un malabarismo político*, Instituto de publicaciones navales, Buenos Aires, 1981.

Clarke, James; *Atlantic Pilot Atlas*, Adlard Coles Nautical, London, 1996.

Cameron, Jane; *The Falklands and the Dwarf*, Picton Publishing Limited, Chippenham, 1995.

Campos Menéndez, Enrique; *Los pioneros*, Emecé, Buenos Aires, 1994.

Chester, Sharon R.; *Antartic Birds and Seals*, Sharon Chester, California, 1993.

Charter, Tony; *The Falklands*, The Penna Press, St Albans, 1993.

CARI; *Malvinas, Georgias y Sandwich del Sur, perspectiva histórico jurídica* (Tomos I y II), Secretaría Parlamentaria, Direccción de Publicaciones del H. Senado de la Nación, Buenos Aires, 1992.

CARI; *Malvinas, Georgias y Sandwich del Sur - Diplomacia argentina en Naciones Unidas* (Tomos I al V), ed CARI, Buenos Aires, 1995.

Carlevari, Isidro J; *La Argentina* Ergón, Buenos Aires, 1977.

Cisneros, Andrés & Escudé, Carlos; *Historia General de las Relaciones Exteriores de la República Argentina"*, (tomos I a XIII), Grupo Editor Latinoamericano, Buenos Aires, 1999.

Bibliography

Connor, Ken; *The secret story of the S.A.S.*, Weidenfeld Nicholson, London, 1998.

Costa Méndez, Nicanor; *Malvinas, esta es la historia*, Sudamericana, Buenos Aires, 1993.

Lukoviak, Ken; *A soldiers song*, Secker & Warburg, London, 1993.

Connor, Ken; *Ghost Force*, Orion House, London, 1998.

Cairns, P.J. & Hopkins, A.G.; *British Imperialism 1688-1914*, Longman, London, 1993.

Cairns, PJ & Hopkins, A.G.; *British Imperialism 1914-1990*, Longman, London, 1993.

Childs, David; *Britain since 1939*, Mac Millan London, 1995.

Coronel Maldonado, Luis E; *Lord Ponsonby y la Independencia del Uruguay*, ed. Proyección, 1987, Montevideo.

Casellas, Alberto; *Antártida, un malabarismo político*, Instituto de Publicaciones Navales, Buenos Aires, 1981.

Canclini, Armando; *El fueguino*, Editorial Sudamericana, Buenos Aires, 1998.

Davies, TH and McAdam, JH; *Wild flowers of the Falkland Islands*, Bluntisham Books, Bluntisham, 1989.

Dodge, Bertha; *Marooned*, Syracuse University Press, New York, 1979.

Darwin, Charles - *Voyage of the Beagle*, Penguin Classics, London, 1989.

Destéfani, Laurio H.; *Historia marítima argentina* (Tomos I, V y VI), Departamento de estudios históricos navales, Buenos Aires, 1988.

Destéfani, Laurio H; *Famosos veleros argentinos*, Instituto de Publicaciones Navales, Buenos Aires, 1967.

Dolzer, Rudolf; *The territorial status of the Falkland Islands (Malvinas)*, Oceana Publications Inc, New York, 1993.

Del Carril, Bonifacio; *La cuestión de las malvinas*, Emecé, Buenos Aires, 1982.

De Massiac, Barthelemy; *Plan francés de conquista de Buenos Aires, 1660-1693*, Emecé, Buenos Aires, 1999.

Del Carril, Bonifacio; *Cómo se perdió la paz en 1982*, La Nación, Buenos Aires 4-4-99.

Durnhofer, Eduardo; *Malvinas: la premeditación en el despojo británico de 1833*, Documentos, Buenos Aires, 1989.

Daus, Federico y Rey Balmaceda, Raúl; *Islas Malvinas, geografía, bibliografía*, ed. Oikos, Buenos Aires, 1982.

Destéfani, Laurio H; *Las Malvinas en la época hispana*, Corregidor, Buenos Aires, 1981.

Dirección Nacional del Antartico; *Antártida*, Instituto Antártico Argentino, Buenos Aires, 1992.

Del Carril, Bonifacio; *The Falklands Malvinas case*, Ciga, Buenos Aires, 1982.

Duroselle, Jean Baptiste; *Tout empire perira*, Armand Colin, Paris, 1992.

Etchebarne Bullrich, Conrado; *Doce años después*, La Prensa, 24-7-94.

Dimbleby, David & Reynolds, David; *An ocean apart*, Random House, New York, 1988.

Etchebarne Bullrich, Conrado; *Nuevas ideas*, Revista Bienvenido a Bordo, Septiembre, 1999.

Dimbley, Jonathan; *The last governor*, Warner Books, London, 1997.

Etchebarne Bullrich, Conrado; *Two hopes a couple of missunderstandigns*, Buenos Aires Herald, 19-3-99.

Doise, Jean & Vaisse, Maurice; *Diplomatie et outil militaire*, Duroselle, Paris, 1987.

Etchebarne Bullrich, Conrado; *Una nueva relación Argentino-Británico*, La Prensa, Buenos Aires, 16-9-94.

Etchebarne Bullrich, Conrado; *Americanos del Sur en el Siglo XXI*, Emecé, Buenos Aires, 1989.

Etchebarne Bullrich, Conrado; *The Falklands*, Britain & Argentina, Oxford, 1977.

Bibliography

Etchebarne Bullrich, conrado; *A useless unilateral cold wan*, Buenos Aires, Herald, 30-9-96.

Edwards, Roger; *The other side of the Falklands*, Roger Edwards, Hampshire, 1993.

Etchebarne Bullrich, Conrado; *Un cambio favorable*, La Nación, 5-10-96.

Escudé, Carlos; *Gran Bretaña, Estados Unidos y la declinación Argentina*, Editorial de Belgrano, Buenos Aires, 1988.

Estebán, Edgardo; *Diario del regreso*, Sudamericana, Buenos Aires, 1999.

Escudé, Carlos; *El realismo de los estados débiles*, Grupo Editor Latinoamericano, Buenos Aires, 1995.

Etchebarne Bullrich, Conrado; *Las colonias de la Reina del Plata*, La Nación, Buenos Aires, 24 de agosto de 1997.

Etchebarne Bullrich, Conrado: *Historia de la Iglesia Católica*, La Prensa, Buenos Aires, 24 de julio de 1994.

Fothergill, Alastair; *Life in the Freezer, a natural history of the Antartic*, BBC Books, London 1993.

Fraga, Jorge A.; *Malvinas, evolución de la cuestión desde la guerra*, Revista Militar, Buenos Aires, abril-junio 1995.

Fraga, Jorge A.; *La Antártida, reserva ecológica*, Instituto de Publicaciones Navales, Buenos Aires, 1992.

Etchebarne Bullrich, Conrado; *Las Malvinas por dentro*, La Nación, 12-3-95.

Foulkes, Haroldo; *Los Kelpers*, Corregidor, Buenos Aires, 1961.

Foulkes, Haroldo; *Las Malvinas, una causa nacional*, Corregidor, Buenos Aires, 1978.

Etchebarne Bullrich, Conrado: *Las malvinas japonesas*, La Nación, Buenos Aires, 6-8-95.

Etchebarne Bullrich, Conrado; *Conducta mafiosa de los kelpers les impide a Argentina comprar tierras*, Ambito Financiero, Buenos Aires, 20-7-99.

Etchebarne Bullrich, Conrado; *Las Malvinas no son un caso aislado*, La Avispa, mayo 1996.

Falkland Islands Government, The Department of Agriculture, Annual Report 1996-7.

Fernandez Gómez, Emilio Manuel; *Argentina: gesta británica* (Tomos I y II), ed. LOLA, Buenos Aires, 1995.

Fontana, Jorge Luis; *Viaje de exploración en la Patagonia Austra*, Talleres de la Tribuna Nacional, Buenos Aires, 1886.

Fernández Gómez, Emilio Manuel; *Argentina: Gesta Británica*, Literature of Latin America, Buenos Aires, 1993.

Falkland Islands Government, Census Report 1996.

Ferro, Marc; *Colonization, a global history*, Routledge, London, 1997.

Forbes, John Murray; *Once años en Buenos Aires*, Emecé, Buenos Aires, 1956.

Foucher, Michael; *Fronts et frontieres*, Fayard, Paris, 1991.

Franklin Bourne, Benjamin; *Cautivo en la Patagonia*, Emecé, Buenos Aires, 1998.

América Latina, Editorial de Belgrano, 1998, Buenos Aires.

Graham-Yooll, Andrew; *Pequeñas guerras británicas en*

Miller, Rory; *Britain and Latin America*, Longman, London, 1993.

García del Solar, Julio; *La contribución de las Naciones Unidas a las negociaciones entre la Argentina y el Reino Unido*, Buenos Aires, 22-6-95.

Graham-Yooll, Andrew; *Pequeñas guerras británicas en América Latina*, Editorial de Belgrano, Buenos Aires, 1998.

Guyer, Roberto; Veto inglés por la Antártida, Clarín, Buenos Aires, 1-12-99.

Hastings, Max & Jenkins, Simon; *The battle for the Falklands*, Michel Joseph, London, 1983.

Headland, Robert; *The island of South Georgia*, Cambridge University Press, Cambridge, 1992.

Hudson, Guillermo Enrique - *Las aves del Plata*, Hispanoamérica, Buenos Aires, 1974.

Hernández, José; *Las Islas Malvinas*, Joaquin Gil, Buenos Aires, 1869.

Hastings, Marx de Sinkins, Simon; The Battle for the Falklands, Chaucer Press, London 1993.

Hastings, Max & Jenkins, Simon; *La batalla por las Malvinas*, Emecé, Buenos Aires, 1984.

Headland, Robert; *The island of South Georgia*, Cambridge University Press, Cambridge, 1984.

Hunt, Rex; *My Falkland days*, David & Charles, Devon, 1992.

Hough, Richard; *Captain James Cook*, Hodder & Stoughton, London, 1994.

Inda, Enrique; *Los sobrevivientes del estrecho*, Marymar, Buenos Aires, 1992.

Izaguirre, Mario; *Estado actual de la cuestión Malvinas*, Instituto de Publicaciones Navales, Buenos Aires, 1972.

Inda, Enrique S.; *Los sobrevivientes del estrecho*, Marymar, Buenos Aires, 1992.

Lawrence, James; *The rise and fall of the British Empire*, Little, Brown & Co., London, 1994.

Kasansew, Nicolás; *Malvinas, a sangre y fuego*, Abril, Buenos Aires, 1983.

Lanús, Juan Archivaldo; *De Chapultepec al Beagle*, Emecé, Buenos Aires, 1984.

Lukowick, Ken; *A soldiers song*, Secker & Warburg, London 1993.

Lista, Ramón; *La Patagonia Austral y viaje a los andes australes*, Editorial Confluencia, Buenos Aires, 1999.

Lawrence, James; *The making and unmaking of British India*, Abacus, London, 1998.

Lee Marks, Richard; *Tres hombres a bordo del Beagle*, Javier Vergara, Buenos Aires, 1994.

Landaburu, Coronel Carlos Augusto; *La guerra de las Malvinas*, Círculo Militar Biblioteca del Oficial, Buenos Aires, 1988.

Mackinnon, Lauchlan Bellingham; *La escuadra anglo-francesa en el Paraná*, Ediciones Hachette, Buenos Aires, 1957.

Moneta, José Manuel; *Cuatro años en las Orcadas del Sur*, Peuser, Buenos Aires, 1994.

Miller, David; *The wreck of the Isabella*, Leo Cooper, London, 1995.

Mayer, Jorge; *La lucha por las islas - El caso malvinas*, Academia Nacional de la Historia, Buenos Aires, 1997.

Migone, José Luis; *Treinta y tres años de vida malvinense*, Instituto de Publicaciones Navales, Buenos Aires, 1996.

Mc Farlane, Anthony; *The British in the Americas*, Longman, London, 1992.

Mc Lean, David; *War, diplomacy and informal empire*, British Academic Press, London, 1995.

Matassi, Pío; *Probado en combate*, Halcón cielo, Buenos Aires, 1995.

Middlebrook, Martin; *The fight for the Malvinas*, Viking, London, 1989.

Middlebrook, Martin; *Task Force*, Pengin Boofs, London 1987.

Moir, Geoffrey; *The history of the Falklands*, Chris Print, Croydon, 1995.

Moyano, Carlos; *Exploración de los ríos Gallegos*, Coile Santa Cruz, Imprenta de la Tribuna Nacional, Buenos Aires, 1887.

Munro, Richard; *Place names of the Falkland Islands*, Schachketon Scholarskip fund, London 1998.

Murphy, Gervase; *Christ Church Catedral*, Jance Bidewell, London, 1991.

National Geographic; *Atlas of the world*, Washington 1981.

Nolan, Conor; *Fishery Statistics*, Falkland Islands Government, Stanley, 1998.

Oliveri López, Angel; *Key to an enigma - British sources disprove Britisk claim to the Falklands Malvinas Islands*, Lynne Rienner, London 1995.

Bibliography

Olrog, Claes; *Las aves argentinas*, El Ateneo, Buenos Aires, 1995.

Oliveri López, Angel; *La clave del enigma*, Grupo Editor Latinoamericano, Buenos Aires, 1992.

Prieto, Adolfo; *Los viajeros ingleses*, Editorial Sudamericana, Buenos Aires, 1996.

Perich, José; *Indigenous extintion in Patagonia*, Vanic, Punta Arenas, 1996.

Poncet, Sally and Jerome; *Southern Ocean Cruising*, Sally and Jerome Poncet, Beaver Island, 1991.

Poncet, Sally; *Antartic encounter*, Simon & Shuster, New York, 1995.

Poncet, Sally; *Destination South Georgia*, Simon & Schuster, New York, 1995.

Plager, Silvia & Fraga Vidal, Elsa; *Nostalgias de Malvinas*, Javier Vergara Editor, Buenos Aires, 1999.

Prosser Goodall, Rae Natalie; *Tierra del Fuego*, Shanamaiim, Ushuahia, 1978.

Pettingill, Olin Sewall; *Another Penguin Summer*, Charles Scribners sons, New York, 1975.

Ralling Christopher; *The voyage of Charles Darwin*, BBC, London, 1978.

Richards, Philip; *Oil and the Falkland Islands*, British Geological Survey, Edinburgh, 1995.

Roper, Patrick; *Holiday in the Falklands Islands*, Falkland Islands Tourist Board, Ashdown Press Ltd, 1990.

Rowland, Charlenne; *Department of Agriculture - Annual report 1996/1997*, Falkland Islands Government, 1997.

Ridout, Molly; *The real live Falklands*, Molly Ridouts, Stanley, 1992.

Roger, Edwards; *The other side of the Falklands*, Drift Publications, Hampshire, 1993.

Ralph, Richard; *Stanley, a guide for visitors*, Falklands Islands Tourist Board, Stanley, 1997.

Ripa, Julián; *Inmigrantes en la Patagonia*, Marymar, Buenos Aires, 1987.

Rodriguez, Horacio y Arguindeguy, Pablo; *El corso rioplatense*, Instituto Browniano, Buenos Aires, 1996.

Rizzo Romano, Alfredo; *Derecho Internacional Público*, Editorial Plus Ultra, Buenos Aires, 1994.

Sáez de Vernet, María; Diario.

Saguier Fonouge, Carlos; *Mis recuerdos de las islas Malvinas*, Revista Timoneles, Buenos Aires, octubre 1999.

Sewall Pettingill, Jr. Olin; Another Penguin Summer, Charles Scribner's son, New York, 1975.

Strong, Roy; *The Story of Britain*, Hutchinson, London, 1996.

Strange, Ian; *The striated Caracara in the Falkland islands*, Ian Srange, New Island, 1995.

Smith, John; *Those were the days*, Falkland Islands Trust, Bluntisham, 1989.

Summers, Ron & Mc Adam, Jim; *The Upland Goose*, Bluntisham Books, Bluntisham, 1993.

Strange, Ian; *Wildlife of the Falkland Islands*, Harper Collins, London, 1992.

Smith, John; *Condemned at Stanley*, Picton Publishing, Chippenham, 1985.

Sprince, Ivan; *Corrals and Gauchos*, Falklands Conservation, 1992.

Slatta, Richard W.; *Gauchos and the vanishing frontier*, University of Nebraska Press, Lincoln, 1993.

Sierra, Vicente D.; *Historia de la Argentina* (Tomos IV, V, VI y VIII), Editorial Científica Argentina, Buenos Aires, 1984.

Southly Taylyour, Ewen; Falkland bland Shores, Conway Maritime Ltd, London, 1995.

Solari Yrigoyen, Hipólito; *Malvinas, lo que no cuentan los ingleses*, El Ateneo, Buenos Aires, 1998.

Strong, Roy; *The story of Britain*, Hutchinson, London, 1996.

Smith, John; *An islander's diary of the Falklands occupation*, John Smith, Stanley, 1984.

San Martino de Dromi, María Laura; *Gobierno y administración de las Islas Malvinas 1776-1833*, Ediciones Unsta, Tucumán, 1982.

Shackleton, Sir Ernest; *South*, The Lyons Press, New york, 1998.

The Falkland Islands Gazette, The Constitution of the Falkland Islands, Stanley, 20.8.97.

Tanzi, Héctor José; *Compendio de Historia Marítima Argentina*, Instituto de Publicaciones Navales, Buenos Aires, 1994.

Thatcher, Margaret; *The Downing Street years*, Harper Collins, London, 1993.

Tilman, H.W.; *The eight sailing books*, Diadem Books, London, 1995.

Vairo, Carlos Pedro; *Los Yamana*, Zagier & Urruti, Buenos Aires, 1995.

Wilkinson, Rosemany; Diary of a farmes wife, Lyon Lithographic, Hampshire, 1992.

Wilkinson, Rosemary; *More humourous tales of life on a Falklands farm*, Black Shup Books, Falklands, 1993.

Wigglesworth, Angela; *Falkland People*, Peter Owen Publishers, Woreester 1992.

Woods, Robin W.; *Guide to the birds of the Falkland Islands*, Anthony Nelson Ltd, Oswestry, 1988.

Wolsey, Shane; *Old Falkland Photos*, Peregrine Publishing, UK, 1990.

Woodward, Admiral Sandy; *One Hundred days*, Harper Collins, London, 1992.

West, Nigel; *The secret war for the Falklands*, Little, Brown & Co., Polmont, 1997.

Zorraquín Becú, Ricardo; *Inglaterra prometió abandonar las Malvinas*, Editorial Platero SRL, Buenos Aires, 1982.

*Esta publicación se terminó de imprimir en el mes de marzo de 2000
en los talleres gráficos Edigraf S.A., Delgado 834, Buenos Aires, Argentina.*